The

Jack Colman grew up in a s.... .u.ai community in the middle of the North Yorkshire Moors. His first job was picking potatoes on the local farms and he has since been an antique furniture restorer, a grain tester (yes, that's a real thing), a plasterer's mate, a football coach and a corporate lawyer. He is married and lives in Poland. He can be found on Twitter @_JackColman

C1 879936 60

The Rule

JACK COLMAN

HARPER
Voyager

Harper*Voyager*
An imprint of HarperCollins*Publishers* Ltd
1 London Bridge Street
London SE1 9GF

www.harpervoyagerbooks.co.uk

This Paperback Original 2015

First published in Great Britain in ebook format by Harper*Voyager* 2015

A catalogue record for this book
is available from the British Library

ISBN: 978-0-00-812068-9

Set in Sabon by Born Group using Atomik ePublisher from Easypress

Printed and bound in Great Britain

For my wonderful mum, Mary, who never once doubted this would happen.

Prologue

I

In the midst of the darkness, Gunnarr's eyes snapped open.

The hairs along his forearms stood raised like the hackles of a snarling wolf. Muffled voices were hissing at each other from somewhere across the room. Quietly, Gunnarr reached a hand out from the covers and felt the warm absence that his parents had left in the furs at his side. The air felt chilled, and thick with disquiet. Something had happened. He could sense it.

Closing his eyes, he lay very still and tried to listen to his parents' words, but their voices were low and rushed, and he could follow only snatches.

'... now they've decided they ...'

'... and you think death will solve ...'

Gunnarr jolted as if shaken awake from a dream. Death, he thought, and a gleam of a smile spread across his lips. Gunnarr Folkvarrsson and his warrior father were no strangers to death.

The first time he had still been a boy, not yet five. He'd stumbled across a nameless corpse floating in a swell by the shoreline, staring up at the clouds. Of that he remembered

1

mostly the queerness of the dead man's face, all swollen like a sow, front lip eaten away up to the nose.

A year later, on a spring day with a biting breeze, he met death for a second time. Again he'd been down by the near-black sea, the freezing-cold surf roaring with anger at his feet. His grandmother was leading him across the coastal rocks, looking for shellfish, when she made a strange sound and collapsed. Gunnarr had waited patiently for her until the tide was almost in before someone came and carried him away.

His parents had quietened their voices to breathy whispers, perhaps fearing they might wake him. For a moment, Gunnarr contemplated going to his father's side and declaring that he could soon find the old kindling axe and be ready for whatever might be needed of him. But his father, he had learnt, was quick to temper whenever he addressed the topic directly. He would call Gunnarr a child and tell him he knew nothing, but he was wrong. True, those encounters from his early childhood had been tame affairs; the first he had come upon too late, long after death had done its work, and the second was but the quiet expiry of life from an old and wasted body. The third, though, had burnt its way deep into his mind. For that was when he had seen the strike of death's hand; the vicious snatch that rips a life away with the eyelids still blinking.

It was the first time he had been taken on a hunt with his father and uncle. Winter had come early that year, bitter and fierce. The grass had turned brown, and his mother had wrapped him in thick furs to guard against the searching wind. A group of seals they had stalked for most of the morning had become spooked and scattered into the waves when just yards out of range, so the group was returning to town unsuccessful, and in a black mood because of it, when they heard shouts from over by the smoke house.

Gunnarr did not see what had caused it, but he had never forgotten what followed. His father and the rest broke immediately into a run, sweeping Gunnarr along with them. He remembered his uncle screaming curses in a voice louder than thunder, and glancing up into the distance to see a man some twenty yards away hacking his sword double-handed into the half-turned neck of Agni Alvisson. Gasps went up like startled birds, and a crowd of onlookers swamped in and smothered Gunnarr's view.

The rest was a mess of trampling feet and women's screams. There had been one deafening clang of metal, which Gunnarr remembered well, and a rush of grunting movement almost bundled him over. When he recovered his balance, he found his father, uncle, and their friends facing down a group of frozen-eyed men who were cautiously backing away, leaving one of their number spluttering on the floor at his uncle's feet, while a silenced crowd looked on.

That had been a real death. Almost too real, for the man had had time to say a lot of strange things before his wounds drained him, and his blood had smelt sickly as it steamed amidst the mud and rotting oak leaves. Agni Alvisson's head, grinning up at the sky, lay a few feet to one side. Gunnarr's friends told him it had continued to scream in agony even as it landed on the ground, some three yards away from its body.

There were other memories of death besides those, of course. The wails of his aunt and the silence of his father on the day that his uncle had died. The time he caught his father rinsing his sword in the stream, and the way Folkvarr had turned around and placed a sly finger to his lips and patted Gunnarr on the head as he walked inside. Countless other times where the only detail Gunnarr could recall was the billowing heat of the funeral pyre on his cheeks as he pushed and pointed with the other excitable children. Nothing that compared to those first three, though. Perhaps tonight, he thought eagerly, he would finally find something that could challenge them.

He might have lain there for longer in the dark, enjoying the mischievous sensation of hearing what he was not supposed to hear, of knowing about his father things he wasn't supposed to know, but Gunnarr's eyes jumped open again when he heard a new sound amid the rustles and the whispers: a sob from his mother, fearful and desperate.

A protective impulse drove a shiver across his shoulders, and his grin vanished. Casting his furs aside, he stared into the black until he found his parents standing beside the far wall. The wicker door of their single-roomed hut stood an arm's width ajar, with a dull sheen of moonlight drawing a pale line across the floor. He thought he heard voices outside.

'Father?' he called into the gloom, and his parents' conversation immediately hushed. As they looked across to face him, Gunnarr noticed that his mother was clinging very tightly to his father. Had it been lighter, he would have seen tears in her eyes.

'Go back to sleep, Son,' his father said, after a brief pause.

Gunnarr ignored him and rolled up onto his knees. 'It's almost dawn already,' he said with enthusiasm. 'I can get the fishing things ready.'

For some reason the words caused another sob to escape his mother's lips, which she tried to suppress by clamping both hands over her mouth. Confused, Gunnarr saw her give his father a gentle push, and with a sigh the older man moved across the room to his son. As he stepped through the shard of light, Gunnarr noticed that his sword was at his waist.

'Is there a battle?' he gasped excitedly.

'Go back to sleep,' his father said again. 'I'm only going out to check the traps.'

'Let me come!' Gunnarr urged, but his father shushed him and pushed him firmly back down into the furs. Gunnarr tensed against him, giggling playfully.

'Do as I say, please,' his father said gently. More gentle than he would normally have been. His eyes looked very big in the darkness. Then there came a booming voice from outside the walls.

'Do it now or we fire the house. The choice is yours.'

It cut through the still night air, very close by. Gunnarr jumped, and his mother scurried across the room and dropped down beside them, again pressing herself against his father's chest.

'Who is that at this time?' Gunnarr asked, scowling with mature disapproval.

'Just drunken idiots on their way home,' his father replied dismissively, and his mother did her best to nod with reassurance, but even her young son could see that her usually bright features were strained.

'You're a good boy, Son,' his father added suddenly, and he brushed his lips across Gunnarr's forehead, before standing to resume his rapid conversation with his wife.

That uncharacteristic show of affection numbed Gunnarr like a blow to the head. He looked up at his parents, and for the first time noticed the glimmer of moisture on his mother's cheeks.

'I'm going out there with you,' she was saying passionately.

'No my love, what about the boy?' he heard his father reply.

Again Gunnarr found his eyes drawn to the crack of moonlight in the doorway. Rolling silently out of the covers, he crept his way towards it, leaving his parents in their oblivious embrace behind him. He inched the door further from its frame and peered into the shadowed clearing, feeling the night breeze tighten the pores across his face. Leaves whispered ominously in the trees swaying over his head.

'Go back inside, lad,' a voice called from the blackness, and Gunnarr could just make out their half-hidden forms, cloaked in shadow. Five of them.

'Is it not a little late to be calling on my father?' he asked tentatively, moving forward out of the doorway. 'We're to be fishing at dawn.'

One or two of the men laughed callously, and Gunnarr turned to them in confusion.

'What do you want?' he challenged.

'Enough of this,' an angrier voice growled from the right, and Gunnarr shuddered as one of the shapes moved briskly towards him. 'I say we take the boy as well.'

'No!' shouted another, and rushed forward to intercept, restraining the aggressor with an arm across the chest. 'That is not what is called for.'

Through a mist of uncertainty, Gunnarr realised that he recognised the voice. 'Egil?' he asked hesitantly.

'Yes,' Egil answered, with heavy reluctance. 'Greetings, Gunnarr.'

'Egil,' Gunnarr began, 'I'm sure if you wait until tomorrow we'll be calling on you. I can play with Hákon and the boys—' He stopped abruptly as he felt a gentle hand on his shoulder, and turned to find his father standing calmly behind him.

Egil hurried forward and spoke with hushed urgency. 'This time I cannot help you, old friend. It's my own cousin's name at stake.'

'I know that,' Gunnarr's father replied, with a voice of indifference. 'But you can protect my wife, and my son.'

6

'Father, what is happening?'

'Yes Folkvarr, I can,' Egil responded, ignoring Gunnarr, 'but there is a sword at your side. For every number of them you take, they will take one back from you.'

Again Folkvarr sighed heavily, and then he placed a hand on Egil's shoulder. 'Please, a moment with my boy?'

Egil's face became regretful. 'Of course.' He retreated back into the gloom, deliberately avoiding Gunnarr's searching gaze.

Folkvarr turned and dropped to a knee, so that he and his son's eyes were level. Gunnarr was whimpering, his expression distraught.

'Fight them, Father, don't let them hurt you!'

'Gunnarr—'

'Or run, into the forest, please!'

'Gunnarr, enough!' his father said sternly, and he shook the little boy's shoulders until he was silent. 'I want you to take my sword inside, and go and hug your mother until she tells you to stop. Remember, she brought you into this world and protected you when you were weak. Now you are strong, it is your turn to protect her.'

Gunnarr's mouth shot open, but then he felt the weight of his father's instructing eyes and dropped it closed again. With practised, unquestioning obedience, he scrunched up his face and nodded silently.

There was a moment of still as the two of them looked at each other for a final time. Folkvarr's eyes were wide, almost apologetic. Gunnarr bit his jaw closed and determinedly returned the gaze long enough for one stray tear to roll down to his chin. Then he turned dutifully and carried the heavy sword in both hands towards the house, feeling the snatched brush of his father's fingertips across the back of his head before he stepped out of their longing reach.

Once inside, he located his mother's whimpers in the darkness and, rather than crawling onto her lap and sinking into her breast, he sat upright beside her on the floor, placing an arm across her shoulders and letting her fall gratefully against his tiny frame. Together they flinched as they heard a brief flurry of sound, like stones being hurled against sand, and then a ruffled silence returned almost as soon as it had faltered.

After some moments, Gunnarr gently dislodged himself from his mother's now feeble grip and crawled hesitantly over to the doorway. Egil was there still, standing patiently over a motionless shape on the floor.

'Come here and help me carry him, Gunnarr. One day you will understand.'

II

She would always follow too closely, so eager was she not to be left behind. Perhaps in later years Gunnarr would recall that about her with a faint smile, but as a boy of twelve he was conscious of it only as the snatch of her fingers on his feet and the tickle of her breath against his calves as they crawled through the dew-laden grass.

It was a clouded spring morning, with still a touch of winter in the air. Together they worked their way along a tufted ridge that bordered a red-brown stream, following the rushing water up a gentle gradient inland. Gunnarr led, as he always did, eyes forward and alert, barely feeling the thistles that scratched across his knees as he went. Kelda followed gamely. She was weaker than the boys, and he could hear the determined little grunts that she let out as she struggled to keep pace. There were times when she would rise up onto her knees and peer back at the town walls as they receded further into the distance, but she would never voice the uncertainty that Gunnarr saw growing on her face.

After a short time of slithering down and scrabbling up the rises and falls of the riverbank, they reached the shelter of a thicket tangled with brambles, and lost sight of the stream. Gunnarr drew to an abrupt halt and cocked his ear skywards, feeling Kelda's chin thump softly off the sole of his foot as he did so. She exclaimed aloud, but must have sensed his scowl even with his head turned, for she quickly fell silent again. Gunnarr listened to the wind once more and heard the voices clearly above the rush of the stream, one gruff and sounding in short, sharp bursts, the other quieter and less frequent.

He broke off and turned back to Kelda. She was watching him with her mouth ajar, brown eyes gleaming with excitement. Her teeth looked very small, and Gunnarr was reminded that she was much younger than he was. A 'little girl' the boys called her, and would name Gunnarr the same whenever they caught the two of them together. But the boys had wanted to stay in town and watch the dog fight, and Gunnarr was not the type to waste a day standing in one place. Whatever the others might say about her, Kelda would never let him down when there was adventure to be had.

'Stay quiet,' he warned her under his breath. 'It will mean death if they find us.'

She smothered her smile instantly and locked her lips closed.

Gunnarr studied her with a stern expression. Her plait had come half undone and her hair was wisping around her head. It had been raining only a short time before dawn, and her woollen clothes were plastered with mud. 'Your mum is going to be angry again.'

Kelda rolled her shoulders and smiled once more. 'I don't care.'

Gunnarr did not return her grin. 'You remember the signal?'

She nodded quickly and rolled into a sitting position. Casting about briefly, she plucked up a blade of grass, stuffed it between two grubby thumbs, held it to her lips and blew. It made a blunt, hissing sound.

'You can't do it,' Gunnarr complained.

'I can,' she insisted, and continued to blow into her hands, until Gunnarr reached out and snatched the grass away.

'Just follow me and stay quiet.'

Through tunnels in the long grass he led her, weaving through the roots of the bushes on trails made by foxes and river rats. A few days past, Eiric had come home boasting of seeing a mother wolf and six cubs lying at the water's edge. Gunnarr had left town that morning looking for burrows in the river bank, his aim being to take the pups and skin them so that his mother could make them all hats. He'd brought Kelda with him because he needed someone to snatch up the babes while he threw stones at the mother. But that plan had vanished when they'd heard people talking by the river, somewhere just upstream.

The low voice sounded once more, louder this time, and Gunnarr realised that they must be close. He turned and wriggled back to Kelda.

'Who is it?' she whispered. He could hear the breath rushing in and out of her chest.

'A thieving band from the uplands, most like,' he replied grimly. 'Could be as many as twenty of them, waiting until nightfall to snatch any beast we don't bring inside the walls.'

Kelda drew a sharp intake of breath. 'What should we do?'

Gunnarr gave her a reckless look and patted the short skinning knife that hung at his waist. 'If I have to fight them, their numbers will tell eventually. They'll be starving, just like everyone else, so if I'm caught they'll likely roast me over their fire. You they'll carry off to bear their children.'

Kelda caught his hand. 'Let's go back.'

Gunnarr shook his head.

'What then?'

'Egil would want us to ambush them and drive them off.' He reached across into the nearest bush and handed Kelda a stick about the length of her arm. 'When I give the signal, you come out waving your sword and screaming as loud as you can. They'll think us an army, and flee.'

Taking the stick, Kelda looked down at it in her hand and nodded hesitantly. Her eyes flashed a sparkle of enjoyment. Gunnarr smiled at her and fell forward onto his front to crawl off again.

Within a few yards he heard the low voice talking once more, and this time he could make out words.

'Stupid, stupid ...' the voice was saying, over and over again. The words were punctuated by the sound of splashing footsteps as the man stamped about in the water somewhere below Gunnarr's line of sight.

Gunnarr slowed his pace, his heart beating solidly against the ground beneath him. The undergrowth was thinning, but the sound of his limbs as he dragged them through the foliage seemed to be louder than ever. He realised that he could not hear Kelda. For once she had stayed back, watching as he pressed forward.

Within two more yards he breached the cover of the last bush. Once he did the long grass died away into tough, cropped shoots. His head and shoulders had emerged on an elevated ridge that overlooked the water, although from how high up he could not say. The men were still hidden from view somewhere beneath him, but the low voice continued to talk, almost incessantly.

'Look at this, stupid, stupid ...'

It was only when his face was barely inches from the edge of the bank that Gunnarr for the first time felt a stab of unease. He glanced backwards. Kelda was watching him from the bushes, her face frozen with anticipation. He shook away his thoughts and went on. Pushing with his toes, he eased himself forward until the grass parted from his vision and the bright water flashed up at him from below. His eyes swallowed in the scene, and his breath died upon his lips.

A man was standing below him at the edge of the water. He was facing the opposite direction, hands on his hips, as if deep in thought. Gunnarr was so close that he could see grains of dirt in the man's scalp where his hair thinned at the back of his head. Though he was clad in a brown woollen tunic, the man's shoulders were shaking as if through cold, and at intervals he would place his hands into his hair and clutch at it as if intending to pull it free.

It was not to him that Gunnarr's eyes were drawn, though. Instead, he found himself looking in the same direction that the man was staring. There his gaze fell upon the second man, the high-voiced one, and the sight caused Gunnarr's hands to clench involuntarily around fistfuls of grass.

The second man was nearer to being a boy. He could not have been much older than Gunnarr. He was lying on his back in a shallow point in the middle of the stream, naked, his pale skin very bright amidst the greyness of the river rocks. He could almost have been bathing, but the rushing water was surging against the crown of his head and pouring over into his open eyes and mouth, and the boy was not in the least bit conscious of it.

A splash of movement sounded from below, and Gunnarr almost jolted with shock as the man began to stride across to where the boy lay. For once the man's lips had fallen silent, and the sound of the water sloshing around his feet was the only noise to mask that of Gunnarr's heartbeat. The man came to stand over the boy's body and stooped to peer down at it, like a hunter studying a paw print. He gazed at the corpse for a long while, his lips pursed questioningly, and then Gunnarr realised that a knife was in the man's hand. With a sudden movement, he dropped to a knee in the water and began jerking his arm back and forth in a swift cutting motion.

The sight caused Gunnarr to lock rigid with shock. He clamped shut his jaw and tried to avert his eyes. And as soon as he did, he knew immediately that he had been found.

He must have made a sound. Some rustle of grass, or snap of a twig. With dread, he rolled his eyes back towards the scene, and found the man crouched frozen over the body, his head up and alert and his eyes roving slowly across the river bank directly below where Gunnarr lay. Gunnarr could see the man's face for the first time. It was not one he recognised. It was the kind of drained, hollow face that displayed every bone, every muscle that moved beneath the skin. His complexion was the colour of week-old bruises, and his thin brown hair hung so closely to his face that his ears protruded through it. His eyes were creeping steadily upwards, seeking someone out. For a heartbeat Gunnarr was trapped with indecision. Then his muscles twitched and came alive again, and with a burst of sound he found himself bolting from his hiding place and scrambling back towards the bushes.

He found Kelda blocking his path, waiting for him, her face barely inches from his own.

'Kelda, go back,' he urged.

For a moment he saw a flicker of confusion pass across her face, the shadow of an uncertain smile giving way to a crease of concern.

Footsteps started splashing through the water down below.

'Run back!' he told her again, his voice almost a shout this time, and finally her eyes flicked past him and back again and she seemed to understand.

She clasped his hand. 'Come on!'

But Gunnarr hesitated. The ground around them shook as a weight leapt against the bank beneath their feet. Kelda screamed and skittered backwards. She grabbed for Gunnarr's arm again, but he shook free of her grasp and fixed his eyes on the edge of the bank.

With a thud, a hand snapped up over the side and clutched hold of the grass. It was trembling with effort, the nails clawing down into the soft earth. With a crack of broken branches, Kelda was gone, vanished into the undergrowth, but Gunnarr realised that he was not going to follow. Thoughts, or memories, were racing through his mind so fast that he did not know what they were, but he knew that he had to stay. He rose to his feet and stepped forward towards the river.

The man was halfway through hauling himself up over the bank, the top of his head cresting the side, but he must have heard Gunnarr's movement and feared an attack raining down from above while he was helpless, for his hands pushed free of the bank and he crashed back down into the water.

Slowly, Gunnarr continued forward. As he leaned out cautiously over the side he found the man staring up at him from below, his body tensed, ready to spring forward or dart backwards at the slightest flinch. They studied each other's eyes for a moment, and then the man's features stretched into a twitching grin.

14

'Greetings, little friend. What are you doing up there?' His voice was speaking different words to his eyes.

Gunnarr placed a hand on the ground and came warily down the slope to the stream floor. The man watched every step, twisting his neck to follow the movement. Behind him, the body still lay in the water like a log. Gunnarr's eyes must have flicked towards it, for the man also glanced quickly around at the sight, and then turned back to Gunnarr with a short awkward laugh.

'I know you, I think,' the man said, as Gunnarr reached the fine shale gravel that bordered the stream. 'You're an Egilsson.'

'Folkvarr was my father,' Gunnarr corrected instinctively, with such conviction that the man shrank his chin into his neck and gave a smirk.

'That's right, Folkvarr's lad. Too fair to be Egil's own. What are you doing up here, boy?'

Gunnarr glanced again at the pale figure lying in the water. Blood was bubbling out of a dark vent in his chest and rinsing down his thighs in long brown streaks. Gunnarr gathered his breath. 'You should not have done that.'

The man glanced around at the body again and then eyed Gunnarr with a sideways look. 'How long were you up there?'

Gunnarr offered no reply, so the man continued.

'He's my son, of sorts. I've fostered him as Egil has you, kept him fed when I've had scarcely enough for my own. He liked coming up here with me.' He stopped there, as if that were explanation enough, and pressed a positive smile through closed lips.

'You should not have done it,' Gunnarr repeated.

Like water, the smile drained from the man's face. His eyes hardened. 'And who says so?'

Gunnarr answered without hesitation. 'The rule.'

15

The man spat. 'Egil's rule.' He seemed to be finished, and then the next words erupted as a shout. 'And what's that got to do with me? I never supported his claim. He was a man just like me once.'

Gunnarr shifted his weight. The temper had revealed itself, and now the man seemed to loom over Gunnarr, darkening like gathering storm clouds. The bloodied knife had appeared in his hand, apparently plucked from the air.

'What were you doing to him?' Gunnarr asked.

The man stared at Gunnarr for a moment and then turned over the knife in his hand, speaking more softly. 'Opening his chest to the sky so that his spirit might escape, like the old ways for the dead. The old ways that all men of Helvik used to follow,' he added in a louder voice. 'Your father's rule is taking that away from us as well.'

'He's not my fa—' Gunnarr began, but that was all that he had time to say.

In a flash of movement the man sprang forward and snatched hold of Gunnarr's arm. Gunnarr heard himself yelp and flailed out with his free fist, battering muscle, but the man dropped the knife and latched onto that arm as well. The wiry strength of his grip lifted Gunnarr from his feet, sapping his power away. The man's face was ablaze with madness. His fingers drove so deep into Gunnarr's arms that it felt like they were bending his bones. Agonised, Gunnarr twisted violently in the air, wriggling half loose, and from the side of his vision saw the stream rushing up to meet him. He hit the icy water with a clunk, and pain jarred through his bones as his hip came down upon a jutting rock.

The pain caused him to croak and convulse. His body sought to double over into a ball, but the man was kneeling on top of him, snarling in the thrashing spray as he sought to lock Gunnarr's arms down against his sides. Gunnarr screamed and kicked out at the man's groin, but he could generate no force. His strength was leaving him, his heart hammering against his ribs. He rolled onto his side, turbid water sloshing up to rush down his throat, and there on the river bank he saw the dead boy's clothes lying in a ragged heap across the stones. A cry came unbidden to his lips.

'Help!'

A hand clubbed down against his nose and mouth, trying to smother his cries, but Gunnarr twisted his neck free again.

'Help me!' His words came out high-pitched and shrieking, crying out to anyone that could hear. His throat felt like it was tearing. With a shout of his own, the man kicked Gunnarr hard in the ribs. The last of his air was driven from his lungs, and his cries turned into an empty gasp.

From somewhere far off behind him, there came a ringing shout. Someone was roaring at the top of their lungs. Gunnarr grunted with hope, and the man's head jolted upwards at the sound. And yet it was a shrill, thin voice. A girl's voice trying to sound fearsome. A little girl. Kelda, Gunnarr thought. She had come back for him.

A hidden energy flared in his chest, and he fought with renewed vigour to break free. The man was distracted, his grasp relaxed only slightly, but it was enough for Gunnarr to squirm loose. Still doubled over with pain, he tripped onto the river bank and dragged himself clear of the water.

Kelda was scrambling down the bank and arriving at the water's edge, her delicate features scrunched with aggression, seemingly unafraid. She looked pathetically small, a child playing a game, as he had been only moments before. Gunnarr's heart went out to her as he watched her play her

17

role so dutifully, waving her stick left and right as she roared, just as he had told her to.

'Run!' he tried to call to her, to beg of her, but his voice was an airless whisper. He could only look at her, and before his eyes he saw the change that came across her face as she took in the scene properly for the first time. In the space of a heartbeat he saw the game become reality, her bravery turn to foolishness, and her innocence revealed as weakness.

Her cry fell silent when she saw the intent in the eyes of the man who still knelt in the middle of the stream, glaring at her. The stick fell forgotten from her hand when she turned her head to the boy in the water, whose mouth was gaping further and further apart with the weight of the liquid filling it, as if he was screaming in silent anguish. But it was when she turned to look at Gunnarr that the last of her resolve finally snapped, for there she must have seen something that she never had before: fear in his eyes.

Her face and body seemed to go limp. The focus drained from her eyes and they glazed over with terror. Gunnarr tried to drag himself towards her, but he was not half as quick as the man, who saw the girl's senses leave her and surged eagerly from the water to take advantage. Kelda did not so much as react to his movement, like a hare transfixed by a stoat, and the man caught hold of her easily, a hand on each of her shoulders. For an instant he paused, thrown by her lack of resistance. Then he released an awful sound, like a beast about to gorge away a yearning hunger, and dropped to his knees at her feet.

'Gunnarr,' Kelda murmured quietly, as the man started tearing at her clothes, but otherwise she stood as still as a carving.

Gunnarr had plenty of time to choose his spot. The man was engrossed, intoxicated, his head bowed and hands shaking as he fumbled with the ties on Kelda's smock. His ears were deaf to footsteps. The knife that he'd discarded as he wrestled Gunnarr to the ground was forgotten, or at least it had been until Gunnarr had retrieved it from the shallows. Even Kelda did not give Gunnarr away, so numb with fear that she barely seemed to notice his creeping approach even when he stood barely a yard from her face. As he stood looking down at the man's shoulders, Gunnarr could hear his ragged breathing, coarse and urgent. He raised the knife two-handed over his head, and dragged it downwards with all of the strength he could muster.

The man erupted upwards with such force that Gunnarr was hurled backwards into the stream once again. Only a quiet groan escaped the man's lips, but his neck arched as if he was being pulled by the hair, and his mouth opened so wide that the skin on his face might have ripped.

Gunnarr stared up at his work with morbid fascination. The knife had entered just beside the right shoulder blade and there it remained, almost hilt deep. He was certain that that would be enough, that the man would soon sink to his knees, but he did not. Instead he whirled in fury, and his eyes found Gunnarr lying in the water at his feet. A crazed expression burned on the man's face. He began to lumber forward. Gunnarr scrambled to his feet and drew the curved skinning knife from his belt.

'Kelda, go back,' he said, his eyes never leaving the man that stood poised in front of him. And this time she listened.

When they eventually found him, as the evening shadows began to fall, he was still standing exactly as he had been when Kelda left him, ankle deep in the water, knife in hand. But this time his tunic was ripped open from neck to navel. His skin was as pale as salt. Drops of blood dripped from his white-blond hair and daubed his trembling hands. And his eyes were staring only at the corpse that lay face down at his feet, half in and half out of the water.

Expecting to find two dead boys and a killer to trail, the search party had set three hounds upon the scent. The first that Gunnarr knew of their arrival was the slate-grey bitch that came sniffing around the corpses and licking at his fingers. He looked up and found Egil striding hurriedly towards him through the water, his black cloak streaming from his shoulders.

Ten or so other men had come with him. One of them carried Kelda on his back. She was shouting and pointing needlessly, for they had all seen him by now. The boys had been allowed to come as well, it seemed. Hákon, Fafrir, Bjǫrn and Eiric were all there, running to keep up with the others. All of this Gunnarr witnessed only fleetingly, and then inevitably his eyes would return to the bloody pile at his feet.

Egil hugged him when he reached him, but Gunnarr barely noticed. Breathless and excited, the boys clamoured around him, all speaking at once, but he heard only some of their words. Someone gently eased the knife from his grip. He did not feel it go.

Hákon, the oldest of the boys at fifteen, stepped across Gunnarr's vision and dropped to his knees beside the corpse, leaning very close so as to demonstrate that death and gore could draw no fear from him. He studied the body with a stern face, crinkling his nose slightly.

'Gods, Gunnarr,' he exclaimed, peering upwards, 'you've made a right old mess of him!'

Gunnarr stared down at the corpse, the countless stab wounds that had left the man's back a mire of red and pink. 'He would not die,' he said quietly.

Egil placed an arm across Gunnarr's shoulders. 'Sometimes a man will move even when the life is gone from him. But you are too young to be learning that.'

'You were that busy stabbing him that you didn't give him chance to die!' Hákon jibed. The other boys started to giggle.

Egil's stiff voice broke in and cut off their titters. 'Do not tease your brother.'

'I didn't,' Hákon protested, with a rebellious smirk. 'I teased Gunnarr.' He sauntered off to study the other body. The rest of Egil's sons followed him, gawping and exclaiming.

An old lame horse had been towed up the trail with the men. When the time came to leave, darkness gathering, they wrapped Gunnarr in a blanket and lifted him onto its back, seating Kelda up in front of him and Bjǫrn behind to keep him warm. Egil himself led the beast by the mane, the hounds padding along just in front, while Eiric scurried along at his father's side and asked questions about death and dying, which Egil answered with brusque, direct replies. Fafrir and Hákon marched along some twenty yards in front of everyone else, half-jogging to make sure that it was so, two silhouettes shrinking into the sunset.

For much of the journey Gunnarr leaned back against Bjǫrn's chest and dozed, his chin resting on top of Kelda's head as she did the same against him. When at one point a misplaced step from the horse jolted him half awake, he heard his name being spoken, and realised that Egil was in conversation with one of the other men. He kept his eyes closed and listened.

'We are all happy to find him alive, Egil, but we cannot ignore the fact that we also found two that were not.'

'Aye, and one of them the killer of the other,' Egil replied dismissively.

'Are we sure of that?'

Egil huffed with annoyance. 'Of course we bloody are. Thorgen's relationship with that boy was well known. Just ask his poor wife.'

'Hákon says that Thorgen was using Rolf as a woman, and that Gunnarr was watching them so that he could learn what to do with Kelda.' It was Eiric's young voice. Both men ignored the comment, and Egil went on.

'We have Kelda's account to vouch for Gunnarr. He's a boy of twelve, not some blood-hungry cur. Today is the first time he's killed anyone, and the poor lad has scared himself half to death in doing so.'

'I didn't know that your rule made exceptions for youths.'

Egil's voice quickened. 'Randulf, our kingdom has only one rule, and I was the one that devised it. Do you think I'm likely to have forgotten what it says? When Thorgen killed Rolf, it was him that broke the rule. Gunnar witnessed it, and he punished the culprit. He has upheld the rule, not broken it.'

The man named Randulf persisted. 'I still don't think you can just ignore that this happened. People will ask questions.'

'What do you want me to say, Randulf, that I will put my own son to death? Our people have barely made it through winter without starving. They have more pressing concerns.'

Randulf sighed. 'You might at least punish him of sorts. To teach him, and the townsfolk, that his actions were at best reckless.'

'I'll do no such thing,' Gunnarr heard Egil reply firmly. 'Life has never been easy for Gunnarr. He lost Folkvarr in the time before there was a rule, and so he understands why we have need of one. Brave is what his actions were. And our town needs men brave enough to do what is right.'

They reached the town after darkness fell. A crowd had gathered just inside the gates to wait for their return. Night torches had been lit around the walls. By the glow of their orange light Gunnarr found his mother standing beside Kelda's. She smiled cheerfully and raised her hand in a wave. Though she loved him more than any other, she had a trust in him that meant she was always the last to worry about his safety. The expression on Kelda's mother's face, though, could not have been greater in contrast. The sight of it cleared the sleepiness from Gunnarr's head, and filled him with a sudden urgency.

Egil came to a halt with the horse and the mothers started to make their way over. Hands reached up and guided Gunnarr down from his seat, and as soon as his feet touched the ground he turned around to face Kelda. She was still half asleep, her eyes wrinkled against the glare of the torches, but she pushed her lips into a conspirator's smile when she looked at him.

'I'm sorry that you'll get in trouble now,' he told her.

Kelda made a face, and was about to reply when her mother arrived and took her sharply by the arm.

'Just look at the state of them,' she exclaimed, standing back to gaze in horror at the two children. 'I'm sorry Frejya, this is no reflection on you, but I will not have the two of them playing together any more, I just won't.' She jerked Kelda by the arm and started dragging her forcefully away, continuing to scold her as they went.

'Goodnight, Kelda,' Gunnarr stepped forward and called after her.

Kelda looked back over her shoulder and darted free of her mother's grasp. Reaching quickly inside her smock, she produced something from her pocket and placed it between her hands. Just before her mother wrenched her away again, she snatched her thumbs up to her lips and blew. A whistle pierced out into the night's sky, as clear and pure as any birdsong.

Chapter One

The outrider approached at a gallop, hair billowing, and reined to a skidding halt at Egil's right hand. His horse's mouth and nostrils were covered in strings of white mucus. Blood ran down its pasterns from kicking up the sharp mountain stones.

'How many?' Egil asked gravely, reaching up to take hold of the bridle.

The scout's name was Torleik, a son of Egil's cousin. He slid down from the steaming mount with a thud. 'Enough for me to see that there was little use in counting them all.' His mouth twitched briefly into a quivering smile, but he swallowed with uncertainty halfway through, and it did not return.

Egil tugged at the horse's noseband as it snorted and threw its head. 'Do they march?'

'They make camp, just beyond the ridge. The rearguard is still arriving.'

Egil nodded brusquely, and turned away. Slowly, he let his eyes wander up the beaten highland path that wound into the mountains until it was lost, trying to take it all in. The horse shied again and he lost patience with it, thrusting control of it back to its rider with a growl of annoyance.

'Father. Steingarth?' he heard his second son, Fafrir, venture from behind him, and other voices murmured in concurrence.

'Aye,' Egil sighed, turning back to Torleik, 'what of Steingarth and the other hill settlements?'

'Fallen, I suppose,' Torleik answered, still breathless from the ride. 'Of prisoners I saw no sign, but there is smoke to the north-east, and I think I saw some to the west as well, where Blendal sits.'

Egil sucked on his lip and spat on the ground. Only a fool could have expected different. That black part of the night before dawn had brought wails and clangs and rumbling footsteps tumbling down off the slopes, as if all the barrows had opened and the ghouls were running riot in the darkness. Now he knew that something far more threatening awaited them beyond the horizon.

It was approaching mid-morning already, the sunlight still pale with immaturity. Egil stood just below the summit of the first of the foothills, at the elbow of a sharp twist in the road where a weary old hawthorn tree grew so stooped that the children would run up and down its trunk in summer. At his back were his most trusted men. They had dug out their shields and tough leather armour, the swords and spears of their fathers, and now they were waiting, tense and restless. In number, they were no more than ten: his sons, old friends, wise heads. As he turned around to face them they pressed inwards with anticipation, but Egil looked off beyond their eager eyes and instead gazed down at the paltry town some five hundred yards in the distance below.

Helvik. His town. He'd become an old man quickly during the years of his rule, and his sons were pushing for him to name a successor and step aside, but Helvik was still his town. She sat miserably on a scrap of bleak coastline, hunched around a wind-battered bay that bordered the green seas of the north. From a distance, her surrounding pasture looked bleached and poxed, her wooden stockade all sunken and damp and mouldy. So few buildings sat within her walls that outsiders might call her a village or an outpost rather than a town. To Egil, she resembled a tired old grandmother clutching a gaggle of children within her feeble arms. And as he looked down upon her, it was as if he could see her dying quietly before his eyes.

'Father, we cannot just stand here. We must act!'

It was Hákon, eldest of Egil's sons and growing more assertive by the day. He wore the rusted coat of ringmail that had belonged to Egil's own father, though it looked to be too broad for his shoulders. The other men, Egil could see, were becoming just as restive, but he was now sufficiently old that his silence ought to have been able to hold an audience as well as his words could. He rolled an admonishing look in Hákon's direction, and resumed his contemplation.

For years his town had been dogged by sickness. It was mid-autumn. The women should have been in the barn winnowing the barley, the boys and girls out in the fields pulling turnips amid the gentle warmth of a benevolent sun. Instead, the sky was choked with rain clouds, as it had been for the past three harvest seasons. Any crops that had scavenged enough sunlight to grow now lay rotting in the fields. Once, Egil's people might have relied on the fruits of the sea to sustain them, but the fish that once had teemed in the cold clean waters were gone, hunted to exhaustion or tempted away by some enticing current, so that the longboat beached on their shore might as well have been driftwood. The scrawny beasts that sniffed around the fields did not have the meat on their bones to make them worth killing, though killed they would have to be once winter came, or else lost to the cold or starved out on the frozen grass. It was set to be the worst famine of all those that Egil could remember. And now this.

'They could be here at any moment,' Hákon pressed. 'We must at least tell the men to arm themselves.'

Egil gave a weary smile. 'Hákon, if they heard the sounds that you and I did last night and they still haven't thought to arm themselves, then they're not the sort of men we need.' He sighed, and his feet crunched in the gravel as he turned once again to gaze up into the barren hills. 'Bjǫrn,' he said, without turning around. 'Go down and fetch Meili.'

Wordlessly, his youngest son detached himself from the group and started back down the rutted road towards town. Egil could hear the other men muttering under their breaths, and waited for Hákon to speak. In fact, it was Fafrir who responded.

'Father,' he queried gently, 'one man against what some say is the largest army ever to have marched?'

Egil crunched around to face them, and opened his hands. 'One man against thousands is a poor contest,' he agreed. 'But sending a hundred against the same number would gain us little, and lose us much.'

While they waited, Egil studied their faces. Uncertainty lingered in some of their eyes, but they were all loyal men who trusted his experience and remembered how he'd served them in the past. Yet in truth, he thought, what do I know? This was as new to him as to any of them. No invading force ever bothered with Helvik, even if they did find a waystone that acknowledged it. Theirs was a realm that had not needed to raise an army in living memory. And yet Helvik had seen no shortage of blood.

Egil ran his eyes along the group standing before him, remembering then that most of the good men, the truly good men who he would want by his side at a time such as this, were already dead. They may not have had food for their children, but the soldiers of Helvik had always had their pride. A history of feuding clans had savaged the population, until it became ingrained within the culture of the town. Year upon year, the slightest of insults against family honour were ruthlessly punished. Blood paid for blood. Brother avenged brother, cousin avenged cousin. There was always someone owed vengeance. Helvik had seemed intent on becoming a town of widows.

Thoughts of those days, of the decimation of his generation, brought the same memory they always did to Egil's mind. He glanced to his right and found where Gunnarr Folkvarrsson stood nearby, keeping a respectful silence. So tall he was now, white-blond hair and a broad face of wind-weathered skin. Folkvarr's sword was under his arm, and Egil looked at it and remembered the night when blood ties had forced him to watch his truest friend slain before the eyes of his wife and only son. It had been the last that Egil could tolerate; as soon as he was named ruler of Helvik, he made one desperate bid to preserve his people.

As an isolated realm, raging sea on one side and towering mountains the other, Helvik had developed a society far different from the other kingdoms occupying the same sprawling continent. Its inhabitants had always been free to live as they chose. If they wanted to steal from each other, they could steal. If they wanted to fight each other, they could fight. Men chose their own culprits and their own punishments, and any attempts by the people to live in harmony had no other basis than the unfortunate need for coexistence. Rulers like Egil were followed purely because they had proven themselves most fit to lead. There were no noblemen, no peasants, no slaves. No restraining principles determined by any power that claimed to have greater authority than that of the ordinary autonomous man. No rules. That was, until Egil imposed one upon them.

It was a single rule, known by the townsfolk simply as 'the rule', and every inhabitant had agreed to either leave or submit to its governance. It was simple, self-implementing, requiring no detail, no interpretation, no single enforcer. Its wording was plain: 'No person of Helvik may kill another person of Helvik. Any person who breaks this rule is no longer a person of Helvik.'

From that day forward, a line was drawn under the events of the past. When old grievances surfaced and the call of the sword was too strong, the rule stopped the blight of vengeance from spreading. Those who broke the rule lost their place in society, and so became liable to be struck down in retribution by any person wishing to claim it; for the rule said nothing against taking the lives of those who were not persons of Helvik. Thus, such punishers were protected from recrimination, for in the eyes of the rule they had done nothing wrong, and any who wished to retaliate against them would have to break the rule themselves in order to do so.

It was Egil's proudest achievement. The years that had passed since that day had not been enough to rebuild a broken population, especially when that time had seen only a handful of decent harvests, but nevertheless Egil had felt that, since the inception of the rule, Helvik had finally begun to pull together. It had started to fight back against the curse that had gripped it for so long.

Yet now it was faced with complete extinction.

The rumours had existed for many moons. Any tradesman who still saw reason to battle his way over the mountains to Helvik carried tales of vast armies sweeping across the northern lands. They were the soldiers of Hálfdanr Svarti, branded 'the Black' by virtue of a mane of hair so dark amongst the fair heads of the north that he resembled a rook among doves, though others claimed his name befit the colour of his heart. Ruler of the neighbouring kingdom of Agóir, he had set about growing his holdings to north and east, and his armies had sacked every stronghold they had come across in a relentless surge of slaughter. Those that resisted were butchered and thrown onto bonfires, their women wrenched to their feet and shackled into slavery. Already the kingdoms of Vestfold and Raumariki, along with great swathes of Vingulmörk and vast Heiómork, had been added to his dominion. Now his nose had sniffed something in the air to the west, and one of his armies had arrived at the doors of Helvik.

A familiar voice dragged Egil from his thoughts.

'I say we strike at them now. They're unprepared, weary from the march.'

Eiric. Egil's second youngest, wilful as ever. Egil looked back down the slope to the gates of the town, and saw Bjǫrn re-emerge with the tall figure of Meili at his side, donning his armour as he walked.

'No,' he murmured. 'First let us see if words can do what iron cannot.'

When Meili arrived, Egil took him aside and held a brief whispered conference, before sending him alone into the hills on Torleik's stumbling horse. Though he was old now, and had to drink more than was good for him to keep the chill from his bones, Meili was still the town's most famous sword. As a youth, he had left Helvik to fight as a mercenary in all the greatest battles of the age, and soon word of his exploits

30

had spread from the sea in the south to the ice-lands in the north. That he had managed to survive was a surprise; even more so was that, once it was over, he had chosen to return to his damp and miserable home, when all the world knew songs that mentioned his name. Whoever the invaders might be, they would surely have heard of Meili. And when faced with him, Egil was certain, they would either feel fear or respect.

He was out of sight beyond the ridge for only a short time. Then the horse carried him back down again with his throat hanging open and his blood drained over his chest. Sheep shit had been forced down his ears. His eyes they had cut out and stuffed into his cheeks like plums.

Egil's arms were shaking as he lifted the old man's body from the saddle. 'To the walls,' he ordered grimly, and his men rushed to obey.

As night fell, all the men of Helvik stood lined along the town's spiked parapet, wrapped in thick felts, watching the northern horizon glow orange with the camp fires of the enemy. They had made a fire of their own too, on which they settled the body of Meili to sizzle and hiss by the water's edge. Not one of them expected to see dawn. Yet the sun rose the following morning and the mountain road lay empty as the mist cleared. Egil sent some boys out to bring the rest of the livestock inside the walls, and then the gates were barred and bolstered.

They came that same morning, though not in the manner that Egil expected. One of the younger men gave a shout, and as Egil craned against the parapet he picked out a solitary figure ambling down the mountain track. The stranger took his time, stopping often as if to take in the sea view, until he came down off the heights and made his way right up to the gates. He drew to a halt well within the range of a spear, and called up at the walls, barely bothering to raise his voice.

'I'll see the leader of this place, please.' Then he settled down on the damp earth to wait.

Many of Helvik's men offered to gut the stranger and take his eyes, but Egil came down off the walltop and ordered the gates unbolstered. The man who paced easily through the entrance had the look of no stranger to battle. He had a barrel chest and sturdy gut, scarred forearms naked to the wind, a wild beard that almost buried his mouth. The only armour that he wore was a faded leather kirtle, but he must have had wealth, for it reached almost down to his knees.

Helvik's soldiers gathered menacingly about him, but the man didn't so much as glance at them. He nodded a greeting to Egil, thanked him for granting an audience, and then spoke plainly to all that could hear.

'My name is Olaf Gudrødsson, ruler of that portion of Vestfold that men now call Geirstad. I share the same blood as Hálfdanr Svarti, and that is my army on your hilltop. Your settlement is the smallest I have faced on my journey, and I've enough men at my back to sack a place ten times the size. We are footsore from days of marching, but if you insist we will attack with all haste, and be clearing away your bodies before the tides change. Should you wish to avoid that fate, have every single thing of value, every scrap of precious stone or metal in this village, loaded up and delivered to me before midday tomorrow.'

Finished, he did not wait for a reply. He turned and walked himself out of the gates again, whistling a tune through his teeth.

Chapter Two

On the bench in the master's chamber of the longhall of Helvik, the oil lamp began to flicker.

Sitting alone on his wooden sleeping berth, Egil lifted his eyes from the packed-earth floor and stared across at the flame. It was dying, spluttering weakly for breath, and the wash of orange light that it cast out into the gloom was slowly shrinking inwards. Egil glanced up through the smoke-hole in the roof, and saw a lighter shade of black. Beyond the walls he could hear the waves falling back out to sea. Dawn, he thought. He put on his cloak, and ducked through the partition door.

On quiet feet, he passed through the dim main hall, listening to the gentle sounds of the sleepers on his right. The logs in the central fire pit were charred black bones with red bellies, as grey on the tops as the heads of old men. He stooped to pick up a fresh piece of wood and dropped it onto the ashes. His two wolfhounds lay on their sides in the glow of the flames. They were motionless apart from their uppermost ears, which lifted to follow his progress.

Night had rolled in beneath an empty sky, the stars twinkling with cold. As Egil slipped out through the doorway, the last of them were fading and the black horizon was faltering to the east. He hitched his cloak closer about his shoulders, and headed towards the light.

His men had not trusted the word of Olaf Gudrødsson, and for the second night in succession they had slept out upon the walls, but Egil had elected not to join them, and sequestered himself in the longhall instead. It sat upon a thin strip of land that reached out into the seawater to form the western arm of the bay, secluded from the rest of the town. Egil wandered down the narrow causeway and turned left along the stony beach, until he reached the place where the town walls met the shore.

Up on the battlements, the air was brisk, a breeze coming in off the sea. Only the sentries were awake, roving their heads back and forth through the blackness. The rest of the men lay doubled up beneath layers of blankets at their feet, steaming like piles of old leaves. Silence hung in the air like a low fog. Only the waves made a sound.

Egil found Eiric and Bjørn within the first fifty yards. He might have been able to locate them by the sound of their snoring alone, for they drowned out any man nearby. They were lying beneath the same few sheepskins, sprawled out carelessly like drunkards. Crouching, Egil shook them with increasing vigour until they came awake squint-eyed and confused. He mumbled something in their ears, and they dragged themselves up and made for the nearest steps. Egil straightened, and continued on his way.

He went slowly, studying the sleeping faces of those that he passed by the weak light of the torches that blazed at distant intervals. Each man he recognised. The sentries muttered simple greetings as he passed, keeping their eyes forward, and he stopped to share hushed conversations with some. They all professed a yearning to put their spears to use. Egil wondered if they could still say the same with the light of day upon their features.

As he crossed over the footbridge that ran along the top of the main gates, he noticed someone stir in the shadows at his feet. By the light of the torches he saw that it was Gunnarr. He was staring up at Egil, eyes wide and alert, a questioning look upon his face. Egil smiled as he made out another form huddled beneath Gunnarr's cloak and realised that Kelda had come up onto the walls to spend the night out in the cold beside her husband. She was sleeping with her head against his chest, her hair covering most of her face. The bump in her belly was so large that he could see its smooth contours even through the thick rolls of bedding. Egil remembered when he married them in his hall, on a night in midsummer when they were barely more than children, and felt all the more glad that he hadn't denied them.

Gunnarr drew his arms out from the covers and made as if to rise, but Egil quickly shook his head to stay the movement. He smiled at the pair again as Gunnarr dug himself back down into the blankets and closed his eyes, and passed on into the dark.

Fafrir was the last to be found. Together he and Egil walked back towards the longhall beneath the greying sky, and by the time that they arrived the other three were already waiting, huddled inside the small antechamber beyond the outer door.

'Why can't we go inside?' Eiric asked irritably.

'I didn't think you'd want to wake your wives,' his father replied.

'Nonsense!' Eiric declared. 'It's about time they were up. These women will sleep all day if you let them.'

He pushed his way through the inner door, and led the rest of them into the hall. The log that Egil had tossed on the fire was bathed in bright new flame, and the room seemed to sway in the vague and murky light. Two identical sets of benches ran parallel to the walls on either side, with raised berths behind them, upon the west of which the women were huddled in slumber. Eiric and Bjǫrn set about lifting the trestles and table top down from the cross-beams overhead, making little effort to dampen their noise. Hákon lounged in the chair at the head of the table, the flames dancing behind his back.

'Isn't that my seat?' Egil reminded him, and Hákon smiled and slid onto the bench beside his brothers.

'Since we're here together, how about some ale?' Eiric suggested, flashing his teeth with a grin.

Egil came around the table to his chair. 'I'm told there's one cask of ale left for the whole town.'

'And judging by your face, this might be our final chance to drink it.'

Egil smiled wearily at his young son's bravado. 'Save it,' he said, 'for when we have something to celebrate. What I have to say now won't keep you long.' He draped his cloak over the back of his chair and then, rather than bothering to sit, rested against the shoulder of it as he made to begin. Before he could start, Bjǫrn spoke up from his left.

'Shouldn't we wait until Gunnarr arrives?'

Hákon huffed. 'I'm certain we'll manage without him.'

Egil flashed his son a disappointed look. 'I didn't ask Gunnarr to join us. At this moment, his wife has far more need of him than I do.'

Eiric ruffled with mock offence. 'Well, you could say the same thing about mine.'

'Except Brynja, unlike Kelda, isn't fit to burst with child.'

'About bloody time too,' Eiric muttered, and he and Bjǫrn sniggered together. They were boys still in Egil's eyes, but each had already succeeded in adding to his bloodline. Their children lay beside their n

right. Gunnarr and Kelda

Egil knew, but Kelda was a s

went harder on her than mo

Without speaking, Egil wa

near the back of the room an

with a heave of exertion. Whe

was carrying a large trunk made

He held it for a moment befoi

then dropped it onto the table t ... bang.

'There you have it,' he said.

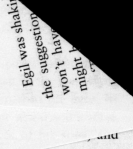

All of his sons came to their feet at once, and stared at the trunk as if they'd never before seen such an object. One of the women tossed in the bedding and muttered some complaint about the noise, but none of the men seemed to hear it. Their silence drew out for a few waiting breaths, and then Fafrir voiced what they all must have been thinking.

'That's it?'

Egil nodded. 'I gathered it myself.'

Fafrir was shaking his head. 'They will say it's not enough.'

'They can say what they like, that's all that there is,' Egil growled, his voice rising in volume. Helvik had never been a place of any magnitude. Its wealth was its freedom, nothing more. What meagre treasures it did possess were scattered around the dusty alcoves of the longhall, odd trinkets and relics from days gone by. Egil had spent the evening going around with the lamp and sweeping up every last one.

With a dubious expression, Hákon lifted the lid of the trunk and stared down at the shadows inside. 'We should ask the men,' he said after a moment. 'Get them each to contribute whatever they have.'

g his head before his son had even finished
. 'Life here for them is miserable enough. I
them give up what small sources of joy they
ave, only to buy more of the same.'

hey wouldn't agree to it anyway,' Bjǫrn stated, slinging
himself back down onto the bench with a thump. 'It's a
glorious fight they want. This paying off our enemies doesn't
sit well with them.'

'Nor I,' Egil responded, 'but we have no need for such
fancies. If all these invaders want is plunder, they are welcome
to it. I will not seek out bloodshed for the sake of a few
bits of metal.'

He sat back down heavily and glowered at the trunk as
if it were the cause of his problems. One after the other, his
sons did the same, apart from Hákon, who remained on his
feet. He stared down at the contents for a moment longer,
and then dropped the lid closed.

'I will fetch someone to carry it to them,' he said, and set
off towards the door.

Egil let him go a few steps before he stopped him. 'Hákon,'
he called reluctantly, and his son must have sensed something
in his tone, for he drew up just as sharply as if he'd reached
the end of a tether. He turned back around, his lips apart
with query. Egil sighed, and leaned forward in his seat. 'I
have found someone to carry it,' he said.

Hákon hesitated for a moment, and looked to his brothers.
They were all watching their father, brows wrinkled with concern.
In the gloom of the sleeping berths someone shifted beneath the
blankets, as if rolling over so as to hear better. The hounds by
the fire had lifted their heads, ears pricked in anticipation.

'Father,' Hákon sighed, coming back towards the table,
'you cannot. If they capture you—'

'I wasn't speaking about myself, Hákon,' Egil said, with heaviness. 'I want you to be the one to take it to them.'

Hákon stopped in his tracks once again. 'Me?' He glanced towards his brothers, and released a breath of hesitant laughter. 'And what might I have done to deserve such an honour above all others?'

Egil felt the familiar tug of sympathy, and did his utmost to suppress it. 'Sometimes as a ruler,' he explained, 'you must demonstrate to your people that you serve them more than they serve you. I will not have any more mutterings that I stood back and sent Meili to his death. But, as you say, if I ride up there myself there is a risk that I may be offering our enemies a gift that they cannot resist. That is why I wish for you to go in my stead.'

Hákon was leaning one hand on the table, his face becoming slowly more drawn. 'And is the risk not nearly as great if I go? I am your eldest son, the next in line to be ruler—'

'I do not recall having named my favoured successor yet,' Egil cut in, and his voice had an edge of reproach to it.

'But still,' Hákon spluttered, 'surely someone else, like Gunnarr perhaps—'

'For the love of the Gods,' Eiric groaned, standing up from the bench, 'I'll bloody take it if you're so scared of losing your eyeballs.'

'No,' Egil said firmly. 'The rest of you have families. I won't put your wives and children through that kind of torment. But that is not why I chose you, Hákon,' he added quickly, seeing his son's face become hurt. 'As you say, you are my oldest son. You are an important figure in this town, and I know that I can trust you as much as any other person in it. Let our adversaries see that we are taking them seriously, but let them also see that no Egilsson is afraid to look his enemies in the eye. You are always asking me for greater responsibilities. Let this be your first of many.'

Hákon shifted his feet on the earth-and-ash floor, and fell silent. His face was downturned, but he was nodding very faintly, so that his tawny hair trembled about his ears. The other boys were watching their brother awkwardly. Behind their exteriors, Egil could see their worry, and as he ran his eyes across them he felt the creep of guilt returning. Their mother would have killed him if she'd seen what he'd just done. But she was long dead, taken by a sickness one morning when the boys were still children, without showing the slightest sign of ill-health. Before her there'd been another one, more children, but they were all gone too, and it seemed like more than a lifetime ago now. His sons were all that Egil had left. And now he was sending one of them into the very heart of danger.

'Come,' he said quietly, climbing to his feet. 'Let us not keep them waiting.'

There were only a handful of horses in Helvik, most of which belonged to Egil's household. They strapped the wooden trunk onto the old bay pony that the boys had learnt to ride on, and gave Hákon a separate mount to lead it up the hill. The sun had risen from behind the headland, and the higher it rose the quieter Hákon seemed to become, but he managed some swagger as he bade farewell to his brothers. As he came finally to his father, Egil slapped him on the back and boosted him up into the saddle.

'Make sure that they know this is everything we have. Tell them that we require nothing in return other than that they move on from this place. And if they don't appear willing to do that, then you remain calm but firm. Say that we have no wish for bloodshed, but at the same time, these are our lands and always have been. We will not sit idle while they're taken from us.'

Hákon gathered his reins, and gave a stern nod from the saddle. 'I'll make you proud, Father,' he promised.

'You did that long ago,' Egil told him. 'Now off you go, and we'll speak when you're back.'

By the time he rode out from the town, all the men were awake and watching Hákon from the walls. Egil climbed up to the battlements to join them, and stood above the gates until his son had meandered up into the cloud and disappeared from sight.

When he returned to the longhall, the women were up and squatting around the fire, frying flat barley bread on battered old pans. Egil took his with one of his grandchildren on his lap, but he found he had scant appetite, and the child devoured most of it. Bjǫrn was snoozing on one of the cots, sitting up against the wicker wall with his mouth hanging open. Egil thought to pass the time by doing the same, and retired to the walled-off section at the south end of the hut that was reserved for him and his woman, should he ever find another. It had its own fire pit, but it wasn't yet cold enough to light it. For a time, Egil thrashed about upon the sheepskins in his berth, but the waves outside sounded almost deafening, and there was too much light coming in through the smoke-hole for him to properly close his eyes.

Midday came, and Hákon did not return. The women were busying themselves on the work benches that ran along the east wall of the room, rolling wicks for the lamps from cottongrass gathered earlier in the year. Fafrir, Eiric and Bjǫrn sat murmuring in low voices around the table. Egil tried to join them, but their conversation felt trivial and forced. He went outside again and spent a while watching

41

Fafrir's son leading Eiric's son and Bjǫrn's daughter, both still young enough to be tottering on their feet, from rock pool to rock pool. He hoped they were as oblivious as they looked.

For the second half of the afternoon, he returned to the wall above the gates and stood staring up into the hills. Come evening, he was still there. The wind had forced a chill into his bones. The wild sky was orange in the west and darkening to soot in the east, like iron lifted out from the coals, and still Hákon didn't come home. Egil's men seemed to sense his emotion, and left him to himself. Before long, he was standing alone in the dark.

He returned to the longhall, and found his sons standing anxiously by the doorway inside. Gunnarr had joined them. The women were sitting very still and quiet, and when the children spoke too loudly they shushed them.

'Will you come with me?' Egil asked.

'Yes,' Gunnarr answered for his brothers. 'But Egil, fighting in this dark ...'

'I do not go to fight today,' Egil said quietly. 'I fear that the horse may have wandered off the path.'

They took no light, in case it was seen. Egil led them, almost running in his haste and intent on maintaining that pace all the way up the slope. But as soon as they pushed through the gates, Eiric gave a shout. Egil looked up, and saw a flame floating down the mountain in the blackness.

'Hákon,' he gasped.

Gunnarr clutched his arm. 'We cannot know that,' he warned, but Egil shook himself free and hastened up the road.

The going was difficult. He had to rely on his feet to distinguish between the hard stone of the path and the soft grass when he strayed. Unseen rocks rolled beneath his feet, and his old legs stumbled many times. He could hear his sons following behind, labouring to keep up.

When he was twenty yards away, he looked up and found that the flame had halted. It glowed from a ridge above his eye line, spitting sparks into the air. A horse gave a whicker, and shifted its feet nervously in the gravel. Egil squatted down and placed a hand over his mouth, his ragged breath racing through his fingers.

'Who's there?' a halting voice called.

'Hákon!' Egil cried.

'Father!'

They came together in the darkness, and Egil dragged Hákon from the saddle and wrapped him into an embrace. The other boys raced up to be alongside. Egil squeezed his son fiercely with relief, and then thrust him back to study him in the torchlight.

'I did it, Father,' Hákon said, and there was a glimmer of pride on his face. 'I won us more time.'

Egil was so overjoyed that he hugged his son again before he really heard the words. He drew back suddenly. 'More time? What do you mean, more time?'

Hákon's cheeks fell slowly. He worked his throat as if swallowing a mouthful. 'They want more payment, Father.'

'More? Well they can go and find their own. They've had all that they're getting.'

Hákon clutched his father's hands. 'You haven't seen their army. Or heard the things they've done to other towns, and will do to us too. We cannot hope to withstand them.'

The joy was gone from Egil's face. 'But that was all there was. We have nothing left to give.'

'Then we must find someone who does,' Hákon said, and his eyes were wide with fear.

Chapter Three

Bjǫrn Egilsson came awake gradually, and for a moment didn't remember where he was.

A cool drizzle finer than sand grains was tickling his cheeks. The sky he saw above him was a shroud of grey vapour, so dense that it swirled and mingled before his eyes like smoke drifting from a damp log smouldering on a low fire. His back ached. His left leg felt like it was lying in something wet, and the woollen cloak that covered him was heavy on the same side with damp. He sighed as his senses returned to him, and then freed an arm to elbow his brother.

Eiric was the deepest of the sleepers. It took three attempts to draw a response, and even then he did no more than throw an elbow back. Bjǫrn rolled over and pressed a finger into his eye.

'Wake up.'

Eiric grunted and slapped the hand away. 'Not until there's someone to kill.'

'I heard a gull.'

'Then tell it to bloody be quiet.'

Bjǫrn shook his head with a helpless smile and clambered to his feet, twisting his cloak back behind his shoulders. He

stumbled over to the prow of the ship and leaned against it
for balance as he looked around. The great serpent carved
into the stempost was glaring off into the distance, head
erect, long tongue tasting the air, but at that moment there
was nothing for it to see but fog. It had closed in on them
from all sides during the black night, so that no more than a
yard of ocean was visible in any direction. The water looked
choppy and restless. It slapped against the hull, shunting the
boat from side to side.

Bjǫrn turned and waded towards the stern, stepping carefully through the clutter of stowed oars and sea-trunks and
blanketed men in various states of repose. The mast and sail
were down and packed away, but even if they hadn't been
Bjǫrn might not have been able to see them through the
brume. The men he skirted around were huddled together
as closely as whelps piled against the teat. All of them were
slumbering, apart from one. The man emerged last through
the folds of vapour, seated by the steering-board at the rear,
where Bjǫrn had placed him with the task of keeping them
on a straight course while the others stole some sleep.

'Well?' Bjǫrn asked quietly, as he gained the man's side.
Toki was his name. He was a full-faced, hulking farm lad,
too young to have ever been a sea-farer, but he'd been the
loudest voice prattling away for most of the voyage, and
Bjǫrn had wanted to see whether weariness might finally
shut him up.

Toki slapped the tiller. 'I haven't let this thing so much as
twitch. Wind stayed down so we shouldn't have done much
drifting. Waves have only started getting up since first light.'

'And did you hear that gull?'

'Now and then since the dark started thinning. Can't tell
if there's lots of them or the same one circling.'

Bjǫrn cast a speculative glance up at the hidden sky above. 'A gull is supposed to be a sign that there's land, isn't it?'

Toki shrugged. He knew as little about sailing, especially the long-distance kind, as Bjǫrn did. The glory days of sea-raiding had missed them by a generation or more, Helvik's sense of adventure having diminished along with her strength. Only a few men aboard the ship were old enough to remember how to read the signs out on the open water, how to chart a course through cloud, and they needed their rest more than most. Bjǫrn decided he would probably have to wait until they roused themselves.

He returned to the bow of the ship, and found Eiric snoring gently with his mouth agape like a day-old corpse. A thin swill of water was running up and down the planks, and his brother had somehow managed to sleep through the night with his head in it, the slop lapping up around his ear every time the boat tipped to the steering-board side. If there was that much leakage up by the prow, then Bjǫrn dreaded to think what it was like beneath the bodies in the low belly of the ship. Once, the vessel had been the pride of Helvik, but in recent years it had become more a resented reminder of better times passed. For almost as long as Bjǫrn could remember it had lain up on the beach on wooden stilts, played on by the children like an old horse, and when the stilts had rotted away no one had bothered to replace them. Moss and slime had caked its hull when, in the half-light just before dawn, Bjǫrn and his men came to drag it free from its berth. But it had floated, and there was no time to require anything more. Bjǫrn just hoped that it continued to do so.

With the sole of his boot, he pressed down gently on Eiric's throat until his brother's mouth started working like that of a landed fish and he burst awake flailing his arms. 'Get up,' Bjǫrn said. 'I need your help.'

Eiric scowled and lay there rubbing his neck. 'What do I know? Just keep going straight and try not to sail up Rán's arse.'

Bjǫrn sighed and kicked his brother in the shoulder. The plan had sounded like such a simple one when they'd volunteered to carry it out. Their father needed riches with which to mollify the invaders, but Helvik had none left, some would say none to begin with, and so it had been decided that a group of Egil's soldiers would take their old boat and sail along the coast until they found somewhere that did have the wealth to spare, and take it from them instead. But by now, the start of the third day of their voyage, they had lost the coast, and a measure of their resolve. Bjǫrn needed his father there, or Hákon at least. It had been his idea, after all. But Egil would not be seen to desert the town at such a time. And Hákon claimed that he had to stay where the invaders could find him, for he was the only one they trusted.

Eiric groaned and got up, wringing the seawater from his hair. 'What happened to your gull?' he asked.

Bjǫrn rested his weary head against the serpent's neck. 'Gone. But Toki heard it too. I've heard it said that you can follow them to land.'

Eiric rubbed at his beard and nodded past his brother's shoulder. 'Why don't we just follow that light?'

Bjǫrn whipped his head around and glared into the fog. There was nothing there, only the cloud dancing slowly before his eyes, opening and closing like drapes in a breeze. He spun back around and aimed a punch at his brother's head, but Eiric caught his fist, and pointed.

This time he saw it. He'd been looking too low before, scanning the tops of the waves, but now he realised with

47

shock that the light was in fact high above him, shining bluntly through the haze like a star on a winter's night. It could have been a great bonfire blazing a mile in the distance, or a tiny lantern hanging there just out of reach. But it was certainly land.

Bjǫrn clamped a hand on his brother's shoulder. 'What make you of that, then?'

'Settlement. Must be,' Eiric replied, crowding closer to the rail. 'A beacon to welcome lost travellers.'

Bjǫrn sucked on his teeth for a moment. 'We need to get out of this fog to see what defends it.'

'Drift in at this speed and they'll have the whole army roused before we're even landed. Even a lonely crofter would turn us back.'

'Aye, but if we rush in then there's no rushing out again.'

Eiric shrugged, and his face came alive with excitement. Bjǫrn studied the eager eyes of his brother and gnawed on his lip, hesitating. He glanced around at his men, still slumbering obliviously beneath their cloaks, and then back out at the light, twinkling there like a prize waiting to be snatched. 'What would our illustrious brothers do at a time like this?' he pondered.

Eiric grinned. 'Hákon would be too busy throwing his guts up over the rail to do anything. Fafrir would doubtless propose we turn for home. And Gunnarr would probably suggest something sensible like mooring up the coast until the fog lifts. But we're not as soft or as clever as them, are we Brother?'

Bjǫrn smiled, but his lower lip was still clamped between his teeth, and his face made an expression like a cat baring its fangs. 'I don't particularly want to lose our father's ship. Especially when we're the only hope he has of saving our home.'

'Courage, little brother,' Eiric urged, slipping an arm around Bjǫrn's shoulders and worrying his cloak. 'Let us take this chance to remind the old man that his young sons are worth every bit what his older ones are. Let us make a friend out of this fog.'

Still Bjǫrn delayed. He gazed again at the light. It seemed to be growing clearer, as somewhere the morning sun rose ever further and burned away the vapour. High above them, a gull released a keening cry. Bjǫrn looked across at his brother, and slapped him heartily between the shoulders. 'Wake the men,' he said, and Eiric whooped and ran to obey.

The raiders were up and seated on their trunks in the work of a moment. Those few that owned mail threw it on and then hurried to get their oars in the water with the others. Bjǫrn bellowed at Toki to steer them straight at the beacon, and then found his sword and slung it over his shoulder and took up his shield from the rail. The men at the oars grunted in unison with each stroke, driving the sleep from their limbs. The head of the vessel lifted, as if the serpent was preparing to strike, and they flew over the water like an eagle skimming for fish.

As sudden as a ram splintering through a gateway, they burst out from the fog and found the whole landscape waiting before them. Two hundred yards ahead, great cliffs the colour of bonemeal reared up into the air. An empty beach, open and flat, lay at their feet. And at the top, framed against the streaked dawn sky, stood a solitary building, the largest and grandest that Bjǫrn Egilsson had ever seen. The treacherous beacon burned in a stand at one end of it, twinkling innocently, guiding the raiders to their prize.

Eiric came to join his brother at the prow, and Bjǫrn roared his rowers to even greater speed. A hundred yards out, as their keel began to smash through the rollers, he noticed a single figure scrambling down a cut in the cliffs towards the shore. The man's feet reached the sand, and he began to labour along the beach to intercept the ship. Bjǫrn gave a grunt of admiration, and drew his sword.

The figure was stumbling the last few paces as the ship ploughed its belly into the ash-grey sand. Bjǫrn stood high against the masthead and looked down at him. He was some kind of old and wretched man, clothed in only a coarse brown robe with an old length of rope about his waist. The top of his head was as bald as a skull, but so symmetrically so that Bjǫrn was tempted to think he had shaved it that way deliberately. He went without boots on his skinny grey legs. He was not even armed.

The man peered up at them and opened a nervous mouth as if to speak, but then he seemed to see something that made his neck gulp and the words crumble on his lips. Too late, he realised he had made a grave mistake. He babbled something in a tongue that Bjǫrn did not understand, a beseeching look upon his face, and then turned and stumbled into a run. Before he had made it two paces, Eiric jumped down into the shallows, caught him by the robe, and hacked him into the sand.

'See?' Eiric roared, turning back to the ship. 'Easy!'

Bjǫrn and the others leapt down into the surf behind him, and he led them towards the cliffs at a run.

Chapter Four

On the eighth day following Olaf Gudrødsson's arrival as a noose around Helvik's throat, Gunnarr Folkvarrsson rose at first light. He dressed in hurried silence so as not to wake his wife and mother, before ducking out into the freshness of dawn to check his traps.

It was a routine that, by now, he could probably have conducted before waking. He let himself out through the bolted east side-gate and stalked through familiar parts of the lowland woods, carefully inspecting each snare. Unfortunately, the outcome of his forages had become all too repetitive as well. The land was parched of wildlife, and all his traps were empty. He wandered weary-eyed down to the shore, hoping to have had better luck with the sea.

By the time that the sun was fully risen, Gunnarr was stooped waist-deep in the ocean shallows. He wore an old pair of sealskin trousers to keep some of the water off, and stepped across the smooth ocean rocks barefooted. His hands moved in brisk, familiar patterns, working across the stiff twine of his nets. After a short while longer he sighed and straightened, smearing a dash of seawater across his furrowed forehead as he flicked a strand of hair away with the back of his palm.

His nets were empty, as usual. Once he would have under-gone the laborious process of drawing them in to the shore first, and replanting them elsewhere if unsuccessful, but he had long since learnt that that was wasted effort. The disappointment had been too much to bear. He snatched a section of netting up to his chest and began trying to knot together an area where the salt had corroded through the joints. At another point further along he noticed a darker piece of material from where Kelda had repaired it previously, and he smiled sadly to himself. The poor girl had spent days trying to mend the nets at one time or another, using anything she could find that would tie, even lengths of her own hair when there was nothing else. With so few fish to be had it seemed there was little point to the exercise, but Gunnarr knew that it wouldn't be long before she insisted on taking another look at them to see what could be done. He often wondered whether she had been born with that positivity, or if it had been beaten into her through Helvik's hard schooling.

A movement inland caught his eye, and he raised a forearm across his brow to watch a rider climbing slowly up the hill-side leading out of town. It could only be Hákon Egilsson. As the oldest son of the ruler of Helvik he had been riding the mountain path regularly to 'negotiate' with the invaders. Gunnarr felt that was a generous term for such one-sided bargaining, but this appeared to be one matter in which his opinion mattered little. So many days of ceaseless waiting had allowed the townsfolk time to scare themselves half to death. Many now saw Hákon as their only hope.

Pointing, he called across to the two friends who were also checking their catches at either side of him, prompting them to straighten their backs and wade over to his position. Ári and Hilario were their names. Like most of those in Gunnarr's life, Ári had been with him for as long as he could remember. Hilario was one of the rare few who had come in from the outside, arriving as a boy with a sprawling family of travellers and finding as a man that he did not want to leave, even as the rest of his kin were disappearing over the hills.

'Mine are empty,' Hilario stated as he drew up beside Gunnarr. He was a short, curly-haired man with a face full of expressions. 'Someone's been at the nets,' he concluded. He often chose being robbed over being unsuccessful.

Ári had caught something, albeit small, and he took a knife and skilfully emptied the fish's innards into the water, using his thumb to hold back some of the dark waste flesh. The good meat would be saved for his wife and son, and the innards would make oil for his lamps. He would have whatever there was left.

'How long do you reckon he'll be up there this time?' Ári asked, giving his blade a quick rinse in the water.

'Not long,' Gunnarr replied, still watching Hákon on his ascent. 'I doubt they're as welcoming when he comes empty-handed.'

Hilario ignored Hákon, instead running an inspecting eye along the lie of Gunnarr's nets. 'I suppose we'll be some of the first to know whether he's persuaded them to be patient,' he said eventually. 'He'll be coming down that hill pretty quickly if not.'

Ári sheathed his knife with a click. 'Or not at all.'

The others murmured in agreement. Together they started to wade back to shore, the splashing of water between their limbs steadily increasing in pitch as the depth shallowed off.

'When will you next speak to Egil, Gunnarr?' Hilario asked.

'There's to be a meeting when Eiric and Bjǫrn return from their raid, to discuss a more permanent solution.'

Hilario smirked with light-hearted affront. 'In the old days they'd hold great big gatherings for the whole town to attend. Is everyone invited to this one?'

'I think Egil worries that might become unruly.'

'Well,' Hilario said, as they reached the stony beach, 'if he does happen to ask for my considered opinion, tell him that if we're going to end up fighting, I'd rather it was sooner than later. Anything is more fun than a famine.'

Gunnarr sat, and began to sweep the dirt from the soles of his feet. He could manage a smile at the words, but he wasn't surprised when Ári did not do the same. His friend had been a stern adolescent when Gunnarr was a child, son to a proud old metal worker who had liked nothing better than to spend the day working himself into the ground whilst complaining about the damage that it did to him and the laziness of those that did not do the same. As a boy, Ári had had a man's concerns. Now a man, he showed no sign of taking the opposite approach. Not that he had any choice.

'You have only yourself to worry about,' Ári said dismally, and his face appeared drawn with the strain of the last few days. 'My Tyr is too young to fight, and before long he'll have a little brother to protect as well as his mother.'

Hilario scoffed, striving, as always, to keep the mood light. 'Well, it seems I'm the only one with a bit of sense in this town. There's little enough food and few enough breasts to suckle on around here without having to share it all with some squalling child.' He looked down at Gunnarr, smiling. 'How long for Kelda now? I saw her yesterday; she looked as if she's carrying an army of her own in that belly.'

Gunnarr's bleak expression made way for a brief smile with the thought of Kelda waddling around beneath the weight of the first child she was carrying. 'Before the close of the moon, they say. Poor lad couldn't be born into a worse situation. He'll probably try and climb back inside once he gets out.'

The three men produced a muted bout of laughter, and Gunnarr began to pull on his boots. At dawn it had looked like the day might stay clear, but already the clouds were rolling in, the same colour as the wet stones on the beach.

'Another day for inside work,' Ári said, glancing up at the sky.

Gunnarr sprang to his feet and brushed off his legs. 'I have two tups turned out on the hillside. I may go and bring them in, before they find themselves roasting over an army's camp fire. But that depends on Eiric and Bjǫrn.'

He went over to stand beside Hilario, who was gazing out to sea.

'They're out there somewhere,' Hilario said. 'But I don't see any sign of them coming back today.'

The others agreed. For a few moments they stood and stared out beyond the waves. Of raids they knew nothing, for Egil had put an end to what had been a dying occurrence. Enough lives had been lost on home soil without going looking for fighting overseas as well, and in some cases it had been asking for bloodshed even to put certain men in the same boat together. There had still been deep-water fishing trips though, sometimes even whale hunts, and as sharp-eyed young lads Gunnarr and the others had been stationed around the prow and told to bellow when they saw something. Gunnarr remembered crowding along the rail with the other sighters, waiting for a glistening back to crest the surface with a hiss from its blow-hole and present them with a target they could drive in to shallow waters and strand on the beaches for killing. But that he had seen once, maybe twice. As with everything else, the people of Helvik had soon learnt to give it up.

'Gunnarr?' From behind them, the sound of a female voice interrupted their viewing.

'Fun's over,' Hilario sighed, without turning around. 'Is that wife or mother?'

Gunnarr swivelled and located the source of the sound. A dainty figure waited politely for him at the edge of the beach.

'Looks to be neither,' he replied, with an air of intrigue.

'Aren't you the lucky the one?' Hilario grinned, suddenly keen to take a look for himself. Gunnarr ignored the comment and left them, walking steadily across the shore to meet the woman.

'Forgive my interruption,' she called in a quick, nervous voice as he approached, and Gunnarr smiled away the apology as he made a short study of her appearance. She wore grubby woollen skirts, tattered and muddied around the bottom and flecked with stains across the front. Her limbs were slim, too slim, and though she attempted to hold herself presentably, her posture was slumped with a look of perennial exhaustion. She smiled self-consciously, and Gunnarr realised that she could be very pretty to some, but for the gauntness of her face, the skin around her eyes being dark and sunken from lack of food and sleep, and the element of worry in her expression.

'What can I do for you?' he asked, his voice soft with immediate concern.

'My name is Tyra,' she began, with an effort. 'Do you know me?'

Gunnarr saw her on her knees in a mess of trampled snow, her face wailing with anguish, blood and tears running down her cheeks. 'Yes,' he answered, stirring with recognition. 'You sometimes speak with my wife. I knew your husband,' he added warily, and her eyes flicked immediately to the ground.

'Perhaps you'd like to sit?' Gunnarr suggested, attempting to smother a moment of awkwardness, but she smiled and shook her head.

'I will not keep you long. I wouldn't have come to you if I were not desperate.'

Her hands were shaking, Gunnarr noticed. The nails on her fingers looked torn and brittle, many of them gone completely. He said nothing, waiting for her to gather the momentum to speak, and she did, with sudden emotion.

'It's my neighbour, Brökk; a brute of a man, just like them all.' She faltered. 'Forgive me,' and Gunnarr shook his head and motioned for her to continue. 'He's been taking the vegetables from my land. I dug some drainage for them last year, and they've come on better than most. It would not be so bad, but I have no animals of my own, and no husband to hunt. They are all I have to feed my boy on.' She hesitated, as if suddenly worried that she was wasting her time. 'I was told—well, I know—that you are the man to help me with such things.'

Gunnarr's features had been set since the first of her words. The familiar flush of anger tightened his jaw.

'I know the kind of man that Brökk is,' he said plainly. 'Leave it with me.'

Tyra relaxed visibly, and a proper smile flashed across her features for the first time. 'Thank you so much, Gunnarr,' she exhaled. 'I didn't know what else to do.'

Gunnarr waved away her thanks, feeling his anger doused slightly by the relief that he saw on her face.

'Please, my son would like to meet you,' she continued, and held out her arm, prompting a grubby little boy to dash out from where he had been stationed among the trees at the edge of the shoreline and career boisterously into her hip, almost knocking her sideways.

Gunnarr smiled through the twinge of guilt he felt upon seeing the child, and bent down to bow his head in greeting. The boy briefly reciprocated the gesture, as he had been taught, before being overcome with a sudden bout of shyness and retreating behind his mother's skirts. It was clear where most of his mother's share of food went, but even the child was scrawny and awkward.

'He's not usually this timid,' Tyra said with embarrassment, trying to pull him gently out from behind her, but the boy gave a squeal and fought back gamely.

'Please,' Gunnarr said, 'you must come and eat with us this morning. Kelda has been preparing a lovely stew.'

As he'd expected, Tyra refused with proud determination. 'That is very kind of you, Gunnarr, but we have already eaten this morning. We won't bother you any longer.' She took her son's hand, and started to draw away.

'Me and Kelda will visit you tomorrow,' Gunnarr told her, and Tyra thanked him again. The little boy shouted a brief goodbye, and scurried away into the trees.

'Where are my two favourite women then?' Gunnarr asked loudly as he stepped through the doorway of his house. It was the same home built by his grandfather many winters ago, with various patches of repair and slight modifications. It sat inland to the north-east, nestled on the fringes of the settlement beneath the sheltered canopy of a small group of rowan trees.

He found them kneeling together on the floor in the middle of the room. 'There's one,' he said, grabbing his mother with one hand and pulling her playfully into his shoulder. 'And there's another!' he exclaimed, reaching down to use his other hand to tug his wife gently upwards and kissing her lovingly on the lips.

Both women laughed happily as he held them in the double embrace. They appeared to have been carding odd scraps of wool and arranging the fibres on top of each other for felting. The square shape laid out on the floor looked to be the perfect size for wrapping an infant in.

'Well that's not going to fit me,' Gunnarr commented, and his mother Frejya thumped him in the stomach. She was shorter now in her old age, and these days to hug her was more like hugging a younger sister than a parent. Strands of grey were beginning to highlight her dull blonde hair and faint webs of blue capillaries had crept across her weathered red cheeks. Yet her eyes were as quick and mischievous as ever, with deep laughter lines extending from the corner of each.

Kelda, to Gunnarr, looked just like she always had. In his eyes she would always be a girl of barely ten winters, with mud in her hair and bruises on her shins. She was almost as short as Frejya, with hair the colour of wet sand, and smooth, pale skin. She had crawled into Gunnarr's heart as a child, without him even noticing, and though she was very much a woman now, more likely to chide his immature behaviour than join in with it, the memory of adventure had never left her face.

'What a lucky man I am to have not one, but two wonderful women to return home to,' he sighed cheerfully.

His mother leant out from his embrace to speak directly to Kelda. 'Such charming words. Do you think there's a chance he didn't catch anything?'

Kelda laughed, and Gunnarr raised both arms above his head and released the pair of them with mock indignation. 'How's my big strong boy?' he asked, stooping down to cup an ear against Kelda's swollen belly, and then, after a brief moment, coming back up again to answer his own question. 'Sleeping, as usual, lazy git.'

'Gunnarr!' both women scolded.

'He can't hear anything,' Gunnarr protested. 'How else would he put up with your nattering?' He smiled away their reproachful faces and took a seat on the floor beside the felting. 'What's been the topic this morning?'

Before the words had even finished leaving his mouth, he regretted the question. The women looked at one another, and then Kelda replied glumly, leaning heavily on her husband's shoulder as she lowered herself back down into a kneeling position.

'Same as every morning, Gunnarr.' She did not say any more. There was no need to. Silence followed her words. Gunnarr exhaled stiffly through his nose and hung his chin a little, as if unable or unwilling to give a reply. Frejya moved closer and placed an arm on the back of his head.

'My son will protect us, Kelda,' she said, with the unwavering confidence that a mother has in her child. 'He has never once let me down, not even when he was a boy.'

Gunnarr's cheeks flushed with affection and embarrassment. 'I have to go out,' he announced, rising and kissing his mother and then his wife firmly on their foreheads, before going to the back of the hut to change his trousers.

'Where to?' Kelda asked casually, returning her eyes to her work.

'Brökk Haldensson has been stealing food from the widow Tyra and her boy,' he replied, hopping briefly as he dislodged the clinging trousers from each leg and searching momentarily for the second pair before snatching them up. 'I told her I'd go and speak to him.'

'As in speak to him with words, or speak to him with a sword?' Kelda enquired with familiarity.

'Sword,' and she heard him fitting it under his arm.

60

She dropped the wool back down into the basket. 'Brökk Haldensson is one of Hákon's closest allies, Gunnarr. You're not going to have a friend left in this town.' She sought out Frejya's eyes, trying to encourage her to offer some support.

'You can't change him, dear,' Frejya said with resignation. 'He's always hated bullies.'

'Brökk has never been my friend, and Hákon and I have not seen eye to eye since we were children,' Gunnarr said as he appeared at Kelda's side once more. He fastened the drawstring of his trousers and took a drink of water from his mother. 'Besides, women like Tyra have no one else to protect them.'

'You do know who her husband was, don't you?' Kelda reminded him, peering upwards so that she could study his reaction.

Gunnarr faltered for a moment, and then focussed his attention on retying his waistband, as if the comment mattered little. 'He was a bad man, who deserved more than what he got, and she of all people should have the scars to remind her of that.'

'But does she know that it was you?'

Of course, Gunnarr thought. How could she forget?

The quiet woman named Tyra had barely been known to anyone in the town. Her husband had made sure of that. He'd kept her like a beast, by all accounts, broken and obedient, penned up for any time of the day and night that she was not working, mastered by him and him alone.

As it was for most of the townsfolk, she had first come to Gunnarr's attention on the day that a man, a boy in fact, barely fifteen, had made the mistake of offering to help her carry whatever it was that her husband had sent her out to fetch. It was said that she had hurriedly refused, but thanked him politely. Too politely for her husband's liking. He had beaten the pair of them to within a yard of death's door.

Tyra had barely been seen again afterwards, and from that moment there was growing disquiet about her treatment. But it was not for men of Helvik to tell others how to treat their wives. The father of the boy, whose right eye had turned white and gone blind after the attack, had made noises about claiming one back from the husband, but he was an old man, and he never fulfilled his promises.

It was Tyra's brother who eventually decided he could stand it no longer, and he lost his life for it. The husband had gutted him in front of his sister, kept his body in their single-roomed hut for three days so that word would not get out. Yet, as always, word did get out, and it was then that Gunnarr had come to be involved.

He remembered being awoken from his bed on a freezing winter's morning. Egil himself stood grave-faced at the door, the air still midnight black beyond his head. 'I wanted to be here to restrain you when you found out,' he said. 'So I decided I would bring the word myself.'

As the sky began to grey, they had trudged through the crunching snow in silence. Egil had insisted that it be he that did the act. 'A leader must be seen to enforce the rules that he creates.' But in the chaos that followed, it was Gunnarr that struck.

The husband had heard them coming. His chosen first weapon had been the scream from Tyra's mouth as he cut into her skin with every step the two men took towards him. Fortunately for them, he'd been the type of man that soon grew tired of a stand-off.

Gunnarr could still remember it all if he let himself. The clattering sound as he battered the husband's sword away and sent it spinning from his grip. Hot breath freezing in the air. In the madness of love, or duty, Tyra had rushed forward to protect her man at the last, her babe in her arms. Gunnarr recalled knocking her to the ground. Her cries of pain and sadness and relief. A frightened look in a cruel man's eye. Blood, almost brown in the pure white snow.

He knelt down and kissed his wife gently on the lips. 'I won't be long,' he said. He went to get up and leave, but she kept a tight hold of his arm.

'Please don't go and get yourself killed, Gunnarr. Brökk is a big man. You've gained enemies all through the town by involving yourself in other people's affairs like this.'

He remembered her saying almost the exact same words the last time, clutching at his hand in the doorway as the snow melted on her cheeks. He'd been able to withstand her then, and this time was no different.

He smiled and kissed her again on the upper lip, one hand placed protectively across her pregnant tummy. 'Better to be yourself and have enemies, than to be someone else and have friends.'

There was a sound to the left. Frejya was smiling fondly, her features almost cracking into laughter. 'How long have you been thinking up that one?' she asked.

Gunnarr felt the haze of memory melt away and a grin return to his face. 'Nearly three days,' he said, and poked her in the stomach so that she doubled over laughing. He stretched up to his feet. 'I'll be back soon.'

He patted his mother affectionately on the shoulder and strode out through the doorway, just as the rain started to fall.

Chapter Five

Olaf Gudrødsson stood framed against the rumbling sky, watching the horse pick its way over the final few yards to the summit and clack across the stones towards him.

'Greetings, Hákon,' he called, stepping out onto the track.

His visitor plodded a few steps closer, and then stopped and gave a nervous nod. He was dressed in the same ancient ringmail he'd be wearing the first time, though he appeared to have left the sword behind. He stayed on his horse, and his eyes darted around the deserted hilltop. 'Do you have somewhere we can speak?' he asked.

Olaf smiled, and swept an arm out to his side. 'This sodden earth is my bed, the leaky sky my blanket, and what little we have to discuss we can do on this very spot. The wind is strong today, but even a voice as treacherous as yours will not carry as far as your father's town.'

Hákon scowled, but made no reply. He glanced around behind his shoulder, and then slid from the saddle with a splash. Short, Olaf remembered, narrow-shouldered. And yet strangely arrogant.

The visitor did not appear willing to speak, so Olaf made a show of leaning out to one side and studying the rear of

Hákon's horse. 'You didn't bring your little pack pony with you,' he observed.

'I need some more time,' Hákon replied. 'My brothers are yet to return.' He was staring away at the ground to his left, barely parting his lips. Some men might have pleaded the words, but this one looked like he was sulking.

'I had noticed,' Olaf confirmed. He paused, and ran a thoughtful tongue along his teeth. 'You said five days.'

'They must have been delayed. They're not used to being at sea.'

'They're not delayed,' Olaf told him. 'They're gone. They'll have fled while they had the chance.'

'You don't know them,' Hákon responded, somewhat haughtily. 'They will come back.'

A single cloth bag was tied to the horse's saddle. Olaf pointed at it. 'What's that?'

Hákon gave a moody shrug, embarrassed. 'A small offering, to make amends for the delay.'

'Fetch it here.'

While Hákon untied the bag, Olaf glanced up at the huddling clouds. He wore loose brown trousers, grubbied up to the knees with mud, and a coal-black cloak that billowed around him in the wind. Both garments were heavy with damp, and his boots were so sodden that they wheezed like old men every time he placed his feet. On their first night in the hills, he and his men had sat around laughing beside blazing fires. But the rain had fallen near enough constantly ever since, and the thin mountain soil was too rocky and windswept to host any natural shelter.

Hákon crunched across the gravel and held the bag at arm's length. Olaf took it and rifled through. It contained one roll of cloth, two of unspun wool, and a small wooden casket not much bigger than his fist.

'What's in the container?'

Hákon cleared his throat. 'Salt.'

'Salt,' Olaf repeated. He stared down into the bag, the cold wind flapping his wet cloak against his face, and if he'd been alone he might even have chuckled at the lunacy concocted when pride and growing age were thrown together.

After thirty-eight long winters, Olaf Gudrødsson ought to have been sat in his longhall in Geirstad, listening to the crackle of a brawling fire and gazing into a good cup of ale. His battles were fought, his name well known; except here, it would seem. Yet the boy had stirred something within him, he was big enough to admit that. Was it jealousy? A desire to show the upstart how a real man did a job? Or even fear? When a man wakes up content, without ambition, he sometimes fears that the Gods will deem his life has run its course, especially when confronted with one so young and full of vigour. In truth, Olaf sensed that he might never really know the reason why. Why, when his young half-brother Hálfdanr had ridden through his gates and said that he was looking for an ally to help extend his kingdom of Agóir westwards, Olaf had risen from the comfort of his chair and, a few days later, found himself marching through the drizzle at the head of the army.

He dropped the bag into the puddles at his feet, and the roll of cloth slapped into the mud. 'I climbed over these hills with an army of five hundred men,' he said. Hákon made to respond, but Olaf held up a hand. 'When we looked down from up here and saw that town of yours below, most of them laughed. They wanted to raze the place and be done with it, get back to civilisation, but then you came riding up here and told us that if we just held off a while longer, we wouldn't regret it. Fool that I am, I believed you, Hákon. I kept the hounds at heel, just like you asked. And now you come here and reward me with some wool and a handful of salt.'

'It's all that there was,' Hákon protested.

'It's an insult,' Olaf growled, kicking the bag and sending the contents skidding across the wet earth. 'What will my men think of me when they see what I'm worth in your eyes?'

Hákon hung his head like a shamed dog, but he kept his eyes grimly in the tops of their sockets, as if embarrassed to look at the gifts scattered by his feet. 'My brothers ...' he muttered.

'How long do you need?' Olaf grunted.

'Could be today, could be tomorrow.'

'And if their boat is sat on the ocean floor? Did you stop to consider that?'

Hákon didn't appear to have an answer. Again his face took on a somewhat resentful expression, when instead Olaf might have expected to see deference, even trepidation. Not used to being spoken to that way, Olaf concluded. That was the problem with being isolated in a place like this: a boy could grow up having never come across a real man to measure himself against, and spend the rest of his life in the misguided belief that he was equal to, even better than, everyone else.

'I think this discussion is over,' Olaf finished. 'Go back to your town, and tell your men to prepare themselves.' He began to turn his shoulder.

'Would it cost you so much just to wait one more day?' Hákon asked helplessly.

Olaf looked back at him, and then raised an arm to point northwards. 'Perhaps you should see how my men answer that. They've been sat up here in the pissing rain, with no fires, no shelter, scarcely any food. At the moment, they'd happily risk life and limb for the prospect of a dry bed.'

'And if you remembered my offer, you would know that there's no need to!'

Olaf paused. A gleam of intrigue brightened his eyes. His boot squelched as he squared himself with Hákon again. He held his tongue, until his guest felt the need to fill the silence.

'I am in line to be the next ruler of Helvik,' Hákon continued, his voice falling back to a murmur. 'Wait until my father names me, and I will give you this land, Olaf. All that I ask in return is that you endorse me as the man to rule it, as your earl.'

Olaf scraped away the hair that had blown across his face, and studied Hákon with a curious expression. A smirk was playing at the corners of his mouth. 'Walk with me,' he said.

He led Hákon a short distance back along the track to the ridge that marked the start of the descent. The sky overhead was so dark that it might have been dusk, and already Olaf could see the thin grey drapes of rain blowing in over the bleak hills to the east. He looked down at Helvik, dwarfed by the landscape around it, and spoke without switching his gaze.

'There is a world beyond this place, Hákon, that I sense people here may know little or nothing about.' He waved a careless arm through the air, as if smearing dirt across the scene that lay before them. 'I never cared for land, in truth. Small men need big kingdoms, just as ugly men need fine clothing.' He glanced across to his counterpart. 'Yet land I have, Hákon. Fertile land, bigger than any you've ever seen. I gave half my kingdom away to a brother half my age, and yet still I have more than I need. Look at your lands, Hákon,' he invited, nodding down the slope towards the leached and sodden pasture. 'To be honest, I'm not sure I want them.'

Hákon scowled out towards the shoreline. The first band of rain blew across them in a sudden gust, rattling against their clothing. 'Then why don't you leave?' he muttered.

Olaf chuckled, adjusting his cloak so that it faced the rain. 'Because, although I may not always choose to behave like it, I am a king, Hákon. And, aside from any agreement I made with my brother, a king must protect his reputation. A lot of my people were very surprised to see me leave Geirstad. What will they think if I return without taking the prize?'

'You just said yourself that the prize is not worth taking.'

'It isn't. If I'd known what awaited me here, I wouldn't have come. But I've marched a long way now, and I have to salvage something. I know there must be more than wool and salt down there, and I mean to take it.'

Unexpectedly, Hákon turned on him. At first Olaf thought that he was shaping to attack, and his hand went instinctively for his dagger, before he saw the look on Hákon's face, and realised that he simply meant to make an appeal.

'Wait until I'm ruler,' Hákon urged. 'I will see to it that you and your men march into Helvik and take anything you want, without so much as having to draw your swords, so long as it is I that is in control when you march out again.'

Olaf looked at him closely. 'You are forgetting one important thing, Hákon,' he said. 'I like drawing my sword.' He turned, and started squelching back up the slope.

Hákon stumbled after him. 'You told me we had an arrangement.'

'I told you I'd consider your arrangement, provided you delivered me a boatload of riches in the meantime.'

'And the boat will come, if you just give it a chance!'

Olaf spun around, so suddenly that Hákon shirked backwards and almost stumbled. He came upright slowly, face abashed, and Olaf looked down at him musingly. The rain was falling steadily now, painting Hákon's dull hair dark. He had a beard of sorts, though it grew mostly around his jawline and beneath his chin, and the rainwater ran down his smooth cheeks and gathered within it. In height, he was short enough for Olaf to bite him across the bridge of the nose.

Harmless, Olaf concluded. What did it matter to him if the man wanted to play at being ruler? By then Olaf would be back in his hall, sinking his eighth draught of Geirstad ale and awaiting the pig as it turned on the spit. Hálfdanr, though ... His brother had already trebled the size of his kingdom, and was showing no sign of relenting. Who could say how he would react when he arrived in the newest part of his realm to find this one lounging around, calling himself an earl? But now was not the time to bring up Hálfdanr.

'What makes you think that your father is ready to step aside?' Olaf sighed, glancing impatiently at the rain.

Hákon's face lifted with hope. 'He is old. And all this is making him older.'

'Old men cling to power as they cling to life.'

'It's expected of him to name a favoured successor before he becomes incapable. I will demand that he do so. The townsfolk will then have to decide whether to endorse his proposal.'

Olaf rolled his eyes. 'When?'

'There's to be a meeting of my family when my brothers return with the ship. I will press him to make his choice then.'

'And why are you so sure he'll choose you? You sound like a pain in the arse to me.'

Hákon smiled nervously. 'It's always that way. Rulers always name their eldest son, and the people always follow the ruler's decision, for stability. He's already preparing me for the role, not least by choosing me as the one to treat with your army.'

Another dry smirk tugged at Olaf's mouth. 'And a wise choice that's proving to be.'

He sighed again and pulled at his cloak, glancing around him as if searching for a distraction. Sheets of rain were sweeping across the hills. The horse had not even moved, save to lower its head as the water pelted its back. Olaf could feel Hákon watching him eagerly, following his face as a dog does a bone.

'I don't know, Hákon,' he said. 'It sounds complicated to me. I'm humouring you, because I acknowledge the lengths that you've gone to to help me. But the truth is, I don't really need you.'

Hákon's neck jerked. 'Without me, the boat wouldn't even have sailed,' he spluttered. 'Can you imagine the effort it took to persuade my father to send away half our fighting men when an army is camped at our door?'

'I can,' Olaf allowed. 'But don't think my men have been land-bound so long that they cannot sail that ship of yours themselves. What is to stop us from sacking the town tonight and then leaving you in charge anyway, as a token of thanks?'

Hákon swallowed heavily. 'I would not wish to see my people harmed.'

'It will turn into a battle either way,' Olaf said, releasing a tired groan. 'If your people can choose you as ruler, they can choose to disobey you when you order that they stand aside and allow their homes to be ransacked.'

'No,' Hákon contended, 'there are many in the town who are already loyal to me. I can persuade them and my family that this is the only solution. Any who defy me ...' He considered for a moment, then shrugged. 'You may deal with as is necessary.'

Olaf exhaled, and lifted his face to the heavens. He closed his eyes and let the raindrops thunder against his eyelids.

71

'Fine,' he sighed, and he heard Hákon draw a sharp breath and his feet jolt in the gravel. 'But I will be taking the women,' he added.

When Olaf opened his eyes, Hákon was as pale as a winter's moon. His jaw was half open as if it had been frozen that way, his eyes wide and fixed. 'You failed to mention that before,' he murmured.

Olaf shrugged. 'I only discovered today that salt and wool is the best you can offer.'

'You said metals and trading goods.'

Olaf's face creased into a bemused smile. 'Since when are women not trading goods? I know of men in the east who will pay a fortune for a fair-headed woman. You told me your wife is dead.'

'She is,' Hákon whispered.

Olaf clapped him on the shoulder. 'Then don't trouble yourself, Hákon. There are plenty of women to be found. You'll discover that once you're an earl.'

The expression of horror lingered on Hákon's face. Then his jaw became firmer, and his eyes seemed to harden as some stronger emotion resurfaced. He nodded once and then, almost in a daze, he began to move back to his horse.

'I'll give you two days, Hákon,' Olaf called after him, but he didn't even seem to hear. He dragged himself into the saddle, turned the horse, and rode, hunched-shouldered, back down the path.

When he was gone, Olaf looked down sadly at the roll of cloth lying in the muddy water by his feet. He picked up the items and re-packed them into the bag, and then carried it over his shoulder as he wandered back over to the ridge to gaze down at the little town cowering beneath the rain. The sky mumbled with distant thunder. And far out on the grey sea, he saw a ship.

Chapter Six

The meeting was to be held in Helvik's longhall. Gunnarr was summoned just before sunset, and as he ducked through the inner doorway he found that all guests but for Egil were already present, seated around the trestle table between the doorway and the fire. The room was filled with fragrant pine smoke and the smell of wet turf from the roof. The two hounds were in their usual place by the fire, but the women, it seemed, had been requested to make themselves absent, for they were nowhere to be seen. Lamps had been lit along the benches, colouring the place with a warm orange light.

As soon as they noticed him, Eiric and Bjǫrn jumped up from the bench with a shout.

'Gunnarr!' they chorused, and came out from the table to greet him. They were clad still in their battle armour, salt crystals clinging to their beards. As Gunnarr embraced them, he smelt sweat wafting out from their clothing, and ale vapours drifting from their mouths.

He followed them back to the table, and sat on the bench at their side. Across from him, Fafrir was seated next to Hákon. They both must have sensed some occasion, for each was dressed finely in clean woven kirtles, thick furs resting on their shoulders. Neither man spoke, nor even bothered to meet Gunnarr's eye. They had been his friends once. As children they would play together often, while their fathers talked and drank and slapped them across the heads if they became too loud, but that was in the days before the naming of Egil as ruler of Helvik. Power had changed Hákon and Fafrir far more than it had changed their father.

An illustration of the fact stood by the fire a few paces from Hákon's left shoulder. At some point during the summer, Egil's eldest had seen fit to appoint himself two personal protectors to shadow his every step. Few saw the need for them, and many had commented that his father always seemed to survive without such aid. One was named Álfr, a stocky little man with a broad, flat nose. The other was Brökk Haldensson. His gaze was particularly hostile, though it emanated from only one eye, for his left one was swollen almost shut.

A half-empty jug of celebratory ale had been slopped over the table near the centre. Eiric snatched it up and began filling a beaker. 'Well, Gunnarr,' he said cheerfully, 'I hear you've been making friends while we were gone!' and he and Bjǫrn turned to laugh brazenly at Brökk, who bristled but remained silent.

Gunnarr smiled with embarrassment, ignoring the disdainful looks from across the table. 'I don't see any missing limbs, so I take it the raid went well?'

'It was like sport, Gunnarr!' Bjǫrn snorted, with a demonstrative thrust of his arm that shunted the table. 'We stumbled upon a colony of old dotards. They seemed to think curling up and crying would protect them better than taking up a sword!' He nudged Gunnarr and handed him the beaker. 'I haven't had near as much fun in years. You should have joined us!'

Before the conversation could continue, Egil stepped lightly into the room from his partition at the rear. Only Gunnarr stood to acknowledge him, the four sons being relaxed and informal around their own father. He wore a plain woollen kirtle, dirty white, and a brown felted blanket around his shoulders. His greying hair was thin and straight, the skin of his face mottled with sun blotches and beginning to sag slightly around the jaw. The lines of his features crinkled with pleasure as Gunnarr greeted him, and he bowed his head cordially in response.

With a slow grace of movement, he seated himself in his chair by the fire at the head of the table, and smiled silent greetings to everyone. He motioned for Eiric to pass him the ale jug and, before helping himself, offered some to Hákon, who flatly refused with a stern flick of his fingers.

'Well then,' Egil commenced, in a voice that commanded attention, despite its wavering tone, 'thank you all for coming. I have called this meeting to discuss what is to be done to safeguard the future of this kingdom. It is a matter that concerns the whole town, but as the ruling family I believe it is for us to devise the solution that may guide our people. That is why I asked that only our household be present.' He rolled a mildly irritated glance towards the two men standing at his side. 'With a few exceptions, it would appear.'

Pausing, he took a long draught of his ale and held the beaker out for Eiric to refill. 'In truth, I fear that it may be a short discussion, for our options are few, and my own mind is more or less decided. The army we face is far larger, and doubtless better furnished, than we are. They might have attacked us already, were it not for the clever words of your brother Hákon, without whom we may not even have been afforded the chance to hold this meeting.'

Hákon kept his eyes on the table, but his shoulders broadened slightly, and he nodded to himself with a stern expression.

'Your brother,' Egil continued, 'uncovered a weakness in these invaders, which is their lust for wealth. The question we face now is, how do we exploit this weakness to defeat them?' He turned his head across the table, and nodded to Eiric and Bjǫrn. 'My boys; I'm told the raid was fruitful.'

Bjǫrn replied enthusiastically. 'Father, we found a place full of enough treasures to sink a ship on the return journey!'

'Good,' Egil replied, with a fond smile for his youngest son. 'And you lost no men?'

'Not one. Not so much as a scratch on the arse.'

Egil nodded thoughtfully. 'Then that is something we must bear in mind. And our first act should be to deliver your takings to our enemies at sunrise, lest their patience wear thin.' He nodded once in Hákon's direction to address the order to him.

'Forgive me, Egil, but may I ask a question?'

Gunnarr felt every face in the room turn to look at him. Egil gave a slow nod of assent.

'Is it your intention to continue making such payments to these invaders?'

Egil looked down at him from the head of the table, and gave a weary smile, as if he'd been expecting the words. 'What would your response be if it was?'

'That army was sent here with the task of overthrowing this town, and it will carry out those orders. At best, they will only humour us until they have too much treasure to carry back to their homes, and by paying them for as long as their threat remains we hardly give them any incentive to leave—'

'Don't listen to him, Father,' Hákon cut in dismissively. 'He would seek out a war, as he always does.'

'I desire war less than any man here,' Gunnarr snapped. 'But war has found us. I would have us prepare for it, rather than closing our eyes.'

'They are watching us every day,' Fafrir responded. 'Any sign of us preparing for battle and all five hundred of them will be down here burning us out.'

'Then if we are as doomed as you believe, let us focus on putting up the best fight we can! Instead, we send half our army across the ocean in the opposite direction, into other battles, all in order to compensate an invading army for the inconvenience of having to wait in the cold before slaughtering us!'

'If I hadn't made that agreement, you would all be dead already,' Hákon growled.

'We are dead already if we carry on like this!' Gunnarr shouted. 'We just haven't admitted it yet. We must at least give ourselves a chance!'

'There is no chance if we fight!' Hákon hissed. 'If we fight, the town falls. The only option is to keep them at bay with riches.'

'For how long?' Gunnarr replied, but before it could go any further Egil climbed to his feet and waved his hands, silencing both parties with a growl of annoyance.

'My young sons,' he invited, once the quiet had settled. 'You have something to add, I sense.'

Eiric elbowed his brother to prompt him to speak, and Bjǫrn did so willingly. 'Father,' he said, 'even if we do somehow see off this army, what more awaits us in Helvik than famine and misery?' He paused and shrugged, as if inviting someone to answer, and when no one did he continued. 'Me and Eiric have found the most valuable land you have ever imagined, poorly defended, with great stone buildings full of treasures and fields brimming with crops. Let us leave this barren bitch to our enemies if that's what they want, while we sail away and carve ourselves out a new home somewhere better.'

The new suggestion drew momentary silence from the others, except for Eiric, who voiced his agreement and pounded his brother on the back. The two of them turned back to Egil to examine his reaction, and the old man smiled at all of his guests and nodded with an air of finality. Hákon went to speak again, but Egil merely shook his head. He tapped his fingers lightly on the table, and his eyes twinkled with wisdom.

'You have each made good points,' he told them. Sighing, he turned first to Eiric and Bjǫrn, and shook his head regretfully. 'My boys, you talk great sense, but sometimes, I fear, it is proper to do what is right, rather than what is best. We must not leave the land of our ancestors to our enemies without so much as raising a sword to defend it.'

Eiric whispered something in Bjǫrn's ear, but no protest was made now that Egil was making his decision.

He turned next to Gunnarr. 'In contrast, Gunnarr, your solution rests heavily on the brave, perhaps honourable, notion that when a man's home is threatened he must fight to protect it. But it would not be very honourable, I think, to risk the lives of my people where it can be avoided. By delaying the inevitable for as long as we can, we give the Gods every opportunity to intervene in our favour.'

'The Gods favour the brave,' Gunnarr muttered, but Egil silenced him with a disapproving look.

'The Gods cannot favour a corpse, Gunnarr.' He stood, with the groan and effort of an old man, and placed both hands out to lean on the table. 'I am sorry that this meeting was so brief, and revealed to you so little you did not already know. I am weary today, and there is little use in arguing the merits when, at the moment, there appears to be only one route we may take. The sea raid was easy, and successful. We shall continue them, and to subdue our enemies with treasure, until another path is shown to us. And should an attack nevertheless come, we shall defend this place down to the last. That is my decision.' He bowed his head to them, and turned for his chamber.

'Father?'

Hákon's voice was stark in the quiet room. He was staring at his hands on the tabletop, circling one thumb with the other. Egil placed a hand on the back of his chair, and shuffled back around to face him.

'Yes?'

'There is one more matter that I wish to discuss.' He glanced up quickly and nodded to the chair. 'I would suggest that you sit.'

Egil's face lengthened with foreboding. Without taking his eyes from Hákon, he lowered himself back into the chair, so slowly that it barely creaked beneath his weight. Thick blue veins stood out from his hands as he gripped at the ends of the arm rests.

'We are living in dangerous times,' Hákon said, still without lifting his eyes. 'You are a brave and respected man, but you don't have the strength you once did. None of us know what will happen here in the days to come. I think, for the stability of the town, we should discuss now who you will name as your successor. In case you are deprived of the chance in the future.'

The air went as still as a void. The quiet roar of the flames seemed to grow in the fire pit. The water that dripped from the smoke-hole thudded against the floor like the slogging footsteps of a giant. Egil resettled himself on his chair, but his face didn't move an inch. 'Very well,' he said.

Hákon turned his head down the table, and opened his mouth as if waiting for something. 'You may leave now, Gunnarr,' he prompted, nodding to the door.

'Stay where you are,' Egil's low voice growled. 'If you would have me discuss the succession, Hákon, then all of your brothers must be present.'

Hákon bunched his mouth, and he turned back to his father with a tight smile. 'All of my brothers will be present. But Gunnarr is not my brother.'

Egil frowned to himself, taking a small sip of ale. 'You know full well that I have watched over Gunnarr Folkvarrsson ever since his father died,' he said, his eyes holding Hákon's gaze easily. 'He became a member of our family that day, and he remains one now.'

'He does not even carry our blood!' Hákon snapped, and Fafrir began to murmur his agreement, but Egil gave a tired groan and held up a hand to stop them.

'It takes more than the right kind of blood to be a ruler,' he said impatiently, 'and if I am to discuss the future of this town, I will not do so without Gunnarr being present to contribute. He is a fair and moral man, who protects the weakest and restrains the strongest. That is exactly the job of a ruler.'

'He's a meddling bastard who needs to mind his own affairs,' Brökk growled from the corner of the table, before Hákon could restrain him.

Egil's reaction was startling. 'Silence!' he boomed, in a voice that thundered off the walls, and he snatched up his beaker and hurled it at Brökk, striking him across the temple and showering the rest of them in spray. 'Hákon,' he roared, turning on his son, 'if you insist on bringing your half-wit men in here uninvited, you will make sure that they keep their bloody mouths shut!'

Brökk dragged a sleeve across his face and muttered a grudging apology, and Egil fixed him with an icy glare that made him shrink.

'In fact, get him out of here,' Egil decided.

'Father—'

'Get him out! He comes into my home and insults my family.'

Brökk didn't wait to be ordered. Hákon and Fafrir stood so that he had space to brush past the table and walk himself resentfully out of the building. When the door closed again, Egil was glowering from his chair, breathing heavily with passing rage.

'I made,' he started, and then motioned impatiently for Eiric to pass him his own cup of ale, so that he might drink to clear his hoarse throat. 'I made a mistake in accepting your request, and I have changed my mind,' he said quietly. 'There will be no talk of succession today, nor any other day in the near future.'

'Father!' Hákon spluttered, but Egil's tone was iron-firm.

'We are facing the biggest threat that Helvik has ever witnessed,' he told them, turning specifically to Hákon. 'Now is the time for us to pull together under one leader. It is not the time to squabble amongst ourselves while we discuss who should be the next one.'

'There should not even be a discussion!' Hákon gasped, looking skyward with exasperation. 'As the first-born son, I should be the one entitled!'

'Hákon,' Egil warned, 'for a man whose family's kingdom is about to be taken from them, you seem awfully keen to inherit it.'

'I am keen to save it! You must heed me, Father, you are making a grave mistake.'

'My decision is made, and be it a mistake or not, that is the end of the matter!' Egil shouted. His chest heaved up and down with the exertion of the exchange. 'This is my army. It is I the men serve, and if this is to be our final battle, then it will be I that leads us into it.' He slumped down into this chair, and made a banishing gesture with his hands. 'Now leave me in peace and go and do a circuit of the walls. Gunnarr, you stay.'

Hákon muttered something under his breath and lurched to his feet. Gunnarr stood and let the other men file past him, ignoring the insulted faces of the two oldest sons. The doors crashed as Hákon kicked his way through them, and as soon as they slammed closed his angry voice could be heard drifting away in the still evening air.

Once they were alone, Egil beckoned Gunnarr closer to the fire, and clasped his hand tightly.

'I apologise for the way they spoke to you,' he said, his slightly laboured breathing audible in the now empty room.

'That isn't necessary,' Gunnarr replied. 'And even if it were, it is not for you to do.'

Egil poured the dregs of the ale into Eiric's beaker. His hands were shaking, the amber liquid sloshing over the table. 'I know that it is hard, but you must try to get along with my eldest boys,' he advised heavily. 'This town is too small a place for you to be at odds with them.'

'I sense they have no wish for me as an ally,' Gunnarr replied, and then his own voice hardened with concern. 'You must watch Hákon, Egil. I see him becoming twisted by this lust for power.'

Egil smiled and leaned out to toss a log onto the fire. 'As usual, you worry too much, my boy. Hákon is just afraid, as we all are, and he doesn't know how to control it. I may be an old fool in many things, but I know I can trust my own son.'

He picked up the beaker and handed it to Gunnarr, and then patted him warmly on the knee. 'Now,' he said, his face creasing into a smile, 'tell me, how's that mother of yours?'

Night came and went amidst the hiss of falling rain. By the time that the pastel light of morning was spreading across the hills, Olaf Gudrødsson was squatting on his haunches at the side of the mountain road, picking through one of the sacks of offerings that slouched on the ground beside him.

The contents of the bag clunked and rattled as he sifted his gnarled hand through. Carefully, he selected a small piece, a simple disc made from burnished bronze, and squinted at it through one eye in the slowly lifting gloom of daybreak. Satisfied with the appearance, he lifted it quickly to his bearded lips and squeezed it gently between his teeth, nodding with approval and spitting out the taste of wax polish as he tossed it back into the bag and selected another item.

'What's this for?' he asked, holding up the new article so that the men gathered eagerly around him could study it. It was two flat rods of bronze, one slightly longer than the other, joined in the centre at right angles.

'How should I know?' Hákon replied irritably. He wore his furs hitched up around his ears against the cold, and his eyes were shadowed with poor sleep and ill-temper. 'It all melts down, Olaf.'

His beneficiary hummed and nodded in recognition. 'Alright,' Olaf said eventually, tossing the piece carelessly back into the bag and coming back up to his feet. He studied Hákon for a breath or two, narrowing his eyes as if seeking to see beyond the features of the face. 'Now tell me who your father named as ruler instead of you.'

Hákon's tongue caught momentarily. 'What do you mean?'

Olaf lowered his chin and gave a wry smile. 'I can smell a king, Hákon. You can read a king from his walk.' He rattled the bag of goods by his feet. 'You are a sack-bearer.'

A look of agitation crossed Hákon's face, and he massaged his right hand with his left. 'He delays, that is all. Your presence has made him think that he should put off the decision,' he added, somewhat accusingly.

Olaf frowned, and stroked his moustache around pursed lips. When he spoke again, any familiarity was gone from his voice. 'Then it has been pleasant meeting with you, but it seems our dealings are over.' He slung the sack over his shoulder and turned abruptly to leave.

'Wait!' Hákon urged, as Olaf trudged away. 'Give me just a short time more and I can eliminate the competition. The claim will be as good as mine!' His voice was reckless with desperation.

Olaf stopped and dropped the sack. He turned back, smiling. 'I thought you told me that there was no competition? That it was simply a case of waiting for the old man to get round to it?'

Hákon swallowed. He opened his mouth, but the words didn't come.

Olaf allowed his face to become stern. 'I've seen worse liars than you, Hákon, but they were always hanging before me from the lowest branch by then. Here's something to remember: when I'm shit at doing something, I stop doing it.' He turned his back and bent for the sack once more, gesturing for his men to collect the others.

'He'll be gone within days!' Hákon insisted.

Olaf kept walking.

'And in the meantime we will send another ship to bring you more like this. They found a rich land the last time, and only they know how to return there.'

Again Olaf stopped and looked back, this time with a doubtful expression. 'You'd kill one of your own brothers?'

Hákon shook his head quickly. 'He's not my brother. He's just a man that my father is fond of.He I'm working on a way to rid us of him.'

Olaf shrugged his shoulders. 'Sword in the back.'

Again Hákon shook his head. 'If only it were that simple. My father has a certain rule—'

Olaf silenced him with a look. 'It is that simple, Hákon. If I was in your position, I wouldn't be over-complicating matters.'

A chilling breeze was beginning to whip inland off the waves. Olaf's eyes lingered on Hákon for a moment longer, and then he hitched his cloak about his neck and moved off with the rest of his men. As he did so, he called back over his shoulder.

'Here is your last piece of generosity, Hákon. I will accept one more payment from you. If you aren't ruler of Helvik by the time that ship returns home, you never will be.'

Chapter Seven

Rain teemed down in the darkness, with a sound like a thousand charging horses.

Gunnarr sat out by the door of his house beneath the shelter of the short roofing overhang, listening to the storm battering the canopy above and the leaves hissing angrily in the breeze. Droplets as heavy as pebbles plunged heedlessly into the drowning earth all around him. In the distance, the town was nothing more than a presence beyond the black, battened down and cowed into stillness.

A creak from just beside him turned Gunnarr's head, and the wicker door crept open as Kelda stepped through, surrounded by a thick piebald blanket that parted like waves around the smooth bulge of her abdomen.

'What are you doing out here?' she asked gently, and tiptoed over to seat herself across his lap. Her hair was wavy, her eyes half-closed with sleep.

'I've started to think I should be keeping a watch at night,' Gunnarr replied, tucking her under his arms and kissing her forehead.

'Yes,' Kelda said lightly, 'and then they'll come marching down here in the middle of the day and you'll be fast asleep.'

Gunnarr chuckled, hugging her against his cheek. 'Is the other one asleep?'

'Snoring away, just like her son, dear old thing.'

'Shouldn't you be resting too?'

'Not without my husband,' Kelda said flatly. 'The baby needs to spend some time with his father.'

'Is that so?' Gunnarr replied. 'Well then, here I am,' and he worked his hands underneath the blanket and placed them against her bump.

'Your hands are cold,' she gasped.

'Was that you or the baby speaking?'

She smiled and prodded him with her elbow, and then settled down to rest her head against his neck, closing her eyes. For a time Gunnarr sat there in silence, listening to her breathing amidst the backdrop of the rain, feeling the graceful rise and fall of her chest. He spoke his next words in a whisper, in case she was already asleep.

'I feel like he should be kicking or something, if it's nearly time to come out.'

Kelda smiled and shifted her weight slightly. 'He's very relaxed.'

'And how are you feeling? Any sign that he's nearer?'

'No,' she said calmly. 'Maybe I can convince him to hold off altogether for a season or two.'

Gunnarr detected a hint of emotion in her final words. 'Don't worry,' he soothed, and stroked his fingers through her hair.

'How did Egil seem last night?' she asked. 'All this must be taking its toll.'

Gunnarr sighed and leaned back against the wall. 'He seems to think that something will save us, if we just hold out for long enough. I'm not sure he knows what it is, though.'

Kelda was silent for a moment, thinking. The rainwater dripped from the roof in a hundred different tones and pitches. 'Maybe we should leave, Gunnarr,' she suggested quietly. 'We used to say we would, do you remember? There must be somewhere safer than here.'

'Don't worry,' he repeated, rubbing her shoulder.

Her warm breath huffed against his neck. 'Have you any more useful advice?'

'Yes. Never pull a horse's tail.'

He felt her face scowl. 'Very reassuring,' she said, and went to slap him reproachfully across the chest, but he caught her wrist and held it still. With his free hand, he gently tilted her chin until he was looking into her eyes.

'I won't let them anywhere near you. You know that I won't.'

Her face softened with tenderness. 'It's not me I care about,' she whispered. 'What about you?'

'I will be next to you. I won't leave your side.'

'You won't?'

'How could I?'

She relaxed then, and gave him a squeeze. Gunnarr kissed her and resettled her under his shoulder, and she lay there with her arms around his neck as if he were a spar in the middle of the ocean. Within a short while he could feel that she was dozing, her breath becoming deep and paced. Her arm twitched every so often as she lived out some dream that Gunnarr wished he was part of. He sat beneath her warmth, enjoying, for once, the smell of the rain, and eventually she stirred and let out a contented sigh.

'I could lie like this forever with you.'

Gunnarr smiled and kissed her hair. 'Did Frejya ever tell you her story about the lovers and the cave?'

The words took a few moments to filter into Kelda's drowsing mind and, after a long pause, she shook her head.

'There was a young couple so in love that they couldn't bear the thought of being apart. Their greatest fear was the day that death would come and separate them. One day they met an old woman, who said there was a cave up in the hills where they would find a way to live forever, and so never have to face being parted. The lovers immediately went off searching for it, and when they found it they walked down into the dark, damp depths, and found the old woman there waiting for them. There was a pool of water bubbling up from the ground. The old woman told them that drinking from it would make them live forever, but as they stepped eagerly forward she warned them that it would also mean that they could never leave that cave. But the young couple were so in love that they didn't care, so long as they were together, and so they both drank deeply.'

He paused to check whether Kelda was still awake.

'And?' she requested, with a gentle shove.

'And,' he continued, with a smile, 'on a still night you can still hear them wailing from the cave mouth, begging for a death that will never come, so they don't have to spend another moment together.'

He held his breath to listen for Kelda's reaction. She brought her head up to look at him with a face of disgruntlement. The hem of his tunic had printed a pattern across her face, just above the eyebrow.

'Why would she tell you that story?'

Gunnarr laughed. 'I don't know. To teach me that you need more than just love to keep you happy?'

'What more do you need than my love, Gunnarr Folkvarrsson?'

'Nothing,' he assured her.

'Would you choose to live forever with me in a dark and horrible cave?' she demanded, with a hint of sleepy playfulness on her face.

'Have you not seen our house?' Gunnarr replied.

She laughed, a loud, careless laugh, and hugged him tightly, happily. Gunnarr found that he was profoundly aware of how different it felt. All her hugs of late had been out of fear. As her laughter faded away into sighs, he tucked her beneath the blanket and whispered into her ear.

'You and I have always been together, since before we can remember. I could never grow tired of you.'

The night drew on, and he didn't want to carry her inside in case it ended. He remembered the times, even as a child, when she would arrive at his house in the middle of the night, having run away from her mother. Frejya would let her in and she would slither straight under the covers beside Gunnarr, cuddling him while he lay there rigid. He could scarcely remember what the nights were like without her.

Before long, the fresh rain vapours began to lighten his head and he felt himself tumbling towards sleep. It seemed that his eyes had only just closed when Kelda shook him awake.

'What's that noise?' she asked.

She was sitting up in his lap, ear cocked to the sky. Gunnarr stayed still, studying her features as he listened. He could hear only the rattle of raindrops, seeming to draw in closer as he focused on them.

'I can't—' he started, but she shook her head irritably.

'There! Hear it?'

This time Gunnarr did pick up something through the darkness. It was the echo of a faint wail, almost like the call of an owl.

Gunnarr looked at Kelda in puzzlement, and then he felt her stiffen with shock as the sound came again, nearer this time, clearer. It rose up through the air and then died off slowly into silence. Kelda's hands shot to her mouth, and her eyes widened in horror. It was the sound of a woman's scream.

Gently lifting his wife from his lap, Gunnarr rose to his feet and took a couple of hesitant paces out into the rain. He strained his eyes into the thick darkness between the trees, as the water pelted against his scalp and seeped up between his toes. Gradually, he picked up the sound over the clattering of the raindrops, and realised that it was a constant noise. An agonised, ghostly wail.

His concentration broke as he heard Kelda let out a terrified moan, and he whirled around to face her. She was hovering half in, half out of the protection of the doorway, clutching the blanket tightly across her chest. Her face was frozen with awful realisation.

'She's calling your name, Gunnarr!'

Gunnarr looked from his wife to the darkness in confusion, and then took a determined step towards the sound, but Kelda sprang forward and clutched at his arm.

'Please wait,' she shrieked. 'Listen!'

There was a new sound now, punctuating the screaming. A rhythmic, heavy splashing. Footsteps. They shuddered out through the darkness, slow, plodding footsteps that gained volume with each laboured pace, as the person staggered closer and closer through the muddy ground.

Kelda's grip on Gunnarr's arm became tighter with every sound, and then a moan escaped her lips as a woman appeared through the trees directly ahead of them. Her skin was as pale as moonlit death. The rain had left her hair smeared wild and tattered across her anguished face. In her arms she carried a small boy, his head lolling back over her elbow so that his mouth was open to the sky. It was Tyra.

She sobbed as she saw them there waiting for her, and took two further steps before collapsing to her knees on the sodden earth. Gunnarr broke from his trance and rushed out towards them. He hoisted the boy up with one arm and took Tyra's shoulder with the other, dragging her stumbling towards the shelter of the house. Kelda had the blanket drawn up across her face, so that nothing below her quivering eyes was visible. She stumbled backwards to make space. Gunnarr laid the boy down carefully just in front of the doorway, and as he did he realised with despair that a dirty red smear had been left on the shoulder of his tunic and down his right arm.

He glanced questioningly up at Tyra, and saw that she was covered in it. It was coated up both of her arms, half-diluted by the rain, and had stained deep into her woollen skirts, almost black in the darkness. She followed Gunnarr's gaze and looked down at herself in horror for the first time. Kelda quickly took her in and tried to wrap the blanket around her.

The boy was long dead. Tyra must have known that even before she carried him to them. The wound was high on his chest, a finger length tear between where two half-starved ribs stuck out tightly against the skin. His complexion was pale and drained, his lips tinged with blue. Gunnarr took a second blanket from Frejya, who, woken by the commotion, had appeared in the doorway, and wrapped it swiftly over the child's torso to protect Tyra from the sight. The wind and rain had picked up in ferocity, and Gunnarr found that he was almost shouting to be heard.

'Who did this, Tyra?' He had seen that type of wound enough times before to know it was no accident.

Tyra knelt down heavily beside him. Her hands were shaking violently. She swept them through her hair as she attempted to control her tears for long enough to speak, and a smudge of blood passed from her wrist to her forehead.

'My poor boy,' she sobbed, never taking her eyes from the child. 'He was starving. He took one of Brökk's goats. He gave it to me like a gift, so proud of himself. He was only trying to protect me, Gunnarr. He was too young to know any better.' She broke into fresh tears and started to stroke her son's hair, and the two other women dropped down beside her to try to bring her some comfort.

Gunnarr felt his face tighten. 'Brökk did this?' he asked, searching out Tyra's eyes and repeating the question. 'Brökk did this?'

She stared back at him, her pupils very wide. 'Right before my eyes.'

'Gunnarr!' Kelda cried desperately, but he had already gone inside. When he emerged in the doorway, he carried his unsheathed sword, and his face was ugly with aggression.

'Go inside and keep warm.'

'Gunnarr!' Kelda begged again, but he was already striding out into the darkness.

Brökk's house lay towards the western corner of the town. Gunnarr stalked straight there along the same path that Tyra had stumbled down with the body of her son, the rain soaking his tunic against his skin.

As he emerged from the trees and reached her weary old house, he first went across and closed the door that she had left open in her haste. A churned sludge of mud and blood lay across the entrance, shades of black in the near-complete darkness. Gunnarr remembered a similar mess of blood and snow. His grip on his sword tightened.

Brökk's home stood just across the way. Even the building he lived in was clumsy and encroaching, dwarfing the timid structure of Tyra's hut. No light shone from inside. There came a soft creak from Gunnarr's left, and he whipped his head around to find faces poking out through a crack in the doorway of a neighbouring property, watching him. He roved his eyes slowly across the other buildings, and noticed more spectators lurking in the shadows, some animated, some shamefaced, all silent. And all doing nothing. He hesitated no longer.

Making no attempt at stealth, Gunnarr marched up to the front of Brökk's building and, without breaking stride, kicked straight through the wicker door, splintering the wood and driving it from its feeble hinges.

'Brökk, son of Halden,' he shouted.

'What?' a voice answered from the gloom.

'You have ten breaths to come and face me outside. Otherwise you shall never leave that bed.'

In fact Brökk came out much quicker than that. He stepped through the smashed doorway and strode confidently towards where Gunnarr waited some ten yards away. Gunnarr noticed that he dragged a sword with him, half disguised behind his right leg, and realised that he must have already been wearing his armour. Brökk's face sneered into a knowing grin of anticipation.

Both made their opening attacks at almost the same moment, two fearsome overhead swings that drove their blades clanging against each other only a forearm's width from Brökk's head. Blue sparks leapt out into the night, and they stumbled backwards with the reverberations. A child's voice gasped from somewhere nearby.

Warily, they kept their distance and circled each other, Brökk's sword held high above the right shoulder in preparation for a downward strike, his mouth already hanging ajar and panting with adrenaline. Gunnarr moved calmly to the right, away from the weapon, his sword held in two hands at waist level, pointing directly for Brökk's breastbone.

With a grunt, Brökk threw his weight into another clumsy swing, but his lead foot slipped as he planted it and Gunnarr sidestepped past the flashing blade, almost losing balance himself. Their feet were beginning to tear up the ground into a slimy mess that threw their legs around beneath them. One slip could be fatal, and Gunnarr was all too aware of the fact to risk another moment.

With a deft movement, he jabbed forward with the tip of his sword. As Brökk sent another overhead swing hurtling down to block, Gunnarr jumped quickly backwards, hearing the blade split the air just in front of his nose and carry right through into the earth with a splash. As Brökk stood rendered momentarily defenceless, Gunnarr stepped forward and sent a flashing strike down into where neck met shoulder, shearing through the main artery and cleaving a diagonal path right down into the centre of Brökk's chest with a crack of splintered ribs.

Brökk's silent mouth erupted with black blood, and his eyes flashed for a moment with surprise. Then his head flopped over towards the wound as Gunnarr yanked the blade free, and the blood came rushing down his shoulder like a bucket had been emptied over his crown. He tumbled down on top of his own sword, his body slapping heavily into the mud. His face lay part submerged, a pool of filthy water gathering by his open mouth. His eyes stared intently at his earthen death bed. Gunnarr spat on the floor, and made no effort to close them.

Chapter Eight

Bjǫrn and Eiric came for him at mid-morning, while the ground was still wet from the rain. Their manner was polite, but somewhat more formal than usual. Gunnarr got up to follow them without waiting to be asked, pausing only to kiss his wife and mother goodbye. Tyra had passed the rest of the night in their hut. She squatted in the corner beside her enshrouded son, and did not look up.

It was a bright but clouded morning, almost the whole of the sky the same shade of pebble-beach grey. They walked south to the sea, and then followed the coast path along towards the longhall, silent but for their feet squelching through the mud. Leaves were beginning to perish from the trees in greater number, and the seawater seemed thicker and slower with the gathering cold, heavy waves flopping down resoundingly against the shore.

Bjǫrn made a couple of attempts at breaking the silence by mumbling bits of conversation to his brother, but he received little more than grunts from Eiric in reply. They stayed out in front and kept their chins on the path, as if it were Gunnarr marching them before him with a spear-point prodding at their backs. At intervals, they passed small clumps of people who broke off what they were doing and stood to watch Gunnarr go by. They spoke loudly into each other's ears whilst keeping their eyes on his face, but Gunnarr paid them little mind. It was nothing they had not seen before.

In a short while, they turned sharply left onto the western headland, and tramped towards the waiting hall. Finally, as they drew up at the entrance, Eiric turned to Gunnarr and flashed him a marvelling grin.

'You've really done it this time,' he whispered, and pushed open the doors.

Gunnarr stepped through into the antechamber, and immediately felt a tension lurking. The hall beyond the inner door was silent, but he knew that there were people in there, waiting. A low cough sounded from inside, a shuffle of footsteps. Eiric and Bjǫrn paused, affording Gunnarr a moment to compose himself, and then they nodded to him and quietly ushered him through.

Egil was seated at the head of the table, the light from the smoke-hole streaming down onto his shoulders and picking him out from the gloom. His eyes looked tired and red, and they were watching Gunnarr with a look of disappointment. Fafrir sat to the right of his father, wearing an expression of self-important distaste. Behind them, Hákon paced angrily beside the fire pit, and it was to him that Gunnarr's eyes were drawn. He did not look back, but it was apparent even from a distance that his limbs were shaking with rage. A final man sat on the bench nearby him, head down in silent contemplation. It was Jörun, Brökk's uncle.

Wiping his feet on the straw by the doorway, Gunnarr gave a quick pat to the dissident hound that padded across to greet him, and then brought himself awkwardly to the foot of the table. He stowed his hands behind his back, and made no attempt to speak. Egil studied him deliberatively for a moment, scraping a thumbnail between two teeth, and then, with reluctance, he began.

'I take it you know about Brökk,' he sighed, resting his elbows on the table and wearily stroking his hair behind his ears.

Gunnarr cleared his throat. 'Yes, Egil. I killed him last night.'

'Insolent bastard!' Hákon sneered, stamping towards the table, but Egil turned quickly, as if expecting the response, and gave him a furious glare.

'Hákon! I allowed your presence here only on the condition that you agreed to control yourself. We have enough to deal with without this matter getting out of hand.'

Hákon held his ground at the edge of the table, like a dog snarling against a fence. His fair skin was pink with heat, his upper lip lifted to reveal his clenched teeth. At the back, Jörun was calmly studying his hands, but he still hadn't lifted his head.

'If I may explain myself, Egil?' Gunnarr requested, once silence had fallen again. 'He killed the widow Tyra's boy.'

'The boy was a thief!' Hákon snapped.

'There is no rule against being a thief,' Gunnarr replied evenly.

'Because there is no rule against dispensing punishment once you catch one! Any man who chooses to take the risk of stealing must face the consequences.'

Gunnarr's voice fell to a lower, darker tone. 'This "man" you speak of had not seen more than five summers.' He turned to Egil. 'He and his mother were starving because Brökk had been stealing their food.'

'For which he had apologised, and promised never to do again!'

Their voices reached a crescendo, and Egil battered the table with his fist.

'Enough!' he shouted crossly, and then again in a more composed tone once both men had fallen silent. 'Enough. This town has seen enough bloodshed over stupid arguments like this to last it many lifetimes, and I am sick to the bones of hearing them, so I will make this quick.'

He scowled to himself with irritation and took a moment to bring his breathing under control. His eyes darted from one man to the other, and the wrinkles of his face were deep-set with a troubled expression.

'You remember, all of you, the problems this town used to face,' and he looked not only to Gunnarr and Hákon, but to his other sons also. 'Entire generations would be decimated by such feuds. We had babies being killed within days of being born, simply because they were next in the bloodline. As a result of that, we all agreed to have one rule to live by and one rule only. No person of Helvik may kill another person of Helvik. Any who does is no longer a person of Helvik.'

With a sigh, Egil turned to speak directly to Hákon, and his expression was almost bored from repetition over the years. 'When Brökk killed the boy, he broke the one rule, and from that moment he ceased to be a member of this realm. The rule only prohibits the killing of members of this realm. Therefore, in killing Brökk, unpopular though it may have been, Gunnarr has broken no law, and he shall not be punished for his act. That is my final decision, and the decision that each of you should have expected.'

Hákon groaned and clutched at his hair. 'He uses the rule as an excuse to dispose of whoever he chooses!'

'The rule is there to be enforced, Hákon, otherwise it would serve no purpose,' Egil stressed, but Hákon shook his head vehemently.

'But who chose him as the man to enforce it?' he yelled, thrusting a finger at Gunnarr.

'Hákon,' Egil moaned, grinding one of his eyes with the palm of his hand, and then using that hand to emphasise his words with a sharp chopping action, 'any person who chooses to break the rule chooses to lay himself open to the wrath of any person who chooses to enforce it. It allows our people to govern themselves.' He opened his palms, devoid of sympathy. 'Your Brökk killed a child. A cowardly act. Dare I say he deserved his fate.'

A throat cleared from the back of the room, and Egil closed his eyes with regret.

'Forgive me, Jörun. In my anger, I forgot you were there. Some men deserve to die, but no man deserves to lose his family.'

Jörun sniffed, and spat into the fire pit. He sat with his elbows on his thighs, his hair in a braid hanging down past his chin. A messy scar ran from the back of his scalp across his neck and down below his tunic at the shoulder. 'Brökk and I were not as close as some,' he said, in a hard voice long ago scorched of emotion. 'I brought this complaint out of duty, because he was my dead sister's lad. But there's something about this that troubles me, Egil, and I know it troubles others too.'

Egil stood to lift his chair around. 'Speak, Jörun,' he invited. 'I am listening.'

Jörun rubbed his forehead back and forth against his knuckle, like a horse scratching on a fence-post. 'This town has one rule, and it says we cannot kill.' He lifted his head, and regarded Gunnarr with his tongue in his cheek. 'How many people has that boy killed, while he claims to be protecting the rule? More than anyone else living here, I'd wager. More than any person who ever broke it.' He looked at the floor again, and worked another ball of spittle around his mouth. 'There's folk who are saying we were safer before the rule. That its only purpose is to provide sport for this blood-hungry ward of yours.'

Egil dropped his chin to his lap, and started to shake his head. 'You are right,' he said, and Gunnarr jolted with shock.

'Egil—'

'You should not have had to act for Tyra, Gunnarr,' Egil said loudly, swivelling his head in the chair. 'She should have had a husband of her own to stand up for her and protect her. She would have had such a husband, had you not killed him two winters ago.'

Gunnarr gasped with incredulity. 'We took that decision collectively. The man was a dog; he broke the rule once, and would have done so again on Tyra herself had we not got to him in time.'

Egil held up his hands. 'I was there, and I remember. I am simply showing you that your actions have consequences. It is the people's rule, Gunnarr, not yours. You must think twice before you take another man's life over a matter that does not concern you, regardless of whether he has broken any rule or not.'

'You just said yourself that the rule needs to be enforced to be effective.'

'Spare me your tongue, boy, I know what I said!' Egil snapped, shocked by the uncharacteristic lack of respect. 'You must not act for yourself when there are others with a greater right to do so.'

'I act because I will not let popularity decide whether wrongdoers are punished.'

'You act because of anger at what happened to your father!'

He shouted the words, showing the might of his voice for the first time. They echoed away into the rafters, and when they were gone no other sound remained. Egil's features immediately faltered with regret. Gunnarr's mouth fell closed. His lips made a reflective sucking sound, and he took a pace back from the table, lowering his eyes.

Egil's face had darkened with anger, at himself and everything else. From his position at the head of the table, he studied briefly the expressions of Gunnarr and his sons, who made no further attempt to speak, before flicking his head bad-temperedly towards the doorway.

'You can all leave now,' he announced, abruptly rising to his feet without wishing anyone goodbye.

There was a brief exchange of glances, and then those present stood wordlessly and filed towards the exit, all but Hákon muttering gruff thanks. Gunnarr stood aside and allowed the others to pass first, catching a murderous glance from Hákon and a long, steady look from Jörun, before himself turning for the door.

'Gunnarr?'

Gunnarr looked back over his shoulder, and found the old man beckoning him back with a swift waggle of the fingers. Obediently, he re-approached the table, expecting an apology. Instead, as he drew closer, he noticed that Egil's face was drawn, as if his chin was heavy with the words he was about to speak.

'There is a raiding party sailing tonight,' Egil said, in a low and controlled tone that sounded forced. He looked Gunnarr plainly in the eye. 'I want you to go with them.'

Gunnarr choked as if thumped in the chest. 'Egil, no! I—'

'It is not a request, Gunnarr,' Egil cut in, closing his eyes against the harshness of his own raised voice.

For the first time in many years, Gunnarr felt utter panic dig its claws into his back. He stumbled around the table and clutched both hands onto Egil's shoulders.

'Egil, please. My son could be born by daybreak tomorrow!'

Egil breathed out through his nose, absorbing Gunnarr's gaze with his soft, grey eyes. There was sorrow on his features, but his jaw was firm. 'Gunnarr,' he said, placing a hand on the back of Gunnarr's neck, 'you know that I love you as one of my own.' Gunnarr started to interrupt, but Egil shook his head and finished his sentence stubbornly. 'No man returned with so much as a cut from the last attack. It is just for a few days, to allow tensions to clear.'

'It is not my own safety I fear for!' Gunnarr hissed, shaking Egil as if the old man's mind were broken. 'I must be here to protect my vulnerable wife at a time when an army five hundred strong is but a moment's march away! All fighting men should be staying.'

'Gunnarr—'

'You cannot compel me to go!' he snapped, reeling away from Egil's touch. 'I refuse to go.'

'Gunnarr,' Egil said again, somehow softening his voice whilst simultaneously increasing its force. 'You are a free man. But you are also a fair man. I would hope that in the light of all the things I have done for you since I took watch over you and your mother, you can grant me this single request in return.'

Gunnarr fixed Egil with a wounded gaze, pained that he would use such an argument when he knew it to be undefeatable. 'But you know not what you do!' he moaned, dragging his eyes away with exasperation, and then bringing them back imploringly. 'Since the day we were married—since before then, I have never once left her for a night, Egil. And now you would have me do so at a time like this?'

'This is not a decision I have taken lightly,' Egil replied. 'A man in my position must often make decisions that injure him deeply.' Now he looked across at Gunnarr, and made a show of seeking out his eyes. 'One day, very soon, you will understand how it feels to have such responsibilities.'

For a moment, Gunnarr was too lost in his thoughts to comprehend. His eyes were on the floor, his head shaking with bitterness, when suddenly his chin shot upright, and he found Egil watching him with an open, deliberate expression.

'You cannot,' Gunnarr gasped.

'I can and I will,' Egil snapped with belligerence. 'It was always going to be you. But it will not be if I lose you before I have the chance to make it so.'

Gunnarr slumped down onto the bench, reeling. The hound came over and rested its chin on his thigh, but he did not even feel it was there. Egil was fidgeting, re-adjusting his stance. The silence was like a gale in Gunnarr's ears.

'Jörun Thoraldsson is a dangerous man, and Brökk's extended family is large,' Egil muttered eventually, and his quiet voice sounded like the one Gunnarr remembered again. 'I chastised you not just to placate him, but to try to make you see how precarious your position has become. And the reason I send you away is my fear that if you do not board that ship tonight, it will be your death we are discussing in this very room tomorrow.'

'The rule protects me,' Gunnarr murmured.

'On the face of it. But whether a person dies fairly at the hands of the rule, or unjustly outside of it, no victim can be returned from where they are sent. One of Brökk's relations may decide that his own death is a small price to pay for ridding the rest of them of you. And even if I were to kill all that carried his blood as punishment, it would still not bring you, my son, back again.'

104

For a long moment, Egil held himself there before Gunnarr's gaze. His chin was quivering, his eyes holding the open but somewhat awkward expression of a tough man giving rare audience to his feelings. Gunnarr had to turn away from him. He looked downwards at the floor, and saw his fists unclenching slowly at his sides.

'Kelda is a strong girl,' Egil said softly. 'She will wait until your return.'

Gunnarr sucked in a deep lungful of air, and put his hands over his eyes. 'You will watch over her?'

'Just as I have since the day you married her.'

'Promise it to me.'

'I swear it to you.'

Gunnarr bowed his head low with acceptance.

The walls of Egil's hall were filled with tightly meshed straw and daub. It was a durable, insulating combination, strong enough to protect from the whipping salt spray of the ocean wind and the relentless driving rain. But it could not prevent words from within permeating through to its exterior. From where he crouched on his haunches outside Hákon detected the sound of Gunnarr making to leave and jumped hurriedly to his feet. There was a particular purpose to his stride as he rushed away into the town.

Chapter Nine

The rain held off for most of the day and the evening was dry and relatively mild. As darkness fell, the great longboat was hauled down to the centre of the bay and settled in the water. Many gathered excitedly about the ship, but apart from carrying aboard the sail, some food, and a few barrels of rainwater, there was little for them to do. The men were required to row, kill, and row again. For that they needed nothing but their own two hands, and an oar and a sword to wield in them.

Egil stood with his ankles in the cold black water, staring up at the serpent-tail sternpost rearing over him. In another town, he might have been required to climb aboard and furnish the ship with a small box of gold, favourite substance of the sea-goddess Rán, so that she might at least treat her victims with kindness should she choose to drag them below the waves in her colossal net. With not even a knuckle of bronze in Helvik, his men would be sailing her waters empty-handed. 'You're less likely to attract her attention this way,' Egil had told them, and they had laughed. He watched them going about their preparations, with the quiet yearning of a man who knows that most of his years are behind him, and ordered those with torches to keep them low behind their cloaks. He may have decided to send away the swords of some thirty fighting men, but he did not want his enemies to see when they were leaving.

With the departing raiders the sole focus of attention, the low fire that burned to the east just beyond the cover of the nearest headland went unnoticed, just as Hákon had intended. He had selected a place between two of the gravelly hummocks that littered the recesses of the shoreline, a shadowed depression shaped like a giant's thumb-print and shrouded with spiny buckthorn bushes that gave shelter from the wind, and wandering gazes. Dressed in common brown cloaks, with the cowls drawn up over their heads, he and his man Álfr crouched low over the flames, their cautious eyes scanning their surroundings.

Approaching footsteps became audible from some distance away, crunching through the coarse lowland scrub. Hákon rocked his weight forward onto his toes, and for a moment waited there poised to spring. He relaxed visibly as he recognised the particular rhythm of the gait, tapping Álfr on the shoulder and causing him to release his grip on his sword. Eventually the footsteps reached them, and Fafrir dropped to the ground across the fire from them. His features were tentative in the flickering firelight.

'Why all the secrecy, Brother?' he asked in a lowered tone, casting a doubtful glance óver his shoulder in the direction of the town. He wore the hat of white fox skin given him by Egil on the day of his marriage, Hákon observed dryly, and could hardly have looked more conspicuous.

'These are dark times,' Hákon replied, leaning back from the fire so that his voice seemed to come out of the darkness itself. 'I thought it best that only you hear the warning I have for you.'

Fafrir leaned forward inquisitively. 'Warning?' Though his years were advanced, his voice still danced with the excitement of a younger brother on an adventure with the older.

Hákon nodded, while Álfr remained in typical silent stillness beside him, as if his brain were incapable of thoughts and able only to receive instructions. 'I'm worried that your position as the likely successor to our father might be under threat,' Hákon continued, in a voice stern with concern. Hidden from the firelight, his lips drew into a smile as he noted the immediate effect the words had on his younger brother's expression.

'My position?' Fafrir asked, seemingly confused. His eyes flicked twice to the left as he considered whether he could have missed something.

'Oh come on, Brother, you surely know by now that Father favours you?' Hákon said, leaning close to the flames for the first time so that his constructed expression of pride was illuminated.

Unconsciously, Fafrir's shoulders broadened a little. A spark of self-importance flashed across his face. 'But what about you, Brother?'

Hákon tilted his head with disinterest. 'I spoke to him some time back. He wants someone with children to form a stable hierarchy, and that is an area in which I do not meet his criteria. Bjǫrn and Eiric do, but they are too young and headstrong. You are the obvious choice.' He smiled warmly once again. 'I told Father you'd have my full support.'

Fafrir shook his head slowly with incredulity. 'Thank you,' he gushed, and then suddenly seemed to decide that he should not appear shocked at the news, attempting to smother his gleeful expression with one of regal composure. 'This has been welcome information.'

Now Hákon shuffled forward, his eyebrows quivering with intensity. 'Yet old information it might yet be,' he said bitterly, 'for that snake Gunnarr has been whispering in Father's ear for many days now, moulding his thoughts with clever words. He is determined to take the position for himself, and our poor father is becoming more and more swayed by his lies.'

'Father would never pick Gunnarr over his own sons,' Fafrir said confidently, though he spoke through a veil of alarm.

'He sees him as his own son!' Hákon hissed, clapping his hands together with a force that was strikingly loud amidst the silent surroundings. Álfr made a casual scan of the area.

Fafrir stared into the fire, troubled, until the heat stung his eyes. Hákon studied his brother intently, and he could almost see the change materialising before his eyes. A newborn pride prickled across Fafrir's chest. Emerging aspirations flashed through his mind. And a position of glory he had scarce dared believe could ever be his danced just inches from his fingertips.

'Well then,' he stated, lifting his wild eyes, 'we must find a way to remove Gunnarr from his considerations.'

Hákon tossed a splintered stick into the fire and watched it flare.

'I think you are right, Brother.'

Across the bay, a night wind was gathering and the waves were beginning to churn. Slowly, the soldiers of Helvik began to dislodge wives and children and clamber aboard the ship, seating themselves on the rows of storage trunks and taking up the hand-worn oars with which they would row with the aid of the withdrawing tide.

Gunnarr could see them boarding through the trees from where he stood just beyond the shore with his mother and wife.

'It's time I was away,' he breathed, and the two women nodded understandingly.

'I'll look after her,' Frejya told him, with the calmness of one accustomed to seeing her son off into danger. 'Be careful, you.'

'Thanks, Ma,' he replied, and she hugged him tightly before withdrawing a few yards to leave him and Kelda alone.

Gunnarr sighed and dropped to a knee, pressing his forehead against Kelda's swollen belly. 'Now, you just be a good boy and wait until I return,' he whispered, and kissed her navel through the coarse wool of her smock.

Smiling fondly, Kelda pulled him back to his feet. 'Maybe now you wish it was a girl you'd been hoping for all this time? You know how impatient men can be.'

There was a shout from the direction of the ship.

'We wait for you alone, Gunnarr!' It was Bjǫrn's gruff voice.

Gunnarr turned back from the sound and raised his eyebrows. 'Yes, I do,' he replied, and they shared a short laugh. Seeing his wife's face momentarily glowing with amusement, Gunnarr's eyes suddenly became mournful with regret. 'I can stay?' he suggested, almost a request, and he pressed his face tightly amongst the warm smell of her neck as he hugged her for a final time.

'We'll be fine,' Kelda told him firmly, pulling back to look at him so that he could draw comfort from her expression. Her lips were pressed together and elevated at the ends, pushing her cheeks into little cushions of skin as she forced an optimistic smile. Her innocent face held a determinedly brave expression that made Gunnarr's heart twist, especially as he felt her hands trembling in his.

'They know the route now. It will not take the time that it did before. If he does come, know that I'm at most a day away, probably already sailing my way back to you.'

She nodded, more to herself than to him. Then she hugged him for as long as he would let her, until he was gone, so quickly that she was unsure whether he had heard her call 'I love you' after him.

As Gunnarr leaned back for the first pull against his oar and felt the boat lurch into movement with the soft cumulative grunt of the men around him, he realised that she had walked all the way down to the shore to wave him off, a small, solitary figure standing forlornly on the beach. He bowed his head against the first gust of spray, and longed to be back with her.

Chapter Ten

They shipped oars with one hundred yards left to shore and glided in like devils riding the first rays of dawn light. Swords were freed as they crossed the first of the white rollers, and men were leaping lustfully into the shallows before the ship had even nosed sand. The mass of heavy footprints that they churned into the beach were swept smooth with the very next wave, by which time they were already scaling the bank. It was as if a ghost ship had materialised on the desolate shore.

Gunnarr ran near the front of the group, the sound of clumping footsteps and clinking ringmail muddying the air around him. Their target was a quaint little settlement only a short way down the coast from the one that their previous raid had drained dry. A smattering of small houses sat peacefully around the harbour, with a grand-looking building overshadowing them behind, the house of a wealthy ruler, or perhaps another home to the curious men with their robes and shaved crowns. Its appearance promised treasure inside.

The raiders entered the town from the north, trampling through a brief lining of trees and emerging onto the gentle curve of a grass-patched earthen road that led them directly towards the houses. Some of the men broke off and crashed through the nearest doors, but the main group, Gunnarr included, continued straight for the centre of the settlement. Gunnarr heard wood splinter and things overturned but no screams, no clashing of iron. The town was still sleeping, utterly defenceless.

Those first few homes they swept through looked to belong to the poor and unwanted, people on the harsh fringes of society who probably did not deserve to be cut apart in their wretched beds. Up ahead the smattered dwellings died away again and the road narrowed through a dense copse of leaning trees that formed what was almost a tunnel leading to the main site of the town. They passed a solitary cow cropping wearily at the bright grass of the roadside. It glanced up at them with disinterest, and then returned to its grazing.

As the town loomed closer, Gunnarr saw for the first time some evidence of defences. A shallow ditch perimeter, wild with tangled grass, protected the inner buildings. It might as well have been there to drain rainwater. With the squat earthen wall that bordered it unguarded, they would be down and up the other side within the work of a few strides. Gunnarr bowed his head and increased his pace in line with the others, trying to jar his mind into focus. Despite his best efforts, he could not help but think of Helvik lying in the same helpless state at that same moment. Invaders could be rampaging through his own home at the exact time that he was doing the same to someone else's. He found himself pitying the victims he was about to make.

They entered the thickest part of the copse, and the weak dawn light was smothered by the trees. Gunnarr became aware of a set of footsteps running faster than the rest, and Skári Finnrsson brushed past his shoulder towards where Eiric and Bjǫrn loped along at the front, carrying his leather helm in the crook of his arm.

'Eiric!' Gunnarr heard him hiss once he was a few yards away. 'Those buildings were all abandoned.'

Some of the surrounding men shortened their strides, but Eiric turned around to mumble something gruffly and did not change his pace. Gunnarr cast a glance to his right, and caught a glimpse of a shadowy figure watching him from between the trees.

Before he could react, his eyelids were blown closed by a whistling burst of air, and a thumping impact against his arm made him stumble. As he regained his senses, he saw with surprise that one of his comrades had crashed to the ground just in front of him. And then ghastly shouts tore into the air all around.

A flash of colour caught Gunnarr's eye and he managed instinctively to throw his shield up just in time to feel a second arrow cannon into the wood and send shudders up his forearm. He heard himself cursing with shock, and whirled as if gripped by delirium. Bjǫrn was shouting something, and someone else was roaring in agony somewhere behind. The trees seemed to part like ragged black drapes, and screaming attackers came pouring out of them from all sides.

Without time to set his feet, Gunnarr swung a clumsy strike at the first man that charged him down. They were armourless, this one even bare-chested, and the tip of Gunnarr's blade tore a deep trough directly across the front of his ribcage. The man gasped and doubled over, losing his footing, and Gunnarr hacked downwards as the unprotected back stumbled past him, snapping the vertebrae like a stick. As he straightened from the blow, another attacker was almost on top of him, but this one was hit in the back by one of his fellow ambushers' arrows just as he drew back to strike, and Gunnarr dispatched him with a sharp slash up underneath the shoulder. Blood spat across the right side of his face, obscuring his vision, and the body of his victim crashed with lifeless momentum into Gunnarr's thigh, forcing him onto his knees.

They were coming in thicker ranks now, screaming like the souls of the tortured dead, and Gunnarr struggled back to his feet, hands full with sword and shield as he tried desperately with his forearm to wipe away the blood that filled his right eye, barely feeling it as his own ringmail clawed scratches into his face. There was a sound from his blind side, and he spun just in time to block a high blow from a dark-haired man with an axe that had been destined for the back of his skull. It took the attacker half a heartbeat to free his weapon from where it had bitten into Gunnarr's shield, and in that time Gunnarr had lopped off his opponent's arm and plunged his blade through the centre of his pounding chest, mashing organs into tripe. Without waiting for the man to fall, Gunnarr lunged two steps further forward and hacked down an enemy who was facing the other direction, and almost smashed his blade into the unprotected back of a third, pulling out of the swing at the last chance as he recognised the figure as Eiric. Momentarily their eyes met, still wide with astonishment.

They had managed to suppress the initial charge, yet men were still appearing out of the trees, far greater in number than the northmen, and now Gunnarr saw through shaking vision that another group was charging down at them from the centre of the town with weapons swirling above their heads. Dead men writhed on the ground all around. Bjǫrn's voice could be heard distantly above the clamour of battle, ordering his men to retreat to the ship.

Before Gunnarr could respond to the call, he saw Hrókr Ormsson driven to the ground by a shattering blow to the head that sent his helmet spinning through the air into Gunnarr's knee. A strikingly tall man bearing a large tree-felling axe stepped over the corpse and began to lumber towards Gunnarr. He was scarcely clothed, long red hair hanging down over his shoulders and thick muscles that now hefted the axe around in a half circle and dragged it towards Gunnarr's head. Half slipping in his haste, Gunnarr staggered away from the flashing strike, and the fearsome man roared and immediately reversed the swing so that Gunnarr's only option was to fall to the ground to duck the onslaught. Before the man could redirect the heavy axe down onto him, Skári sprang forward from somewhere and hacked his sword into the top of the warrior's shoulder. The sound of his collarbone snapping was loud even through the mess of battle noise.

Most men would have dropped, but the shirtless warrior howled with rage and barrelled Skári backwards, bringing the axe around with his remaining good arm and battering the blunt poll into his ribs. While the man's back was turned, Gunnarr scrambled to his feet and flung out a horizontal strike at what seemed to be the only weak point on his body: his neck. The blade tore clean through the flesh with such speed that the head momentarily stayed seated on the shoulders, and then some lingering impulse caused the man's hand to reach for the wound, and his numb touch toppled the head from its berth with a bright spurt of blood.

Gunnarr stumbled forward to wrench Skári, groaning, upright by the armpit, feeling the thud as the headless body pitched to the earth beside him, and then he turned to chop a route back to the safety of the sea. Someone dropped away in front of him, and through the mass of tumbling, grasping, crawling men, he found himself looking straight at Ulfr

Logmarsson, who was standing on the fringes of the fighting, waving his arms and screaming at the top of his voice.

'The ship! They're stealing the ship!'

'No!' Gunnarr gasped, and he dropped Skári's weight as if he were a sack of dung. The blaring of battle seemed to fade into the periphery, the howling natives and his crying comrades blurring into mist. He saw only Kelda with his son in her arms, and a great waste of ocean between him and them. With a snarl, he slashed viciously across the face of the first enemy in his path, and launched into a sprint towards the boat.

Dying men lay strewn across the road, and he trampled over those he could not hurdle. Aggressors stepped roaring into his passage, but he thrashed out at them with crude running blows or barrelled them aside and fled their retaliating lunges. Eventually he seemed to break through the last of them and stumbled out into the open, where the distance between him and the beach seemed to stretch out mockingly before him. He fought back his despair, and ran as he hadn't done for years.

By the time his thundering feet reached the sand the ship was already some twenty yards out to sea. A small group of men at its prow toiled against the tide to heave it through the last of the rolling shallows and into deeper water, while on board three others had taken up oars and were beginning to row, though they were too few to add any real momentum.

Gunnarr could hear footsteps pounding some way behind him but he did not pause to see who was in pursuit. He slung the burden of his shield aside and ploughed straight into the water, hurdling the breaking waves. Over the first ten yards he gained rapidly, but then the deeper water hit him like a wall and sapped the speed from under him, dragging away his legs so that he half tripped into a swim. Determinedly he forced his way forward, Kelda burning in his mind, and he tore the cloak from around his neck as it began to anchor him down.

By then his splashes had alerted the five pushing the boat, and they threw all their weight into a last desperate attempt to get it clear, needing only a few more yards before the tide would no longer resist. Yet they were clearly unarmed, and when they saw the fury on Gunnarr's face two of them broke off pushing and began frantically to scramble up over the sides. The boat started to flounder in the waves as the remaining three in the water tried to scatter to escape Gunnarr's sword.

They did not. He dropped the nearest two with the same first swing, and as the third held up his hands in defence Gunnarr rapped him across the face with the flat of his blade, bursting his nose and leaving him stunned just as the waves caused the ship to lurch shorewards, battering him down under the water.

Gunnarr leapt up to take hold of the rail and heave his waterlogged body over the side, but was forced to release his grip and fall back into the water as a man loomed over him and brought a sword biting into the wood where Gunnarr's hands had been only moments before. The sea was now up to Gunnarr's shoulders, making it near impossible to generate any power with an upward swing, but his strength was renewed as he realised that there were others in the water all around him, comrades, clambering over the sides to board. Someone was caught across the head by the man defending the rail as they tried to climb up, with a blow that made his helmet sing out like a bell, but as the victim splashed down into the waves the others snatched hold of the defender's arms and hauled him over the side.

While they beat the man to choking death in the water, Gunnarr heaved himself aboard with the others, somehow with his sword still in his grasp. An arrow hammered into the wood beside him as he wriggled over the rail, and as he fell against the deck he heard a cluster of other shafts thudding into the strakes behind him. Those that had already boarded had overpowered the rest of the thieves, and one leaked blood between the planks just a few feet from Gunnarr's head. Eiric was dragging Bjǫrn up over the side towards the rear. Others were grappling to get oars in the water, struggling to keep the boat upright as it listed wildly under the weight of the men clinging onto its sides.

The natives were clustering further up the beach, content to see the vanquished off from a distance. Arrows rained down upon the men still in the water, and Gunnarr crawled to join those that leant bravely over the sides and reached out for those that clawed up at them from the frothing red surf.

Eventually the oarsmen managed to get the boat under control and with a swift few strokes it finally began to pull away. The last remaining man in the water was Skári. There was an arrow in his shoulder and a cut on his head that had taken away part of his face. He managed to grasp hold of Gunnarr's outstretched wrist as the boat moved off, before an arrow cracked into the back of his head, driving his forehead into the water with a splash, and a surge of the boat tore away Gunnarr's grip.

Gunnarr sank down onto his back amid the seawater and blood that slopped around the bowels of the ship, gasping through his ravaged lungs. The boat began to pick up speed, arrows at the extreme of their range beginning to fall steadily away in its wake. Dutifully, Gunnarr heaved himself upwards onto a chest to add another oar to the water and they skimmed away, exhausted, empty handed, and with triumphant roars piercing like daggers through their ears.

'Kelda,' Gunnarr breathed. 'I'm coming home.'

119

Chapter Eleven

Kelda awoke with a start. Her heart was beating quickly, as if she'd had a bad dream. She could feel the blood pulsing through the arteries in her neck. Her forehead was beading with a light sweat.

Feeling over hot, she rolled out of the covers slightly, and felt a sensation in her lower abdomen, a faint clench of scratching pain that built for a couple of breaths and then ebbed away. She ran her fingers across the tightly stretched skin, trying to soothe the child with her touch. I knew you would do this, she thought, with a sigh. All this time he'd been obliging and serene. But now, with surely only a day or so left to wait, the boy had picked his moment.

A few feet away she could hear Frejya's low and even breaths, and felt slightly less afraid. Moving silently, she crept across the space between them and gently squeezed under the covers, feeling Frejya recognise her in her slumber and shuffle across to make room.

'Is everything alright, dear?' Frejya asked. She had that quality of never being truly asleep.

'I think it might have started,' Kelda replied.

Wordlessly, Frejya rolled over so that she faced Kelda's back and reached a warm hand around over the swollen belly, probing gently with her fingers.

'Has it just started?'

'Yes, I think so.'

Frejya smiled, and stroked Kelda's hair. 'He'll probably be some time yet. You're best off trying to get a bit more sleep.'

But Kelda could not sleep, even as Frejya drifted off again. She lay silently on her side, listening to the distant waves outside, and every so often the pain would come back, a throb of sensation, and it grew stronger each time.

They were alone, quite alone. It would not have been such a discernible sensation, had Kelda not begun the evening, like the past two, with three overprotective men in her home. Ári and Hilario had rested on stools by the doorway, while Egil himself sat beside her at the fireside, chatting warmly with his old friend Frejya. Each night Kelda had been kept awake by the old man's heavy breathing as he slept beside the embers, or woken at the sound of Ári creeping out to return to his family, leaving Hilario curled up like a deerhound by the entrance. Yet this night, barely had the moon climbed a hand's width since the arrival of her guardians, when firelight had been spotted in the hills. Egil, after pausing to assure the women of their safety and instructing them to stay inside, had wasted no time in calling the men up to the walls.

Where are you, Gunnarr? Kelda wondered, as another tightening wave gently flared through her abdomen.

Silently, she begged her child to have patience.

The next spasm was longer and more painful than the others, and the startled gasp it drew from Kelda was loud enough to wake Frejya again. She sat up among the covers in the darkness and began to speak comfortingly, in a voice that was light with assurance.

They talked for some time about trivial things, Kelda gripping Frejya's hand tightly as each wave passed through her. The very first light of dawn was beginning to shine around the edges of the doorway, but the rest of the town was either sleeping still or standing silent vigil on the battlements. Their own quiet voices and the blowing of the wind through the branches overhead were the only sounds that Kelda and Frejya could hear. For that reason, they both fell silent as the cry of a startled hen pierced through the hut wall from somewhere nearby.

Frejya lifted her ear and listened to the creature hopping and flapping away, clucking with indignation. When it was silent again, she opened her mouth to resume, but before she could speak there was another noise that froze them both: feet sweeping through the fallen leaves towards them.

'Gunnarr?' Kelda gasped excitedly, without thought, and she struggled to sit upright, but Frejya placed a restraining hand against her shoulder and a finger to her lips.

'You know it cannot be,' she whispered, and something in her sudden tautness gave Kelda a sense of unease.

They lay side by side for a few moments longer, listening to the footsteps growing closer.

'It's probably Egil,' Kelda decided, and she began to roll up again to get the fire started, but again Frejya held her down, more forcefully this time.

'Listen,' she hissed, and there was something urgent in her voice.

Flustered, Kelda held herself still and listened, trying to understand what was happening. Immediately, with a pang of disquiet, she realised what it was. The footsteps closing in on them did not pace easily across the ground, as they had seemed to from a distance. They had slowed dramatically, and the sound that they made in the leaves was the slow crunch of weight being carefully placed, by a person not wishing to be heard.

Suddenly there was tension in the room. Kelda rolled her eyes sideways to view Frejya's face, but the old woman's expression was concealed by darkness. Outside the footsteps fell silent. Frejya's grip on Kelda's arm was as rigid as a clamp.

A creak sounded from the front of the room, and both women watched in horror as the door began to creep slowly open. Frejya hurriedly pushed both of them down deeper among the blankets as a spear of thin dawn light surged through the opening and began to illuminate the interior. Through the gap, a single hand became visible. A man's hand, gently easing the door wider with as little noise as possible. As soon as the space was big enough he darted through, outlined briefly as a silhouette in the doorway, and then he swiftly pushed the door shut, dragging them all back into almost complete darkness.

Kelda drove back the desperate urge to scream out in terror, or to challenge the intruder, and breathed as lightly as she could, shrinking her trembling body closer to Frejya's. They heard his feet shuffle carefully across the floor. They heard the air being sucked in through his nose; deep, slow breaths. Then they heard the awful dragging ring as he gently freed sword from scabbard.

Panicking, Kelda squirmed, desperate to scramble wildly for the door, but Frejya held her down tightly, her breath racing in and out against Kelda's ear. They must have made a noise, for the footsteps stopped, and they could sense the man scanning the room, trying to make out their shapes in the darkness.

123

And then that raking pain began to build in Kelda's abdomen again, snaring the whole of her lower body and sending bolts of fire across her hips. Scrunching up her face, she sank her own teeth through the tissue of her lower lip, fighting desperately not to cry out. But the pain was too strong now and it forced her lips apart. The noise she made was no more than a sharp intake of breath, but it was enough. The footsteps came rushing towards them with purpose.

Now Frejya bolted, and she dragged Kelda with her, stretching her shoulder in its socket as they scrambled out of the blankets. Silence was shattered for a moment by the brief flurry of movement, something being knocked onto the floor, but then it seemed to settle again just as quickly as it had broken. The women crouched cowering on the floor just to the left of where they had lain, not daring even to breath.

The intruder appeared to have halted his charge, perhaps confused as to where they had gone. Then Frejya clenched Kelda's wrist as something momentarily blocked off the light that illuminated the edges of the doorway. He had circled back to the exit to make sure they could not escape him.

With a sudden burst of footsteps he came at them again, worryingly accurate, and this time the women's impulses took them in different directions, scurrying apart. Kelda tripped as one of the bed blankets encircled her feet, and she fell to her hands and knees, feeling the skin of her right palm scratched away. Fleetingly her fingertips lingered on a cool, intrusive object and identified it as Gunnarr's skinning knife. She snatched it gratefully into her bleeding palm.

The man had once again retreated back to guard the door and the standoff resumed. Outside the light was strengthening with each passing moment, and as more of it filtered through the smoke-hole in the roof the darkness of the interior began to thin. Soon he would be able to see them as clearly as if there were a blaze roaring in the fire pit.

'Who are you?' Kelda shrieked, maddened with fear.

There was no reply. Instead, the man suddenly flung the door wide open, illuminating almost the entire room with light. It left Frejya and Kelda stunned and exposed, so that for a brief moment the two women could see each other crouching at opposite corners of the overturned room, as well as the murderous figure standing with sword raised in the doorway.

'You!' Kelda gasped, but before she could react further the man slammed the door closed and let the darkness mask him once again.

There was a loud noise to Kelda's left and she shrank away from it and took her chance to bolt for the door, screaming as she felt two hands latch around her shoulders and drag her to the ground just as she had been about to burst through the opening.

He had tricked her, she realised with terror, as the stool he had thrown as a decoy rolled to a halt, and now he was on top of her, his weight crushing against her poor baby. She lay paralysed by fear, too numbed even to fight free, but then there came a violent crash just above her head and she felt him topple off her, shards of sharp fragments showering down onto her cheeks and eyelids. In her struggle to scramble to her feet, she half kicked open the door, and there in the arc of light was Frejya, her frail body stooped over the intruder as she rained down desperate blows at his head with flailing arms.

Before Kelda could get across to help, the man hurled the old woman aside with untamed savagery, sending her crashing against the hut wall. Growling with anger, he rolled up and snatched hold of Kelda once again. She screamed and fought to rip his grip loose, but he hit her, an unrestrained blow with a cruelly bunched fist. It was a sensation she had never felt before and the shock of it alone would have dropped her, even if the force hadn't. Now he was on top of her, forcing her brutally onto the floor, pressing his body painfully against her ribs.

She had not even aimed the knife. Gasping, she felt a spasm suddenly render her assailant's body rigid. His lips produced a surprised grunt, and his fingers tightened for a moment and then started to slowly uncoil from her hair. Only then did she register the feeling of warm liquid running down her forearm and, moaning with disgust, she forced herself to push the blade up further beneath his ribcage, feeling the resistance of his stomach muscles snap away before the point. She turned her head to the side, unable to look at the shocked expression that stared open-mouthed down at her. His body contorted for a few more heartbeats, and then his full weight flopped down on top of her as the last of his breath emptied with a rush, disgustingly warm and wet against her neck.

It took the last of her strength to roll the corpse off her. She crawled for the doorway, her chest and arms covered in blood, still gripping the knife, gasping urgently for air. A searing agony wracked her belly, and the skirts around her legs were soaked with warm fluid.

Chapter Twelve

It was a dark and wretched sky under which Gunnarr and the men returned. Ominous shale-grey clouds folded over one another above the bowed heads of the rowers, like the foothills of a vast rolling mountain that reached its summit directly above the familiar sliver of coast which they drove solemnly towards.

Most of the journey had been in silence, but for the creak of the oars and the occasional flap of the sail, and that was how it remained as they drew towards the shore. Though less than half of their original number remained, they had rowed almost constantly through the days and nights, eager to be away from what they had left behind, and their hands were raw and their backs bent. Away towards the front of the ship, Bjǫrn and Eiric held a hushed conversation in bitter tones. Bjǫrn had wanted to stay on the water and try to make another raid with what tired force they had left, but Eiric had insisted that they return to their home while they still had some men to defend it. There would be widows to pacify, mothers to console, and one of them would have to trudge into the longhall and explain to their father that paying off the invaders was no longer a possibility.

Gunnarr shipped his oar as he noticed others begin to do the same, allowing the ship to glide in towards the beach. Rising through aching muscles to his feet, he turned to face the shore with excitement in his belly, but it soon died back again as he saw the people lining the beach and thought about the news that awaited many of them. He clambered over the trunks towards the prow, and noticed a man wading alone into the water towards them. From a distance he presumed that it was Egil coming to welcome them home, but as they drifted closer he realised with slight bemusement that he was wrong. It was Ári.

Pebbles began to graze against the hull, and Ári stood aside to wait for the boat to halt.

'Ári,' Gunnarr called quizzically from the rail, but his friend seemed not to notice, so he jumped down into the water and waded across to embrace him.

'You must have missed me,' Gunnarr told him as they drew apart, while the other men began to jump off the ship behind.

'Gunnarr ...' Ári said.

There was a look upon his face that made Gunnarr's knees buckle. His throat caught with fear. 'What has happened?'

'Gunnarr ...' Ári said again, but by that time Gunnarr had already pushed past him and was surging through the water to the shore.

In a heartbeat he was out of the freezing sea and lumbering up the beach. Those gathered on the shore parted for him as he blundered past them, and the sympathy on their faces was like a bolt to Gunnarr's heart. He stumbled over the larger rocks and through the thin lining of trees, and then he was sprinting through the town, the pain in his muscles forgotten.

Before he could see it, he smelt smoke in the air, the thin, dank taste of wet timber burning. He faltered for a moment, and then he ran on, and as he drew closer he saw it rising up from behind the roofs that stood before him. It had the lazy, ashen quality of a dying blaze. This time it stopped him, for he could see the buildings around it, the rowan trees gathered closely behind, and he knew from where it came. He dragged himself the last few yards, rushing desperately towards what he was desperate not to find.

The fire had long since burnt itself out. All that now remained were parts of the blackened timber skeleton of the house his grandfather had built. Thin capillaries of flame still sucked gently away at the thicker pieces of wood, crackling greedily. The thatching lay in fine grey ashes around the base, tossed about indifferently by the breeze.

'Kelda.' Gunnarr felt the word form on his lips. He rushed through what had once been the doorway, calling out her name.

Inside, the smoke coated the roof of his throat. There was almost nothing remaining in the wreckage. All that he had owned lay reduced to ash, swirling around his trampling feet. Desperately he searched for some sign of her, kicking aside fallen obstacles, dreading the moment when a darkened clump was revealed to him in the ashes. But she was not there. The fire had ravaged an empty house.

Lifted with hope, Gunnarr stumbled outside again. Ári was walking slowly towards him.

'What happened here?' Gunnarr cried at him. 'Where are they?'

'Tyra's house,' Ári said gently. He struggled to meet Gunnarr's eye.

Without waiting, Gunnarr left his ruined home behind him and raced along the trail towards Tyra's. At first he ran hard, but then an awful sense of dread began to hold back his legs, so that when Tyra's house came into view he stopped still, too afraid to go any closer. He needed to find Kelda's smiling face behind those walls. Helplessly he pleaded for any pain but the loss of her, and forced himself to the doorway.

She was the first thing he saw as he entered. There were other people gathered there, who turned to face him as he pushed through the opening, but she was all that he saw. She lay on her back on a table in the middle of the room.

Gunnarr moved towards her without speaking, deaf to the voices that muffled through his ears, numb to the hands on his shoulders. Her body and face were entirely covered, carefully wrapped in a dark felted blanket, but to him she was instantly recognisable. He knew her exact height from toe-tip to hairline. He could pick out her shape from a crowd of thousands, for she had been made for him alone. He knew that it was her lying on the table, covered up like an object.

The others backed away from him as he silently approached and came to a halt beside her. Taking the coarse wool between finger and thumb, he drew back the blanket to her midriff, and there she was, lying placidly before him with her eyes closed as if she was dreaming. She did not even register that he had come home. It felt strange that she did not smile and jump up to greet him, that she was incapable of even the slightest sign of familiarity, even to him. Gently, he took up her hand and felt the dry coolness of her palm, the strange weight of her arm.

She was untouched by the fire, but he could see from her pallor that she had been dead for some time. Tenderly he traced with quivering finger a line from her forehead down past the tranquil lashes of her eyelids to the tip of her nose, as he had often done as she had lain beside him, except this time she did not smile in her sleep, or playfully try to bite his outstretched hand. Her face was pale and taut. Her lips were pressed firmly together, incapable of producing another cheerful smile, and as he bent to press his forehead against hers and kiss her gently they felt dry and unfamiliar. Amidst the swirl of his thoughts he suddenly faced the last image that he had of her, standing loyally to wave him off from the beach, and he began to feel pressure building behind his eyes.

Someone took his hand, and he turned sorrowfully to find the tearful features of his mother beside him. There were deep scratches across her wrinkled face.

'I'm so sorry, Gunnarr. I tried, I really did.' She wept, uncontrollably.

Gunnarr sank against her, barely feeling her embrace. Across the room he noticed Hilario, and Tyra crying by the doorway.

Then for the first time, as his mother pulled away from him, he realised that she held something across one arm, a bundle of cloths. Frejya held out the shape to him, and he reached out hesitantly to take it.

'He is her last beautiful gift to you.'

Amid the rolls of cloth lay his sleeping son, his face still scrunched and swollen. A broad flat nose the size of an acorn nestled between his cheeks. Wisps of lucent hair adorned either temple.

'The birth killed her,' Gunnarr said with dawning realisation, but Hilario made a sound, and as Gunnarr looked up at his mother for confirmation he found her to be biting her lip and shaking her head, as if fearful of the consequences. She was helpless to hold back a fresh wave of tears.

Gunnarr was suddenly alerted. He handed back the baby with barely another look, and turned back to where Kelda lay. Before he had been lost in her face, but now for the first time he realised that another blanket was wrapped tightly around her torso, binding her from the pits of her arms down to her legs. Hiding something.

131

The others looked on in pitiful silence as he stepped over to her and began to carefully unroll it, slowly at first, before succumbing to urgently tearing its felted threads apart. Before he had even removed it all, he could see that the inner layers were drenched with blood. Sobbing, he ripped through the last sodden sheets, and let out a wounded cry as he found the injury directly beneath his bloodied palms. A thick puncture wound pierced through the delicate skin of her chest, just below the rise of her ribcage. Gunnarr raised a hand to his quivering mouth, leaving her blood smeared across his lips. A sword had stabbed her in the back.

'It was Fafrir, Gunnarr,' Hilario spoke from behind him.

Gunnarr's face remained fixed on the body of his wife, and his expression did not even alter. With a short inhalation, he wrapped the blankets over her again and bent to hoist her up into the cradle of his arms. Turning wordlessly, he carried her out through the doorway and away.

Chapter Thirteen

That night, he slept beside her under a makeshift shelter just to the west of the town. There was a cove there where they had spent many childhood nights hidden away, listening for voices in the echoes of the bursting waves and ignoring the calls of the adults who searched for them among the hillocks. Her body was rigid and cold, not the welcoming warmth he had known. He had begged not to wake.

The thought of setting flame to her precious skin had been too much to bear. Instead, he buried her in the ground, on a rise near the shore that was last to lose the light at sunset. For a while he stood motionless in the sombre glow of dawn, watching her lie obliviously in the grave that he had dug for her, unable to bring himself to throw the wet soil down on top of her face and hide her away for good.

He covered her body and then packed the earth carefully around the sides of her head, some desperate part of him still clinging to the hope that she might yet be revived if he just gave her the chance. Soon only the surface of her gentle face was left, and when he finally did cover it he sprinkled the earth across her features so lightly that she would barely have felt it even if she had just been sleeping.

Once she was buried below him he found himself lying on top of the soil, whispering through it to her as if in a goodbye embrace. He gathered as many stones as he could find and placed them over her with care to keep the animals away. After that he sat for a while, one hand on her grave, staring out at the grey waves. He felt as if he was somehow still connected with her and that if he went away he would lose that, never to have it back. He lingered long past midday, and then reluctantly left her alone.

Black thunder growled in the sky as he finally returned to Tyra's home. Upon hearing his footsteps Frejya rushed out of the door to meet him, her face stricken with worry. She looked suddenly older without Kelda's youthful energy reflecting on her features. Again and again she called Gunnarr her 'poor boy', stroking sadly at his hanging face and hair, but she could think of no words to draw out his pain. She could see the lost look in his eyes, and she wanted him to stay with her and be still for a while, but she surrendered any chance of that the moment she told him that Egil had visited and waited for him long into the night. It was as if the dark thoughts that Gunnarr had been holding at bay had been released with her words.

Now he was stalking away from her, deaf to her calls for him to wait. Both he and his mother knew where he was going. His face was grim, set with purpose. Overhead, the rain began to fall.

As he approached Egil's hall, Gunnarr noticed through the veil of rain that more men than usual were standing protectively at the doorway. He was glad. He knew then that the man that he sought was somewhere inside. As he emerged through the downpour the guards tensed as a group and warily watched his advance. One scurried off inside to warn of his arrival. Gunnarr pushed roughly past the others, ignoring their sympathetic expressions. None made to halt his progress. They enveloped behind him like a sweeping cloak and followed him into the building.

All were there waiting for him inside. Egil, Bjǫrn, Eiric, Hákon, and Fafrir. A smattering of other men that Gunnarr did not even take into focus lingered around the edges. They each stared transfixed at the doorway as he walked his dripping frame through, like fowl facing a fox.

'Get his weapons off him!' Hákon's voice rang out, and some of the men started forward to carry out his order, until Egil's commanding voice bellowed at them to stop.

'Enough of that!' he shouted, angrily scattering the men. He sighed and turned to Gunnarr, and his face was ravaged with grief.

With the rest of the room watching in silence amid the hum of rain upon the rooftop, Egil came slowly forward with his arms apart and wrapped them around Gunnarr's chest. Gunnarr's chin dropped slightly, but otherwise he stood stoically with his arms by his sides.

'My boy. My dear boy,' Egil murmured in a cracked whisper, muffled in hot breath very close to Gunnarr's ear. 'I am torn apart by the sorrow I feel for you.'

Gunnarr remained silent, conscious of the eyes that watched the exchange. When Egil drew back to let Gunnarr study the sincerity on his face, his eyes were red and glazed with moisture, crusted salt beds caught around the inners from tears already cried. Even through the blindness of his anger, Gunnarr found himself stirred by the sight of his guardian and leader so uncharacteristically weakened. His cheeks were pale, bloodless, his bearded chin quivering, and his expression racked with torment. Swallowing, Gunnarr tried to flick his eyes elsewhere, but Egil grasped his upper arms and shook him, almost with desperation.

'Please, my son. Forgive me.' His arthritic fingers were squeezing Gunnarr's arms down to the bone, as if he were trying to drain the anguish from himself.

Inhaling and blinking rapidly, Gunnarr forced himself to return the searching gaze, determined to allow neither tears nor sympathy to cool the spitting lava in his veins. He spoke loudly, so that his voice would not shake.

'I told you not to send me away, and you swore to protect my wife.'

The words were like a physical blow that made Egil shudder. 'Gunnarr,' he gasped quickly, his pleading eyes seeking Gunnarr's out again, 'the guilt I feel for the pain you have suffered leaves me a broken man. Do you not see? But Gunnarr,' he added in a softened voice, placing one shaking hand against Gunnarr's cheek to direct them to face each other, 'my dear boy, there was nothing I could have done.'

Like a snake strike, the words brought Gunnarr's anger back as a fury, and he screamed and cast the old man's touch away from him, more violently than ever before. Some of the watching men's hands jerked for their sword hilts. A younger Egil might have sprung forward and dropped Gunnarr to the floor with a curse of reproach, but instead the room seemed to gasp as he for the first time reacted like a man of his age, stumbling backwards for balance and looking up to face Gunnarr from his resting point with an expression of reeling shock.

'Your son has slain an innocent woman!' Gunnarr cried at him, thrusting an arm towards Fafrir, who flinched. 'And yet you say you could do nothing to stop it?'

Egil's face became wounded at the words. 'I did not know!' he began to protest.

'Then why were you not there? You swore you would guard her for me!'

'I did, Gunnarr, I swear that I did, but we thought that the battle was coming. We were all on the walls. I thought that was the danger!' He worked his jaw, as if choking on guilt, and repeated his words with a sad downwards glance. 'I did not know.'

'But you know now!' Gunnarr shouted, almost losing his balance in his fury, and his arm went out to Fafrir again. 'You know full well, yet still this killer of an innocent woman, a mother with an infant, stands alive before me, as if he were still a member of this town!'

Again Egil's head dropped and his pained expression returned. He opened his mouth, as if reluctant to say something, and then someone else spoke in his place.

'Your wife was not innocent, Gunnarr.'

Gunnarr whipped his head around at the words and glared at Hákon, and then for the first time he noticed that there was a body lying on the benches in the room.

'You remember Álfr, don't you?' Hákon continued, as Gunnarr fell abruptly into silence, and Egil's eldest son took two steps across to the corpse. Without emotion, he took the dead man's head by the hair and lifted it upright, revealing momentarily the features of his former friend, and then letting it fall back to the bench with a resounding bang. 'It was your wife that slew him. He has no fewer than five stab wounds.'

'You lie,' Gunnarr snarled, after a pause, and he turned to Egil for him to refute the ridiculous suggestion. But instead he found the trusted ruler shaking his head mournfully from where he had crumpled to his knees on the floor.

'His body was found in your house, Gunnarr,' he concurred regretfully, seemingly finding it almost unbearable to speak. 'She was covered in his blood.'

For a moment Gunnarr stood paralysed, as if deciding whether he had really heard the words, and then abruptly he shook his head, and his voice this time was a shout.

'Lies! Kelda did not even know this man! Why would she kill him? How could she kill him? Why would he even be in my house?'

'Perhaps your wife had secrets from you,' Hákon was quick to suggest, with a malicious twist of his mouth. 'A lovers' argument that went too far, perhaps? We've all seen it before.'

'Hákon!' Egil rebuked.

'Bastard!' Gunnarr sneered, and lunged for him, immediately feeling himself grabbed by the arms of the two men that had been approaching him cautiously from behind. He wrestled briefly with them, his glare fixed on Hákon, who smiled back with immense satisfaction. Gunnarr stared into that face, saw the blend of hatred and success that glowed in his eyes, and felt the truth of the situation come crawling into his consciousness like the prickling feet of a spider.

'You have arranged this,' he accused. He raised his voice, turning to the others for their support. 'My wife was attacked! She was defending herself and her child!'

'Be that true or not,' Hákon cut him off pithily, 'it makes no difference. You of all people ought to know that the rule carries no exceptions. Your wife killed a person of Helvik, and as such, my brother Fafrir was acting justly and courageously when he took her life from her as punishment.'

The sight of the puncture wound in the soft skin of Kelda's back fought its way savagely into Gunnarr's head, and he wrenched once again at the grip of those that held him, but they stayed firm. Bjǫrn and Eiric watched uneasily from one side of the room. From where he had been standing alone at the back, Fafrir came forward to Hákon's side in a show of support, and nodded with the judgment, almost more to himself than to anyone else.

Egil's voice was barely more than a whisper somewhere off behind Gunnarr's back. 'I see now more than ever that this rule of ours is a crude, cruel thing, Gunnarr. That day when you were a boy, the day up by the river when you first became enforcer of the rule. It was not because you were defending Kelda, or even protecting yourself, that you were spared punishment. It was because Thorgen had already lost the rule's benevolence through what he'd done to that poor child.' Egil paused with regret. 'And Álfr had not.'

The room waited in silence for Gunnarr's response, but none was forthcoming. He was staring at the wall as if looking straight through it.

'But it was wrong of Fafrir to act as he did,' Egil went on bitterly. 'He has appalled me and the rest of his kin to a degree I can barely withstand. He was stupid and naïve, and thought nothing about what he was doing—'

'Like Gunnarr when he killed Tyra's husband?' Hákon challenged.

Egil scowled at his son with disgust. 'Like nothing of the sort. This act was wrong!'

Hákon sighed. 'But not forbidden.'

Gunnarr did not hear any of the exchange. His head was in turmoil. Strangled, choking breaths escaped his mouth as he drowned in the thought of his dearest Kelda, weak and elated from childbirth, forced to stand up and scrap for the life she had shared so peacefully with the world; forced, in the desperate grapple, to mar her fair skin with bruises and spittle and the scratches of fingernails; to know the immediacy of life against death, the sight of the soul fading from the eyes, the rank smell of human gizzard. Things that only a man should have to know. He imagined her scared and alone, flailing with her arms and crying out for him as Fafrir took a fist of her skirt and stabbed her through cruelly under Hákon's instructing gaze. On her dying face, he saw the innocence drift from her eyes to be replaced by betrayal at his failure to protect her as he swore he always would. He heard himself speaking.

'Your brother has put you up to this, Fafrir. And now he has killed you as surely as if he swung the blade himself.'

Fafrir shuffled with uneasy defiance at the words, and Gunnarr saw his eyes flick left and right to examine the strength of those restraining the man who now threatened his life.

'Gunnarr, please, no,' Egil cried, and he began to clamber to his feet.

'Look at me!' Gunnarr demanded, ignoring his ruler's words, and Fafrir swallowed and turned back to Gunnarr from where he stood five or so yards away with Hákon, who glared with confident interest. 'I will kill you for this,' Gunnarr repeated in a simpler fashion, nodding his head as if to check that Fafrir understood. 'I swear that to you on the grave of my wife.'

A movement turned his head just as he finished the sentence, and Egil thrust himself before Gunnarr's vision. The old man was a wreck. His face was sallow and hopeless, as if everything was collapsing around him. No longer a dominant leader or formidable fighter, he stood before Gunnarr as nothing other than a father, and he was scared.

'Listen to me, Gunnarr,' he pleaded, gripping him by the neck of his tunic. 'Listen to me. This has been a terrible, terrible happening, but you must let it lie now. My son's actions were cruel and heartless and foolish, but he did only what someone else would have done if not him.' He paused, trying to let Gunnarr take in the words. A tear dropped off his eyelash. 'Please,' he begged, 'do not take him from me.'

'He has taken everything from me!' Gunnarr screamed, and for a moment he almost began to cry as well, thick saliva bubbling in his mouth. 'Why should I not take it from him as well?'

'For me, Gunnarr!' Egil replied fervently. 'Because I love you both! And if you take this action, then I will surely lose you both.' He fell quiet, as if he barely dared think of such a scenario. The breath raced between them, and Egil felt the fight sag out of Gunnarr a little. He took hold of Gunnarr's head with two hands. 'Promise me you will give up on this vengeance now. Promise me as my son.'

'I cannot do that!' Gunnarr snapped back, but with less conviction this time, and he did not shake Egil's hands from his head.

'Gunnarr, please, promise me!' Egil implored. 'You have a son now, a boy of your own to think of. Do not choose your blood lust over your life with him, as your own father did.'

Those words seemed to sink into Gunnarr with particular bite. He fought to free an arm to cover his face as the tears finally came, but they would not release him, and instead he dropped his head low to the floor. He pressed his forehead forward against Egil's shoulder, and sobbed. With an expression of intense relief, Egil exhaled and stroked Gunnarr's hair soothingly.

'Promise me,' he repeated, his voice softened now to a whisper.

Gunnarr replied quietly. 'I promise you.'

On a sudden impulse, Fafrir came forward from where he had watched with a look of revulsion, and stamped to a halt just in front of Gunnarr.

'Do not beg for me, Father!' he spat, in an insulted tone, and he thrust Egil aside so that he could speak directly to Gunnarr in a brash, self-important voice. 'Your wife broke the rule and I exercised my right to kill her for it. You may no more kill me in vengeance than we may kill you for all your actions of the past.'

Gunnarr gave no immediate reaction. The fight seemed to have gone from him, the helplessness of his situation finally clear. Then, slowly, he raised his head.

'You forget one thing, Fafrir.'

Fafrir rolled his eyes. 'And what is that?'

Gunnarr inhaled deeply. 'The rule cannot bind someone who no longer fears its punishment.'

His movement was serpent quick, but those restraining him should have prevented it. The man gripping Gunnarr's right arm had loosened his hold at exactly the wrong moment. Gunnarr snatched a knife from his belt and punched it hilt-deep into the side of Fafrir's neck before the would-be heir had even opened his mouth to reply.

The action stunned the room. Frozen with shock, all faces watched as a startled Fafrir took three short steps backwards and toppled over onto his back, causing a rupture of sound as his shoulder hit the benches and he came down heavily on the floor.

Distressingly, he climbed easily back to his feet, as if barely injured at all, but his right hand was feeling for the object that protruded from his neck and his face was panicked as he studied the helpless expressions of those watching him.

Wobbling, he turned to his brother Hákon, and must have tried to speak, for the movement tore something inside him and a sudden rush of blood hurled from his mouth like vomit. Still standing, he looked briefly at the splatter on the floor in front of him, and then reached up and quickly pulled the knife free. The effect was instantaneous. A spurt of blood shot out at a right angle from his neck, and he dropped face forward into the mess he had created.

The sound of his body hitting the ground seemed to jolt everybody into action. Egil wailed as if in agony. Bjǫrn and Eiric and some of the other men rushed forward to Fafrir's fallen side and desperately began to try to plug the wound. And Hákon drew his sword with a roar and came directly at Gunnarr.

He would have slain him within a moment. Gunnarr had already been wrestled to the floor, and was helpless to put up any kind of defence. But before the killing strike could fall, Egil threw himself across the room with the speed of a man half his age and tackled Hákon to the ground. The older man was first to his feet too, rolling up in one movement and placing himself protectively in front of Gunnarr, drawing his sword as he did.

Hákon came up slowly to his feet, sword still in hand, and his face was one of disgusted disbelief.

'Hold him!' Egil ordered two of his men, and they hesitated. 'Hold him!' Egil screamed, the veins jumping out of his face in fury, and this time they responded to his command, taking Hákon by an arm each. Hákon shook his head but did not resist.

'How did your loyalties become so twisted, Father?' he asked bitterly.

'Silence!' Egil sobbed, through unconcealed tears.

Behind Hákon, those men that had gone to Fafrir's aid were finally forced to admit defeat, and came to their feet wiping their bloodied hands. Fafrir's blood continued to drain past their heels, and Bjǫrn kicked out viciously at the first hound that came to investigate, sending it whining under the benches. Eiric's sword was drawn, but the direction he pointed it in was as unsure as his allegiances. Those that Egil had ordered to restrain Hákon looked warily over their shoulders.

Egil turned his back on Hákon and faced Gunnarr, now dragged to his feet but still held by the two men who had taken their grip when there had been only one corpse in the room. 'What have you done?' he asked in a quivering voice, with a face incredulous with betrayal. 'You, my most trusted man.'

'Forgive me,' Gunnarr answered him quickly, 'but you have broken a promise to me, and now I have done the same to you.'

'Fool!' Egil boomed, his face crumpled with regret, and one of his hot tears flicked across onto Gunnarr's cheek. 'Do you not see what I now must do?'

Gunnarr swallowed. He could do nothing but stare back with an expression of acceptance.

From behind Egil's shoulder, Hákon's restless voice called out. 'He may not see, Father, but I and every other man here does. He more than anyone has chosen to live by the rule he's just broken. Run him through and let him now die by it also.'

There was a gentle clink of ringmail as Egil moved his hand to place it on the hilt of his sword. A single line formed across his forehead. Again the metallic ringing sounded as Egil's hand returned to his side.

'I do not wish to spill any more blood in this house,' he resolved quietly, without turning.

'Your own son lies a corpse on this very floor!' Hákon cried, disbelieving. 'How can you not wish the same fate for his killer?'

'The killer shall have his fate whether I wish for it or not!' Egil snapped back solidly. 'But not here.' Keeping his eyes on the floor, he prodded one of the men still locked on to Gunnarr's arm and spoke huskily. 'Take your friend and two others. Ride him out to the altar and execute him with a clean strike. He was a good man once. The Gods will be grateful for his sacrifice. Then maybe some good may come from all this.'

'Father!' Hákon again protested, but Egil ignored him and lifted Gunnarr's chin to speak to him for the final time. Some turbulent emotion rushed between the two men as they faced each other, but there was no embrace, no tears now from the aged ruler.

'A leader must be seen to enforce the rules he makes. Before today you were the best man I have known. I will remember you as such.'

'Thank you, Father,' Gunnarr told him before he was led away, and the words would have made Egil's heart leap with joy, had it not been already broken.

Once the building had cleared, Egil walked solemnly to the middle of the room beside Hákon, Bjǫrn and Eiric, and knelt down over Fafrir's corpse. With a soft grunt, he rolled the body over and stroked the blood-stained hair back from his son's face, placing a calloused palm over Fafrir's eyelids until they stayed shut.

'When I awoke this morning,' he sighed, tracing a forlorn finger through the pool of blood that had once been pumping through his son's veins, 'I had as many beautiful sons as any man could wish for. Now I have lost two in the space of a single day.'

Hákon sneered at the words, his face foul with contempt. 'How can you call that mongrel your son after he has done all this?'

Egil placed his hands on his knees and rose back up to his feet, looking across coldly at Hákon. 'I was not speaking about Gunnarr.'

He struck Hákon then, with a fierce backhand blow across the cheek. Hákon's hands shot to his face with shock, his pomp abruptly knocked out of him.

'And that mongrel,' Egil continued, pacing forward and causing Hákon to retreat, 'was right when he said that you were behind this.' He struck again, an open-handed cuff across the scalp, while his other sons watched and did nothing. 'You saw your chance when that drunkard Álfr attacked a helpless woman, and you have constructed these events, even down to the death of your own brother, all so you could lawfully get rid of a man you were jealous of.' Hákon was tripping backwards, his face a bitter mix of resentment and fear, and then his heels met the benches and Egil's hands closed in around his throat. 'I curse you,' Egil said. 'You have made me ashamed of my own blood.'

Hákon's lips were shaking. He opened them to bare his gums in an ugly, watery-eyed smile. 'You can thank yourself for that, Father,' he stammered. 'It was you that made me this way.'

'You made yourself this way,' Egil growled, shoving Hákon so that he was bending over backwards. 'Don't think to lay that with me.'

'Our mother was dead!' Hákon screamed. 'You were all we had! But instead you gave yourself to him.'

'Get out of my sight,' Egil muttered, turning away. 'You are not my son, and you are certainly not my heir.'

As soon as he was released, Hákon howled with shame and hurried directly for the door. Halfway there, he turned back suddenly, his face wild and reckless.

'For once you overestimate me, Father,' he snivelled, in a voice high with emotion. 'How could I have known when I sent Álfr to that stupid cow's house that she would somehow manage to kill him? I didn't plan for it to be like this. But it seems that the Gods' view of the future is alike to my own, old man, whether you like it or not.'

The second part of the remark was lost to Egil. His face had been stunned since the first of Hákon's words. 'You sent Álfr to attack Kelda?'

Hákon laughed, a sound like the caw of a gull. But instead of answering, he simply smiled twistedly, and ducked out of the entrance.

The doors fell closed with a thud. Egil stood speechless, his chin hanging slack from his mouth. He glanced down at his feet, then across at his sons, and then he lurched towards his chair and snatched up his cloak.

'Father!' Bjǫrn called, but Egil did not respond. He threw his cloak about his shoulders and stumbled for the threshold, his old legs shaking even as they ran.

Chapter Fourteen

Bound at the wrists, Gunnarr stumbled through the town, heading west towards the cliffs.

Evening had come on quickly, as it did in the shortening days to winter, and the sky was already reducing to darkness. The rain had ceased. Thorvaldr led, lighting the way with a glaring torch. Beside him rode Stigr, the man whom Egil had put in charge of proceedings. He had the other end of the rope that secured the prisoner tied to his saddle, so that Gunnarr was forced to walk with his hands out like a beggar. Behind came Gulltoppr and Koli. They knew Gunnarr well enough, and had been reluctant even to bind him.

'Will you struggle?' they had asked him, with empathy if not warmth.

Gunnarr had looked at them grimly and sighed. 'Yes,' he said, and that had decided the matter.

As they neared the outskirts of the town, the buildings that they passed began to thin. People stood watching from their doorways at intervals, and Gunnarr felt sadness at the thought of one of them scurrying off gleefully to tell his poor mother. Some called out questions to the executioners but were met with shaking heads. The churning of hooves and flapping of torch flames were the only sounds that any of the party made. Gunnarr noticed that Stigr's palm rested cautiously on his sword.

They exited in single file through the narrow western side-gate, crossed a short stretch of pebble beach, and began a gentle winding climb up onto the cliffs. The wind picked up immediately, causing the torch flame to recoil into a trembling blue orb, with flecks of fire occasionally losing purchase and being ripped off into the darkness. Strips of racing clouds passed before the moon above, obscuring what sheen it might have reflected upon them. Gunnarr felt the darkness swallow him up as the wind cast his hair across his eyes, leaving only the pale tail of the horse that led him within his vision, flicking out occasionally, while the weary torch hovered above it like a failing star. He kept his senses in his feet, stumbling over loose stones that threatened to buckle his ankles.

Eventually the dull clack of stone against the horse hooves echoed away, and Gunnarr misstepped as the ground beneath him flattened off into the soft grass of the clifftop. Away to his left he could hear the waves smashing into the rocks below, and sensed the great hidden void only a footstep or so to his side. His balance shifted with the sensation that he was being sucked towards its emptiness. The riders carried on dutifully with their heads now bowed against the wind and cloaks hunched around their shoulders. The distant glow of the town fires evaporated behind them.

They carried on in that way for what seemed like miles. Gunnarr had been working on loosening his bonds since the moment they were enveloped in darkness. By now, the muscles of his forearms burnt with the strain of constant flexing, but the ropes were too well tied. He went to ground once, a deliberate trip to test the strength of the knot that bound him to the saddle, but it held firm and the skin was dragged from his hip until he regained his feet. Helpless, he continued to follow with doomed obedience.

They passed through a gentle downward section where the ground was soft and sweet with the smell of peat, and then began to climb gradually upwards again. Away in the blackness, some creature of the night kept screeching with joy, or misery. The path began to wear down to scree, and soon any footstep was accompanied by the sound of gravel crushing to dust underfoot. Gunnarr had the feeling that he knew where he was, and sure enough, shortly afterwards the lead horse abruptly drew to a halt and the torch fizzed through the air as Thorvaldr slipped down from the saddle.

'This is it,' he announced briskly.

They had arrived at a large flat rock, as big as the central table in a longhall, and of similar height and dimension. A jagged crack was rendered down the middle of it, through which, in days passed, blood had seeped like an offering into the earth. In the daylight, it overlooked the churning ocean from a raised summit on the clifftop, where the ground seemed to swell as if a shoot as wide as a boat's hull was about to burst through the turf. In the truly ancient stories, it was said that the rock was the knuckle of Ymir, the giant from whose bones all mountains were formed. Gunnarr had little doubt that there were a hundred such boulders about which the same claim was made.

Stigr strode over to Gunnarr as the trailing riders drew alongside, and tested the ties at his wrists. He smiled as he detected the slight slackness, and met Gunnarr's eye.

'Why bother? You have nothing left to live for.'

Gunnarr growled. 'The price of my wife's blood has not yet been paid.'

Stigr shook his head and led Gunnarr towards the stone. 'You should worry about who will pay for your own.' He forced Gunnarr up onto the rock, still tied to the horse, while the other men gathered around solemnly.

'Kneel,' Stigr snapped, and Gunnarr obeyed, lowering himself to the ground. The stone felt worn smooth against his knees. Stigr's sword sprang impatiently from its sheath with a scratching sound. Gunnarr bowed his head, thoughts racing.

With a sting of cold, Gunnarr felt the tip of Stigr's sword angle his chin upwards, so that the two men were facing each other. Gunnarr could just make out Stigr's features, his shape silhouetted by the torch held by Thorvaldr standing slightly behind him.

'You may give us some words for your mother,' Stigr offered.

Gunnarr shook his head.

With a shrug, Stigr drew back his blade, and Gunnarr lowered his face again.

'I think we've been followed.' The words came from Gulltoppr, who still sat atop his horse. His expression was masked, but his voice sounded fearful. 'I can hear footsteps.'

Gunnarr and Stigr shot each other tense glances.

'Everyone quiet!' Stigr ordered. He twisted his ear to the air, his sword keeping his captive at bay.

The two mounted men turned their nervous steeds and scanned about anxiously, but the moonlight was shrouded with cloud, and no man could see anything further than a sword's length away. The wind carried no noise but for the crashing of the waves and muttering of the horses.

'Let us get this over with and be gone,' Stigr said.

All ceremony lost, he shoved Gunnarr back down against the stone and whipped his sword back, heaving it immediately downwards into a strike towards Gunnarr's undefended skull.

Overhead, a burst of illuminating moonlight punctured fleetingly through the cloud. A whinny of panic pierced the air, and the horse that Gunnarr was tied to reared onto its hind legs, wrenching him sideways. The clang of sword hitting stone rang out through the darkness, and bright blue sparks sprang from the impact. Swearing, Stigr whirled to see what had spooked the beast, and came upon a group of armed men only yards from his own. Before any could react, the moonlight snuffed out again, and the fighting unfolded in the darkness.

Shouts erupted from both sides. A horse squealed, and the gasping cry of a wounded man burst out over the noise of lumbering footsteps. Gunnarr heard the swipe of a sword cleaving thin air in the midst of it all. There was a grunt of exertion, a hiss of discomfort. Scrambling up onto his knees, he wrestled violently with his bonds, fighting for balance as the panicking horse dragged him left and right.

'Gunnarr?' a voice called out, somewhere to the left.

'Here,' Gunnarr replied, without thinking, and he instantly heard a rush of movement in his direction as a response, but as he came to his feet to greet his rescuer he met instead a vicious tackle that smashed into his unguarded stomach and sent him sprawling to the ground. Stigr came down on top of him and took a fierce grip of his tunic, forcing a blade against his windpipe and manoeuvring him into a human shield.

'You stay quiet,' Stigr growled, and together they crouched against the floor, listening to the scuffling movements of fighting somewhere in the space just in front of them.

'Gunnarr?' a voice called again. Stigr spun his head to detect the sound and as he did Gunnarr sprang free, managing to catch Stigr with an elbow to the side of the head as he went. He made it only two steps, though.

With a sickening throb of his stomach he felt his third step fail to connect with anything at all, and suddenly he was toppling over sideways. Gasping with shock, he lurched to try and correct his balance, but with his hands tied there was nothing he could grab on to, and then he was falling into empty space, over the hidden cliff edge.

The awful sensation of falling, as if his guts were being wrenched from his throat, lasted only for moments. Before he even managed a scream, the rope snapped taut and his shoulders almost burst from their sockets as his arms were ripped up over his head. There was a snort of fear as the horse he was tied to felt the sudden weight, and then Gunnarr began to slip downwards again as the beast's hooves lost grip on the slick autumn turf.

The shock left him barely able to breathe. He began kicking out madly at the cliff side, desperately trying to find some kind of footing, but his scrabbling feet did nothing but tear away stones and soil which fell with ominous silence. Slowly the rope began to spin, leaving him with his back to the cliff face with nothing to grab for, at the mercy of his ties. One panicked glance revealed the faint white of the churning waters below, breaking themselves against the angled rocks. The ropes that he had worked so hard to loosen began to lose their grip on his wrists.

To call out could have brought death on swifter wings. Instead, Gunnarr concentrated on locking his fingers around the rope. The horse seemed to have adjusted its footing, and the slide downwards had halted. Gunnarr was left to hang helplessly with his legs tingling into the space below, unable to pull himself up so long as his wrists were tied, but with nothing to stop him from falling if they were released.

A clash of swords above concentrated his senses, followed by the dull crack of bone, and then his grip was jolted as someone above tripped against the rope. His right hand slipped free from the tie, and he just managed to lock his fingers wide enough to prevent the left hand from following before he had grasped hold again with his right. Only his strength could hold him now, but his palms were slicked with perspiration.

He must have made a noise. At that moment, a face leaned out over the edge, torch in hand, and exclaimed as it saw him.

'Gunnarr!'

'Pull me up, you bastard!' Gunnarr screamed. He could feel the fibres of the rope slowly sliding through his palms.

Hilario disappeared from view once again, and then Gunnarr almost lost his grip for the final time as the rope started to lurch upwards. He screamed with one last effort, willing his fingers to stay locked, until, just as he could feel the last of the rope between the tips of his fingers, he felt hands take hold of his armpits and drag him up over the side.

Panting for breath, Gunnarr scrambled a few yards further away from the chasm and collapsed onto his front. Then for a long while he did nothing but lie there on the earth, his chest rising and falling gratefully.

When he eventually sat upright, he found Ári and Hilario squatting at his side, smiling with relief in the torchlight. A further man stood over them, one hand clamped over a leaking head wound, and Gunnarr recognised him as Ári's cousin.

'Volundr,' he said, still gathering his senses. 'You are hurt.'

'A scratch,' Volundr smiled, lifting his hand to reveal a narrow lesion. 'Caused by my own flesh and blood, I suspect.' He nodded pointedly at Ári. 'It's not easy, this fighting in the dark.'

Gunnarr fell back onto his elbows and looked about him. 'Were there any more of you?'

'No,' Ári said. 'Just us.'

Gunnarr nodded with relief. A dark shape just to his side was the bloodied body of Stigr. Over him stood the horse to which Gunnarr remained loosely tied by one hand. It was stock still with obedience, though its ears were pressed back and its eyes wide with tension.

'That beast deserves a crown,' Gunnarr breathed, and climbed to his feet to pat the horse, though it snorted and threatened a bite. He could make out two further bodies scattered just beyond, and hear another horse galloping about in a panic somewhere in the distance.

When he returned to squat beside his friends, he found them silent and awkward. Ári was on his knees, cleaning his sword on the ground. Hilario sat with his elbows on his thighs and his head bowed, pulling up handfuls of wet grass.

'Gunnarr,' he began, without lifting his head, 'we want you to know—'

'You do not have to say anything,' Gunnarr cut in. 'Egil told me that he sent everyone to the walls. It was his fault, not your own.'

Hilario shifted uneasily. 'He would never—'

'I told you I don't need to hear it,' Gunnarr said quickly, almost snapping. 'I thank you for saving me. You remain my truest friends.'

Ári sighed, sheathed his sword, and tossed it onto the turf. 'What will you do now?'

'Go back to the town,' Gunnarr said firmly. 'I finish my work there tonight.'

'Hákon?'

Gunnarr nodded.

Ári seemed to weigh his next words carefully. 'And what of the rule?'

Gunnarr's face darkened in the shadowy torchlight. 'Since I broke the rule this day, I am no longer a person of Helvik, and I refuse to be bound by its laws. Especially one that would condemn an innocent woman to die simply for wanting to live.'

'Then you are outside its protection, and you left more than one enemy behind. You will not take more than a dozen footsteps.'

'I will take enough,' Gunnarr vowed.

Hilario cleared his throat deliberately. When the other men turned to him, he was standing on his feet and gesturing to the nearby corpses. 'We are all outside its protection now,' he said quietly. 'These men did not die of old age. All of us have broken the rule tonight.'

Gunnarr shook his head. 'No one need know of your involvement. You can return to your homes and none will suspect you.'

A throaty laugh rolled from Hilario's mouth. 'The alternative being that you killed four men with your hands tied. That might work on Frejya, but no one else. If you were rescued, who but us would have done it?'

Hilario chuckled again, but Gunnarr had been dragged away into serious thought. When he emerged, there was a new look in his eyes.

'Who said I was rescued?' he said. Jumping up, he approached Stigr's body and began to roll it over with the bottom of his foot, pushing it towards the cliff edge.

'Hide the bodies all you want, Gunnarr,' Ári called despairingly, 'come morning they will still be missed,' but Gunnarr hushed him with an impatient wave of his hand.

'I tried to break free,' he explained between pushes, 'managed to kill some before they overwhelmed me. But it was dark, hard to see the cliff edge. Pass me the torch.'

Volundr handed it to him. Gunnarr thrust it handle-first into the ground and, by the grace of its wavering light, took the rope that had once secured him and tied it around Stigr's numbed wrists. Frowning warily, Ári passed over his sword when Gunnarr held out a hand for it, and, with a quick nod of thanks, Gunnarr raised it above his head and swung it downwards, twice. Tossing the sword aside, he rolled the body coldly over the side of the cliff, the impact lost in the crashing of the waves below. Two severed arms were all that remained, tied by the rope to the horse that had both dragged Gunnarr to, and saved him from, his death, now grazing fretfully on the salt-tipped grass.

'He severed my arms, a fatal wound, but then he slipped, and we both went over,' Gunnarr explained breathlessly. He approached the horse and stroked its flank. 'This noble creature should have found its way home by morning. Then there can be no doubt that Gunnarr, son of Folkvarr, is no more, and you will have had nothing to do with it.'

With the flat of his palm, he smacked the creature sharply across the backside and sent it trotting off hesitantly back in the direction of Helvik, trailing the rope with its grisly attachments along behind it.

Gunnarr strode back over to his friends, wiping the sword quickly on the grass before handing it back to Ári, who eyed him with mild unease.

'I am a ghost,' he told them. 'I will drift into Helvik and cut Hákon's throat in his sleep. I will roam the town until Kelda's blood is paid for, and no longer.'

They walked the long road back in silence, feeling their way over the ground once the waning torch finally died. It was still that quietest, darkest part of the night. Gunnarr was lost in his thoughts. He allowed himself to remember coming back to Kelda on nights such as this, jumping under the furs and nestling against her warmth while she gasped and complained about the coldness of his feet. Still he could not comprehend the enormity of never seeing her again.

So submerged was he in such thoughts that he was the last to notice what lay before them in the distance. Only when Volundr clamped a hand on his shoulder and he felt the others rushing by him did he look up and realise what he was seeing.

Ahead, a mile or two away, the bellies of the clouds glowed like coals. Remnants of terrified screams and the clamour of iron meeting iron carried across to them on the wind. Winding down like a fire serpent from some terrible source in the hilltops were hundreds of tiny torches, flickering and shifting in the air, so many in number that it was as if the world's dead had awoken and were marching out of a crack riven in their tomb.

Ári gasped and almost choked on his words, breaking into a run.

'The invaders have attacked! Helvik burns!'

Chapter Fifteen

Flames danced in Olaf Gudrødsson's eyes as he strode through Helvik's screaming streets.

Everywhere around him, his men rushed about in a frenzy of energy, racing each other in the search for prey. Too long he had kept them unoccupied, and the eventual release had driven them near to madness. They were mauling their victims, punishing each as if afraid that the dead would rise up again if not struck down well and truly. Olaf looked on at them torching roofs, smashing possessions, ripping through walls with only their hands. This was their pay for the long marches and the cold boring nights of waiting. They could have taken any fortress in the land in that mood, but Helvik would do. It was only a shame it would be over so quickly.

Movement up ahead caught Olaf's attention, and he watched as a man of Helvik sprang with a roar from his house and twirled an axe around his head and into one of Olaf's marauding soldiers. He wrenched the axe free and used it to bring down a second, and then a third attacker, before finally being overcome and hacked down by numerous blades. Olaf laughed throatily above the noise of battle, and turned smiling to the man walking beside him.

'They put up a decent fight, these men of yours.'

A hooded Hákon nodded seriously and gave no reply.

From the same house a woman suddenly bolted, and she collapsed hysterically onto the corpse of her husband. Olaf gave a nod of satisfaction as his men remembered their orders and stayed their blades, instead dragging the woman kicking and wailing away to be tied up with the others.

Smoke billowed through the air, and Olaf drank in the familiar taste. He scanned around with hunting eyes, feeling strong and dangerous. It was moments like these that gave him his youth back. Geirstad and the ale barrel and the fire were the future, but before that he needed more stories to tell to his grandchildren. Smacking his lips with anticipation, he hefted his sword and strode off to find some sport of his own.

At the time of the attack, Frejya had not been sleeping. Instead she was sitting awake in the darkness, worrying when her only son would return home. Her grandson lay asleep beside Tyra at the other side of the room. The young woman was a mother still at heart. She clung gratefully to the child as if he were her own.

Just as Frejya might have herself drifted off, the child had awoken and started to cry, like a lost lamb calling its mother. Tyra stirred, and Frejya rose to take the baby away before he woke her. She swayed the little boy on her hip as once she had done to his father, blowing softly on his face until he gave a few last sobs and eventually hushed. It was then that she realised they were coming.

She felt them through her bones rather than heard them. They reverberated the ground like a landslide. Hitching the child up to her breast, she moved cautiously to the door and leaned outside with a searching gaze. A burst of flame flashed across her vision in the distance and the first clash of metal rang out into the night.

She went inside and calmly woke Tyra.

'The town is being attacked. We must leave, quickly.'

Tyra's house was a good distance west of the gates, but already they could hear through the walls the shouts outside becoming louder, the howls of the attackers and the screams of the attacked. Frejya took a long length of cloth that they used to wrap cheeses and constructed a pouch fit to tie the baby securely against her stomach, instructing Tyra to help her with the knot. She then pulled on a long cloak of Tyra's late husband's, which joined at the front and covered the boy all but for the head. Frejya handed the possessions she had gathered to Tyra, and hustled her towards the door. In her own hand she carried the blade with which Kelda had killed Álfr, on the night when everything had changed.

They had been far too slow to leave. Even as they breached the doorway, hand in hand, they saw pillaging soldiers charging towards them from the right. Instinctively they reeled away in the opposite direction, their feet slipping on the muddy ground, but no sooner had they run five paces than they heard a triumphant shout from somewhere among the blaze of burning buildings in front of them, and knew that they had been seen.

For an instant they were inert with indecision, and then Tyra let out a whimper and tried to drag them back towards her house, hoping that those they'd seen approaching had veered off somewhere else. Instead, they ran almost straight into them.

There were two of them, ugly, blood-stained brutes. They each gave a cackle of surprise as the women suddenly burst into view right before them. One was reasonably small, with slow, drooping eyes. The other was larger, dressed in a sleeveless tunic which revealed thick arms covered in a dense pelt of bristling brown hairs from knuckles to neck. Steam rose from their shoulders and gaping mouths into the chilled night, giving them a monstrous quality.

Hopelessly, the women turned to double back again, just as the man who had shouted upon seeing them appeared breathlessly around the corner to block them off. The women pulled up short, so abruptly that Tyra slipped and almost went off her feet. The third man smiled with his tongue on his teeth, sounded a hooted greeting to the others, and then closed the trap.

Tyra screamed, and Frejya wrapped a protective arm across her shoulders, glancing around at the two men behind her and one man in front, who were now creeping forwards as if trying to snare a couple of birds without startling them into the air. As discreetly as possible, she tucked her cloak tightly across her front and shifted her grandson around onto her hip with her elbow. She knew all about what such men did to children who were too young to fend for themselves.

Tyra looked briefly at Frejya, her face a picture of fear, and then suddenly she discarded her hand and bolted for the space to one side of the single soldier. Snarling, he caught her easily around her skinny waist, and she screamed in terror and clawed her fingernails down his unguarded face, writhing away from the stench of his leering breath. Grunting with anger, the man threw a short stiff punch into Tyra's jaw, but it did not drop her, and she flailed back with the emotion of a woman who had been hit many times before and had learned how to seal off her body against the pain.

Gripping her knife, Frejya darted to Tyra's aid, only to feel herself jerked backwards as one of the two men behind her threw out a hand and grabbed hold of the fabric across her back. His fingers latched onto the knot of the band tied around her waist, and the force of her inertia against his hold was enough to rip it free. She was spun into a stumble as the material uncoiled and, with nothing to hold him, Gunnarr's baby slipped free and fell hard into the mud with a slap.

Exclaiming with surprise, the droop-eyed man sprang forward in an attempt to snatch the baby up by the leg, but Frejya roared with a new rage and came at the man with her knife, jabbing and slashing and forcing him backwards, escaping under his guard to tear a gash into his cheek.

The soldier's face contorted with fury as blood began to pour from the wound, and he battered Frejya's searching hand away and threw her down into the mud beside the child. He raised his sword high to hack it down into her, but just as he did there was a loud cracking sound and his arm was cleaved in two at the elbow.

The man's sword dropped and fell point-first into the ground behind him. His muscles still contracted into the killer blow, but it was only his stump that moved, and as he gasped and looked with dumbfoundedness down at his wound, a second movement sheered his head clean off his shoulders, swivelling his body down to the ground and revealing the fearsome figure of Egil standing behind, his body still shaped in the follow-through of the strike.

He wore full ringmail armour, an eye-guarded helmet, and an elk-skin-clad shield, and he was a sight to make men watch in awe. Seeing his comrade felled, the man with the bare arms cursed aloud and slashed his weapon at Egil's face, but Egil calmly avoided the blow with a sidestep and flex of his hips, and brought his own blade around to punish the man for the exposure of his miss, cracking the vertebrae at the base of his neck as his weight carried him past.

With barely the time for the old ruler to reset himself, the remaining soldier threw Tyra headlong towards Egil and followed up with an overhead swipe. Reacting instantly, Egil managed to guide Tyra's stumbling body past him with his shield and throw his sword high to block the man's strike with an ear-numbing clash of iron. Both men gasped and fought to hold onto their blades through the reverberations, circling each other breathlessly. Egil watched his opponent's feet, waiting to see the shift of weight as he attacked, but the soldier was experienced enough to wait for the counter, and Egil could not afford to waste any more time.

Feigning with a drop of his left shoulder, just enough to make his opponent switch his balance onto his heels, Egil tucked himself behind the protection of his shield and lunged forward with an almighty sword thrust. He felt the brief snag of ringmail shiver up his sword tip and into his forearm, before the point burst through and into his opponent's chest. With a flick of his wrist, Egil twisted the blade to bore a messy rupture, and then the weight went out of his sword as its victim slid off and fell backwards to die on the floor.

Before the corpse had dropped to the ground, Frejya scrambled across to her grandson. He was unnervingly silent, but as she leant across to look down on him she found he was staring contentedly up at her, a smear of mud across his forehead. Frejya sobbed with relief and gathered him into her arms. Egil reached down and lifted her gently to her feet.

'We must hurry,' he said anxiously, breathing heavily from his exertions.

Frejya hugged him tightly. 'You handsome rogue.'

Egil allowed himself a moment to look fondly at her, and at the child whose gaze had now latched onto him, and he stroked the little boy softly on the head.

'Bjǫrn and Eiric have formed a stronghold at my hall,' he told them. 'If we can get you there you may be able to escape.' He extended an arm across to Tyra and gathered her to him. 'Come with me, and keep to the shadows.'

By the time Olaf made his way down to the shore his men had swept through most of the town, leaving it burning and broken behind them. A section of the stockade had groaned and collapsed, and as a whole it resembled a vast ring of fire, keeping the madness within it from spreading. The majority of the soldiers had dispersed from the main group to work through the individual houses, flushing out survivors or whatever else they might fancy. So long as they left off the women, Olaf let them be and allowed them to get creative. One man stood throwing chickens into a rooftop furnace, laughing as they puffed into flames. Another group were lugging human bodies to a similar fate, in an apparent experiment to see how many would fit onto one pyre. Nevertheless, Olaf still had a reasonable force at his side as he approached the final point of their attack.

'That one, I presume?' he sought to confirm, pointing ahead to a large unharmed building that sat on the west arm of the bay.

Hákon nodded. He remained hooded, and had not yet drawn his sword, but he thought he might do now as he approached his father's house.

Olaf whipped a thumb and finger to his mouth and gave a shrill whistle, reining his men in around him. Together they crept towards the building, staying out of the light.

Inside the gloom of the longhall, Bjǫrn and Eiric Egilsson crouched against the barricaded main door, leaning on struts they had hacked from the banquet table and hammered across the entrance when the first screams had woken them. Two further men held position beside them, the Anundersson brothers, scarcely more than a year apart in age and rarely more than a yard apart in person. Of all Egil's favoured men, only they had reached the muster point.

Huddled by the embers of the fire pit in the main room behind them were the men's wives and children. Tanja, Fafrir's widow, was there also, along with her four-year-old son. The group sat directly on the floor, with the smashed table pieces lying around them. One of the boys of Leofric Anundersson went to feed some former table to the flames, out of habit that a low fire must always be saved, but his mother forbade him with a few whispered words, reminding him of the expense of the wood and the need to rebuild the table once all this was over. Instead the boy contented himself with observing Egil's dogs, which both lay flattened on their stomachs with their chins on their forelegs. Like those of the women, the hounds' faces were fixed with apprehension.

'What do you see?' Bjǫrn whispered harshly to his brother, who had his face pressed against a narrow crack in the door.

'The whole town burns,' Eiric replied grimly, shifting his position. 'There are men out there, but I cannot see them in this darkness.'

'We should get them out now!' Bjǫrn hissed anxiously. An exit had been cut through the daub and wickerwork wall of Egil's chamber at the back of the hall, leading directly to the sea front, where an old fishing boat that was barely seaworthy waited to carry their families to safety. Fafrir's body was already aboard.

'Father said to wait for him,' Eiric replied coolly, not removing his eye from the viewing point. 'The bastards. I can hear them but I can't see them.'

Swearing with impatience, Bjǫrn swept into the main room and whispered something into his wife's clutching embrace, and then returned to his position and resumed his silent wait with the others. They each wore their ringmail, Steinthor Anundersson his helm also, and carried spears for what was sure to be awkward, defensive work. Their shields lay scattered about their feet.

There was a sudden noise, very close by, and Eiric jerked back from the door. He grasped his spear and motioned for the others to do the same, pointing just behind the door and mouthing 'There!' through silent lips. When nothing happened after a few moments Eiric leant carefully forward again and looked through a different crack between where door met with wall. There again was the shape of a single figure, noticeable only from the glint of his armour, crouched so close that Eiric could have grabbed him by the hair had the door not been there. Unaware that he was being watched, the figure was looking carefully over his shoulder, and then studying the door. He raised his arm and touched the wood.

'Father?'

Eiric turned urgently and mouthed 'No!', flicking his chin briefly left and right, and the other men nodded and kept quiet.

'It's Hákon. Please let me in.'

Both brothers recognised the voice in the same instant, and the instinct of kinship swept over them. Hesitating only to nod to each other, they immediately rushed to lever away the bolsters that barricaded entry, sending the nails tinkling quietly to the earth. In the work of a few moments, the barriers were gone. They scrambled to unbolt the door and get their brother inside before any harm could come to him.

As soon as the doors parted, Hákon stepped through, heavily, not bothering to close them behind him. His brothers crowded around him and waited for him to speak, but he could not even look at them. His head was down so that his hair hung around his face, his shoulders slumped.

'Hákon?' Bjǫrn murmured, but before he could finish there was a resonating crack as the doors were thrown wide on their hinges, and soldiers poured in around Hákon at either side.

The suddenness of the charge forced the four defenders stumbling backwards through the inner door, the children squealing in terror. Spears and shields lost, Bjǫrn and Eiric did their best to fall into some kind of defensive position, ripping out their swords as more and more enemies piled into the building before them. Eiric blocked the first intruder's swing and cut him down with a vertical slash that went the length of his chest. Before another blow could be landed, Hákon's voice was booming out around them.

'My family is not to be harmed, that was the agreement!'

The invaders drew back slightly in response, brandishing their weapons at the four men who faced them in the middle of the room. Hákon stepped out between the two sides and glared angrily at the over-eager soldier who now writhed on the floor with his chest carved apart.

'Agreement?' Bjǫrn repeated, his brow furrowed with dawning distrust. Eiric was already cursing in disbelief.

Hákon ignored his brothers, and another man stepped forward from the crowd.

'I am Olaf Gudrødsson—' He broke off as the man wounded by Eiric began to contort violently on the floor, groans of agony escaping from his mouth. Olaf strode over with a sigh of annoyance and stabbed him in the heart, bringing another horrified squeal from the watching children, before returning to the centre of the room to begin again.

'I am Olaf Gudrødsson, and your brother has just saved your lives. Throw down your weapons and you will not be harmed.'

The four kept a grip on their blades. Hákon shifted with unease. Olaf raised his eyebrows, and waited.

'Please, Bjǫrn!' his tearful wife beseeched him.

After murmuring a few words, the men grudgingly threw their swords into a clattering pile at Olaf's feet, Eiric and Bjǫrn watching Hákon with expressions of disgust. Olaf nodded his thanks and kicked the blades across to the men standing behind him.

'Now,' he asked calmly, turning back with a new business on his face, 'where is the old man?'

It was as if he had been summoned by the words. There was a scurry of movement from the back of the hall, causing Bjǫrn's wife to shriek and whirl around, and Egil ducked hastily into the main room through the partition of his chamber. Across his sword-bearing arm he carried an infant child, and with his left he pulled two women behind him. The skin of his face glowed bright from the blood coursing through his veins, but his posture was hunched slightly from a wound beneath his armour. Crimson droplets dripped from the tip of his sword onto the floor. His eyes shone with small triumph.

'Hákon,' he breathed with relief, hurrying across the room towards him, 'thank the Gods you are here also. We must leave now, there are men—'

He stopped only when he felt Frejya suddenly pull sharply on his arm, and only then when he truly studied the faces of the soldiers present in the room did he realise that they were not his own. Cursing quietly, he thrust the baby into Tyra's arms and took up his sword, assessing the situation with darting eyes. One face in particular he recognised. The face of the man who now moved smiling across the room to engage him. The man who had walked into his town a matter of days ago and threatened its very existence.

'Let my boys go,' Egil instructed, directing the order at Olaf with the point of his sword. He held out his left hand protectively to keep Frejya and Tyra shielded, whilst inclining his head and clicking his tongue to beckon his sons and their families to retreat behind his protection. The women and children rushed to do as he ordered, and even the dogs rolled up to follow. Bjǫrn, Eiric and the Anunderssons took two careful steps backwards also, watching their aggressors intently. Hákon did not respond. Olaf merely watched, eyes twinkling with respect for the boldness of the action.

'Come on, Hákon,' Egil said quickly, holding his hand out for his son while slowly beginning to back the others towards the exit. He sighed with agitation as Hákon again made no movement.

'He's with them, Father!' Bjǫrn shouted, but Egil would not hear it.

With the blood-draining ferocity of a cornered animal, he sprang two huge strides across the room and wielded an almighty blow down at Olaf's head. The startled invader just managed to throw up his sword in time to parry, but the force of Egil's strike wrenched Olaf's sword from his grip and buckled his knees. He collapsed helplessly onto his back, bashing his skull against the beaten earth floor, and could only look up in disbelief as Egil stepped over him to rain down a finishing blow that would splinter his ribcage and rip up his organs.

But just as Egil's contorted face had been about to plunge his sword downwards, his mouth suddenly opened into a howl of pain, and his head arched backwards. The usual iron grip of his fingers sprang open and his sword whirled away into the air. His grey hair fell across his face as he looked down at the sword tip that protruded through the front of his chest, before it vanished again, and then he dropped heavily onto his knees and rolled onto his side, leaving Hákon, his face still snarled with the force of his killer thrust, standing over him.

A scream erupted, and Olaf's men just managed to gather themselves in time to fend off Bjǫrn and Eiric as they charged madly for Hákon. Weaponless, the two brothers were forced to fall back from the wall of swords that appeared, and left to howl instead with unspeakable suffering at what they had just witnessed. Two of Olaf's men rushed to the rear of the hall to block off the escape route.

With his face still stretched with shock, Olaf clambered shakily to his feet and stared down with strange admiration at his assailant. He was yet still alive, the old ruler, rolling his head around the room in between little gasps of pain, and Olaf knelt to place a regretful hand on the dying man's shoulder, half expecting it when Egil growled defiantly and tried feebly to strike out at him. Olaf nodded apologetically and returned to his feet.

His men were watching his uncharacteristic show of reverence with startled expressions. Olaf looked around him, still needing time to compose himself, and his eyes fell on the young woman who had entered the room with Egil. She was weeping mournfully beside her older female companion, stricken by the death of her escort. Olaf stared at her in silence, for so long that one of his men had to deliberately clear his throat to jolt him out of his reverie.

'Hákon?' Olaf snapped, re-gathering his senses.

'He left,' one of his men responded.

'Very well,' Olaf muttered. 'Take these lot down to the others, the men too.' As his soldiers rushed to do his bidding, he grabbed the nearest one and pulled him close. 'Make sure no man lays a finger on the young mother,' he said briskly, pointing with little disguise at the woman he had just been watching. Then he turned and marched busily out of the building ahead of them.

As the captives were led off, Frejya saw both Bjǫrn and Eiric drop down and embrace their father, snatching a few last words with him before they were dragged away. When it was her turn to pass where he lay, she too sank down and hugged him sorrowfully. His great sad eyes opened and studied her face.

'My dearest Frejya,' he sighed mournfully. 'I have wronged you so badly this day. Please say that you forgive me now.'

Frejya sobbed. 'What do you mean, Egil?'

One of Olaf's men shouted callously at her and started to drag her away.

'Please,' Egil cried, raising his voice as loudly as he could manage, 'just say that you forgive me.'

Frejya fought free of her guard's grip and dived back to him. 'I do, Egil. Whatever it is, I do.'

She was cuffed and forced off then with a new ferocity, and the hurting group was marshalled out of the door and away.

Egil, ruler of Helvik, listened to the inner door close and rolled onto his back. For a short while he studied the walls of his hall, the way the dancing light of the lamps played across them, and squinted as if trying to record an image of every angle and surface. Finished, he closed his eyes, knitted his fingers, and waited for his heart to give up.

Chapter Sixteen

As dawn gently broke, and the first shards of sunlight began shimmering like fish scales on the ocean surface below, Gunnarr, Ári and Hilario sat within a sheltered cut in the clifftops, staring emptily into the embers of a low fire.

Volundr sat across from them in silence, waiting for one of them to speak. It was he that had lit the fire in the darkness and stayed to act as a harbour which any of those that escaped the town could make for, but when, in the remnants of the night, he had finally heard footsteps climbing up the escarpment towards him, it was only his friends that had returned. Since then only Hilario, free, like Volundr, from the ties of fatherhood and marriage, had even looked at him, and he had done so only to shake his head regretfully.

'We never found their bodies,' Gunnarr finally announced. He glanced up at Volundr, seeking an opinion to add to those already drawn from Ári and Hilario.

'They were already lost to the fire,' Ári repeated woefully, kicking his feet in the dirt. Soot coated his palms and fore-arms, and he passed it on into his hair, uncaring.

Gunnarr thought for a moment, and then shook his head.

'No. I saw not a single corpse of a woman, nor a child. And yet the bodies of the men were everywhere.'

'Look at Helvik, Gunnarr!' Ári burst, pointing down below them to the east to where the smoke drifted like cloud above the skeletons of the rooftops. 'There is no life left in that place.'

'I too saw no sign, Ári,' Hilario grunted from across the circle. 'They could yet be alive.'

Appearing to ignore the words, Ári climbed to his feet and creased his eyes against the low dawn sunshine to study the destruction the invaders had wreaked upon his home. The stockade looked like a black circle scored with a stick around the grey remnants of a bonfire. Only a few parts remained bright and untouched, and those short sections of clean, tall stakes appeared queer and misplaced, like shoots that had sprouted from a damp bag of onions. Bands of gulls had descended among the corpses, drawn by the chance of a rare feast, wheeling and squawking and diving into the smoke. There was no sign of people, no other sound. It was as if the town had been ravaged and left to die, and they had been unable to do anything to save it.

In the darkness, they had run until their lungs dripped with blood, half falling down the jagged slope that led to the bay, ignoring ripping branches and twisted ankles, like moths driven mad in their rush to the candle flame. Smoke began to taint their gulping breaths but they had not slowed, staggering towards the heat and the screams beyond the trees, driven on by the awful cost of being too late.

But they had been too late. They had collapsed down in front of the homes of their loved ones to find them already engulfed in flames, the enemy gone and rampaging across other parts of the town. Ári had charged heedlessly towards the burning doorway, some desperate belief telling him that he could still rescue his pregnant wife and son from inside, but he had been driven back by the ferocity of the blaze, the searing heat evaporating his tears before they even reached his cheeks.

He had wanted to kill and be killed, but his friends had battled to drag him away before they were discovered, and now he understood why. He stared down at where the ashes swirled in a slow dance of desolation in the morning breeze, and shook his head.

'If they are still alive among that army,' he whispered, 'then may the Gods take pity on them.'

Those were the last words spoken for some time. A cold, clear autumn day materialised, with rain clouds in the east. The sun grew higher, the wind stronger, and the smell of soot began to blow across to them on the air. Eventually, Volundr appeared to decide that he was more uncomfortable with enduring the silence than he was with breaking it, and he began to offer up a string of names to Hilario, friends or neighbours, and ask what had become of them. Hilario either muttered or shrugged in reply, reluctant to answer. There was little comfort to be found in the exercise.

'What of Egil?' Volundr finally asked.

Gunnarr looked up with a jolt. He realised that he had not thought once of the old man since the moment they had parted.

Hilario was twisting his head and staring down at the town. The longhall on the nearest headland was one of the few buildings that could be seen through the haze of smoke, and Hilario noted that it hadn't been put to the torch. 'He'll have had more chance of surviving than most,' he said. 'Sometimes they want the rulers alive.' His tone became dour as he finished. 'To what end though, I wouldn't like to think.'

'He's dead,' Gunnarr found himself responding flatly. 'All the men are dead.' He tossed a scrap of bark onto the fire.

Hilario was eyeing him curiously. 'And I suppose you think that's deserved, do you?'

Gunnarr stared at the embers, and shrugged. 'If he'd had it his way, I would have beaten him to the grave.'

Hilario hunched forward so that his face was brought closer to Gunnarr. 'You really can be a half-wit bastard sometimes, can't you?'

A frown leapt to Gunnarr's brow, and he made to respond, but Hilario talked through him.

'Do you really suppose that me and these two are just in the habit of wandering the clifftops in the middle of the night, looking for poor helpless bastards to rescue?' He allowed Gunnarr a moment to dwell on his question, while Volundr shifted uncomfortably. 'You killed his son, right before his eyes, and yet who do you think it was that rushed to my house and begged me to keep you from harm last night?'

Gunnarr fell mute at the words. His eyes went to the floor, and Hilario, seemingly satisfied, rolled over onto his side and closed his eyes.

Gunnarr listened to him shuffling briefly for comfort on the gravelly ground. He felt as if he should have some kind of reaction, but nothing seemed to come. He was numb down to his core, an empty cage of bones. He lay down on his shoulder, and placed his cheek against the ground.

While Gunnarr and Hilario rested, Volundr went down the slope to gather some sticks for the fire. When he returned he found the two of them sleeping, and Ári still standing where he had been, staring out to sea. Volundr went over to try to bring some comfort to his older cousin, but he could think of nothing worth saying, and in the end merely stood there beside him.

The smoke was clearing slowly in the wind. The gang of gulls must have doubled in size. They whirled above the bay below, cawing and cackling and squabbling. Volundr turned to view the procession of them still arriving from far out at sea as if drawn by some secret rallying cry, and as he did so he picked up a movement in the water down near the shoreline.

He placed a hand on Ári's shoulder, and pointed. 'What's that?'

Twenty yards or so from the beach, a dark shape bobbed and splashed in the water. The smoke from Helvik hung above the water like a sea-mist, obscuring all that lay beyond the western headland, but the object definitely seemed to be moving, submerged periodically by the waves but then reappearing again.

'It's nothing,' Ári muttered, after a moment.

Volundr looked at him. 'Ári, it's a person.'

'There's no one left,' Ári insisted.

Volundr ignored him. With a quick few words he roused Gunnarr and Hilario, and they both came up instantly and gathered around to peer down at what Volundr pointed to. It could almost have been a seal hunting in the shallows, but no such creature had visited Helvik's shores in recent memory. The shape began to swim again, sending up bright little splashes with what could only have been flailing arms.

'A survivor,' Gunnarr said, watching the figure struggling to keep its head above water as the tide sought to drag it away from the shore.

Hilario darted away and threw some of the extra wood onto the fire. 'We must go to their aid.'

They made directly for the cliffs and began picking their way down the craggy face, moving at a light jog and watching for loose stones. Before they disappeared below the tree line they could see that the figure had risen up to wade through the chest-deep water. The person had made it some hundred yards down the coast from the town, but the morning breeze was continuing to thin the cloak of smog that masked their escape. Any searching gaze would find them soon.

Hilario led as his band reached the shoreline. They climbed up over a low ridge that enclosed the beach and the figure became visible again, staggering through the knee-deep rollers. Ári made a sudden wailing noise. The figure was still almost one hundred and fifty yards ahead of them, but something made Ári push by Hilario and break into a full run.

'My boy?' he gasped to himself, almost choking. 'My boy!' he shouted, and his feet spun in the sand as he broke into a sprint.

'Tyr!' he screamed, racing towards his son. The boy recognised his father's voice immediately, his chin shooting upwards towards the sound, before he stumbled, ungainly, up onto the beach to meet him. They each sprinted the last few yards, and met each other just past the furthest reaches of the waves. Tyr collapsed exhausted into his father's arms, dragging them both down onto the pebbly sand, so that it smothered Tyr's sodden clothing as Ári wrapped him into a clinging embrace.

From where they watched in horror some twenty yards away, Gunnarr and the others had not dared to shout a warning. So lost was he in his emotions that Ári seemed to have forgotten that he and his son were in full view in the centre of the beach. He knelt up smiling from the embrace and heard clumping footsteps almost on top of him, and before he could spin around he and Tyr both were tackled back into the shallows and thrust under the water.

Ári felt the burn of sea salt rush up his nostrils, and for an instinctive instant he began to struggle, before he picked up something in the tone of Hilario's muffled underwater shout that made him cease to resist. Opening his eyes briefly, he located Tyr through the cloud of sand and bubbles and held his kicking son under the surface, fighting the throbbing urge to breathe until there was a roar of sound and the tide drew back overhead. It allowed them barely the time to gulp in two breaths of air through sand-coated lips.

'Stay still!' Ári gasped to Tyr, hearing Hilario next to him speak the same words, and then the water crashed back over them again.

Gunnarr and Volundr had raced to the cover of the trees at the fringes of the beach. From there they crouched and watched the scene unfold. They had heard the ominous grunts of the oar stroke first, a low and ghostly sound from somewhere within the haze of smoke. Hilario had recognised it quickest, and it was that which had prompted his rush to Ári's side. Yet he had surely been too late. A stone's throw out to sea, just past the jutting point of the bay from around which Tyr had swum, the smoke curtains parted, and the ugly rearing head of Helvik's longboat came lurching through.

The ship was packed to the brim with soldiers, a wall of their shields lining the edge of its body. Each of its oars was being utilised with swift, digging strokes that sent it skimming with the speed of a hunter across the ocean's surface. Gunnarr watched as it moved directly across his vision and followed the coastline west, and he clenched his teeth as it bore down upon where his friends lay barely concealed by the water in the shallows.

'It's too full to be looking for him,' Volundr whispered, and Gunnarr agreed, but he could see men peering out over the sides, examining their surroundings. Unconsciously he crouched a little lower as their stares seemed to meet his eyes.

The boat was moving fast, now directly level with where Hilario and the others had submerged themselves, and out of pure malice the waves seemed to choose that moment to draw back and reveal the huddled shapes lying in the sand. Any moment Gunnarr expected to see a hand thrown out and a shout go up. His heart beat in his ears.

But the ship continued on its course. Some of the men craned their heads around at the shapes on the shoreline, but the oar stroke did not falter. Either they mistook the three inert forms for rocks or driftwood, or identified them as people but assumed with little interest that they were corpses cast into the ocean during the night's battle. Whichever the case, they were far too intent on their work to pay much attention. Soon the boat had disappeared beyond the next headland, leaving behind only an echo of menace.

Gunnarr and Volundr waited until the sound of the oar strokes had faded out of hearing before they risked leaving cover and hurried to the aid of their friends. Senses still blocked by the water, Ári and the others had not yet dared to move. Gunnarr and Volundr dragged the three of them from the waves and helped them hurry across the open shore and back into the cover of the trees.

Once there, Ári slumped down beside his coughing son and fussed over him. The lad's face was fleece-white, his lips blue. He carried the wide-eyed look of one who, for the first time, had realised the fragility of life. Barely was he given time to recover his breath before Ári was asking the question he could no longer keep from his lips.

180

'Tyr, tell me,' he gasped, 'what has become of your mother?'

The young boy struggled to sit up, prompted to deliver a message he had long intended to give. 'She lives,' he cried, through an expression part happiness, part worry. 'All the women are taken captive. We must rescue her, Father.'

Ári looked with startled hope to each of his friends, and then dragged his son into a bruising hug. 'We will,' he promised. 'Before the day is out, we will.'

Chapter Seventeen

Hákon awoke beneath his cloak on an undamaged section of the wall top, feeling as if he had only just closed his eyes.

All was smoke. An odour like burned hog fat lingered in the air, though Hákon knew that it was something else. The landmarks he had known were embers. Former allies lay like felled logs upon the ground, while strangers walked across his vision in their place. A shiver shook his shoulders, and he hitched his cloak around them and stood to move off into what had once been his father's town.

With everything so sunken and featureless, he felt disorientated as he wandered through the spaces that had once been streets. If he turned his head from left to right, he could see from the eastern side-gate to the western with nothing impeding his view. The two gates, the confines within which he had spent his entire life, seemed barely a stone's throw apart. It was like passing through a field of wheat freshly scythed.

The buildings were blackened stumps that reached his waist. Like a giant lifting rooftops, he could peer over the walls at the pathetic space inside. In some of them, maybe by some trick of the wind, the roof and walls had burned down without so much as scorching the interior, leaving Hákon the curious sight of perfectly laid-out homes sitting out in the open amid a black circle of cracked and baked earth. In one he saw a bowl of broth sat atop a stool by the fire pit, as if the owner had just set it down for a moment while he went outside to see what the commotion was. Others had been occupied by Olaf's men, who lay in furred clumps sometimes five or six abreast, like rat pups in a burrow. One home that had been well and truly gutted was cross-hatched at the base by more blackened bones than Hákon cared to count. The stench reminded him of grease spitting in a pan.

The bodies he mostly ignored. If he avoided their faces, they avoided his conscience. At one point he found Ingvarr Knútrsson sprawled out on his belly with his arms outstretched before him, as if he'd just been tossed from an alehouse, which was fitting in a way, because Ingvarr had loved a drink. Further on he saw Jörun Thoraldsson sitting with his back against the one remaining wall of his house. There were no less than four shattered spears in him, two of which occupied his eye sockets, simultaneously dragging his head earthwards and propping it upright. Hákon somewhat regretted not giving warning to those two. Both of them had owed him favours.

Soon enough he found Olaf standing down by the bay, at the root of the road that ran through the centre of Helvik and away into the hills. He wore the only clothes that Hákon had ever seen him wear, coated still in armour and crusted blood, and a stern expression occupied his face as he barked out instructions to those working in front of him.

The women and children of Helvik had been rounded together like cattle and seated on the road before him. Two teams of Olaf's men were working through them with lengths of rope, binding each to the other with tight, practised knots.

Some of the women cried. Others sat numb and frozen. One covered her eyes with her hands and begged for someone to take the corpse of her husband away from her view.

For a moment the sight of them stopped Hákon mid-stride, and he lingered at the back of the group, watching their bowed backs and shivering shoulders. Only when he saw Olaf notice him did he force himself to move confidently forward, quickly stiffening his spine as he approached. A ripple seemed to pass through the captives as he moved into vision, and some of the women started to shout abuse at him as they recognised his treachery. He closed his mind off to it, and it was easier than he expected.

Olaf nodded him a brusque greeting and then turned straight back to his captives. Hákon drew up beside him with his shoulder to the prisoners, trying to think of something to say.

'Where did you sleep?' he eventually settled on, finding himself strangely nervous.

Olaf looked at him sideways. 'Do I look like I've slept?' he replied testily. A movement drew his eye back to the front as one of the women at the rear of the group lurched to her feet and began screaming.

'Hákon, you monster! Help us!'

Dropping his head, Hákon shirked from the sound, embarrassed, and Olaf bellowed for one of his men to shut the woman up. In response, a soldier came forward and clubbed her across the head with his fist with the force he would have used on any man, dragging her back to the ground. More shouts went up in response to the action, causing the soldier to brandish his fist at others amid the rising commotion.

Rolling his eyes with irritation, Olaf hissed and led Hákon away before he caused further distraction. They walked down to the water's edge, leaving the noise behind them. Gulls watched them warily from where they bobbed upon the waves. The sea crowded forward and milled about the two men's feet, as if hungry for the warmth that might linger from the fires. Hákon muttered an apology, which Olaf ignored.

'Arnkell and Dagr and forty or so others will stay here with you,' he said. 'They'll answer only to themselves, but both have agreed to recognise your position as head of the town.'

Hákon swallowed, taken aback by the suddenness of the discussion. 'What will my role be?'

'You'll be ruler, just like you wanted,' Olaf replied positively. 'No man will challenge your position, and any orders Hálfdanr has will be made directly to you.'

Hákon's eyebrows arched and fell. 'Orders?'

'Even earls have masters, Hákon. As of now, all the lands that were formerly Helvik's belong to my half brother. As such, he may want to exercise some control over them. Don't let that bother you. There's plenty of rulers who reign over other men's lands.'

'Puppets,' Hákon corrected, with a disgruntled twist of his head.

Olaf shrugged optimistically. 'A puppet is better than a corpse.' He looked deliberately at Hákon, and smiled thinly.

Hákon rubbed a hand across his face and nodded with acceptance. 'When will you leave?' he sought, clearing his throat as his voice came out croaky.

Now Olaf stooped and picked up a pebble from the sand, studying it between his thumb and finger. 'That is my issue,' he replied, raising his voice with the movement of tossing the stone underarm into the water. 'You were not lying, for once, when you said that this town was struggling.' He came back up the beach a stride to face Hákon. 'Last night my idiot men slew all the horses, save for one found this morning, which I managed to spare. Once they've eaten through them, there'll be nothing much left, so I'd like to be on the road with the slaves by noon.'

'I see,' Hákon began, quirking his mouth with mild surprise.

'But,' Olaf cut him off resoundingly, 'I have a problem, in that I was expecting an extra payment from you before I left, which was never delivered. And this town does have at least one useful asset remaining to it. Therefore, you might have noticed that your boat is gone.'

One glance over his shoulder revealed to Hákon the dark rut scarred into the shore from where the boat had been dragged out to sea, and he turned back with his lips pursed quizzically.

'I needed to occupy some of my more violent characters to keep them from ruining the women,' Olaf explained. 'I sent them out this morning. They'll try their own hand at your sea raids.'

'Our men encountered strong resistance last time,' Hákon cautioned.

Olaf raised one cheek into a confident smile. 'Resistance to your men is sport to mine.' He scratched his head and turned back up the beach. 'We'll be leaving as soon as they return with my final payment.' Without inviting Hákon to follow, he began to stride back up the shingle.

One or two spits of rain had started to drop from the sky, and the wind was picking up. As Olaf drew to a halt once again in front of the captives, they had quietened considerably, apart from the one who had risen to scream at Hákon, who was weeping. All of the ropes were now secured, leaving the women free to be marched away on any notice, and the soldiers hung around the prisoners in groups, awaiting further instruction.

When Hákon arrived alongside Olaf again, the invading leader looked across at him as if waiting for something, and Hákon became unsure whether he had been intended to follow. The rain began to fall in fatter droplets, and Olaf quickly flicked his eyes up at the greying sky.

'I suppose you want to ask about your brothers?' he said, and then he smirked to himself as he noticed the brief look of confusion that Hákon failed to conceal before nodding. In response, Olaf pointed his forehead at the front of the group of captives.

To Hákon's surprise, it was only then that he realised that the foremost women and children tied before his gaze were the familiar faces of his brothers' families. They were gazing up at him, as if they had been waiting for him to look back for the entire time. It was not their eyes that he felt keenest though.

Behind them, Bjǫrn and Eiric sat watching him with brooding intensity, prominent and imposing in their armour among their female counterparts. Bjǫrn was bloodied from a cut on his hairline that concealed his left eye. They were tied to the two other men that had been guarding the longhall, the Anunderssons, whom the invaders had obviously wrongly presumed to be also part of Hákon's family. Their gaze, in contrast, carried apprehension, as if concerned that Hákon would expose them. He did not.

'I'll leave them when we march,' Olaf continued, studying them himself, 'but for now I think it best to keep them tied up with the rest, for your own sake as much as anyone else's.' There was enjoyment on Olaf's features as he spoke the words. Hákon ripped his eyes away from his family and strove not to look back.

'That reminds me,' Olaf added, 'your father's hall.' He could have turned away from those watching at that point, or lowered his voice to a discreet level, but if anything he seemed to speak with deliberate volume. 'It is the only building standing, and I wish to use it with my men, but you may recall that the old man's corpse is still in there.' He studied Hákon closely. 'Do you wish me to keep it for you?'

A coil snapped inside Hákon and his face became a sneer. 'Burn him on a pile with all the rest for all I care,' he spat, and even threw a look at his brothers as he spoke.

Olaf watched the reaction with calm amusement. 'As you wish.'

A shudder passed across the sky, and the rain broke free. The ground began to rattle as water met earth with a sound like a sack of grain being emptied on a flagstone floor. Glancing around briefly, Olaf made off to find shelter and Hákon went with him, slowly calming from his outburst.

'Where will they stay?' Hákon asked, as they moved past the rows of women sitting mute with misery, backs hunched against the rain's chill.

Olaf took a quick look at his captives, as if to check that they were the ones Hákon spoke of, and shrugged dismissively. 'Where they are will do.' He started to angle away to the left to make for the longhall, when his eyes fell upon someone within the group of slaves.

Tyra sat cross-legged on the sodden earth and stared blankly at the horizon, barely seeming to notice as the rain weighted her hair and began to pull it in strands against her face. At the opposite end of the rope that secured her, Frejya sat beside her with a shoulder turned against the rain, concentrated on sheltering the baby under her shawl.

Olaf held his stride and stood to appraise Tyra, so that both women felt his presence and looked around at him in trepidation. Their gaze did not affect him, and he made no effort to look politely away. He barked the name of one of his men and beckoned him over.

'That girl is to stay in the old man's hall with me,' he said loudly, pointing Tyra out so that all could see. 'Untie her and have her brought along.'

The soldier nodded obediently. 'What about her baby?'

Olaf took another glance at the old woman holding the child. She was remonstrating loudly at him, clutching hold of her friend's arm, while the young mother looked fearful and searched around as if for an escape.

'Just the girl,' he said firmly, and then he was away to the building, walking with brisk steps through the downpour.

Moments later, Tyra was being led down to him with her hands still tied, helpless to put up any resistance other than to refuse to use her legs, upon which she was hoisted up and dragged away. The women moaned with distress at the sight. Frejya could only watch, her vision obscured by the rain that bit through into her skin, drenching the blanket in which her son's baby lay. She pressed the little boy closer to her bosom and closed her eyes, as Tyra's desperate cries rang out in the distance.

Chapter Eighteen

Night fell. The rain eased away, leaving the fresh smell of earth and moss in the shrouded air. Down at the sea front the tide crept wavelessly inland like a silent invasion. The gulls had long since quietened and gone off to roost.

Crouched around the feeble glow of a secret fire, no more than a handful of damp sticks, Gunnarr went over his simple plan one more time. There would be no smothering clouds to conceal them from the moon's glow, no crashing waves, driving winds or battering rain to mask the noise of their approach. They were too few in number, and their strength was weakened from having gone over a day without eating. Yet, if they did not act now, they may never get another chance. Gunnarr's words were absorbed by Hilario, Volundr, Ári and young Tyr. Then the fire was kicked into ashes and they were away.

Their path took them down once again to the water's edge, moving carefully without torchlight, so that they had to slide down to the beach on hands and heels, using their limbs to feel out their blackened route. Swords were deemed too clumsy for this undertaking. Those were left on the shore, along with everything else. Each man was stripped to his underclothes, with a single knife gripped in his hand. A hunting fox shrieked from many miles away. They slipped quietly into the chilled, tar-black water.

Gunnarr led them, slowly. Using the rocky outer edge of the west arm of Helvik's bay as his guide, he reached up with both hands and used the moon-glistening stones to pull himself stealthily through the water, like a sea snake closing menacingly on its prey. The others followed in a single line behind him, keeping their luminous faces low against the surface, threading their limbs in and out of the water so as to make no splash.

When they had rounded the point of the bay and Helvik's harbour lay directly ahead of them, Gunnarr halted their progress. After a brief glimpse down at the water's surface, unnervingly opaque in the darkness, he gently raised both hands above his head and allowed himself to sink. He felt his palms submerge and the water's temperature on his face dramatically decrease long before his toe brushed the bottom and he could launch himself upwards again. Deep. Far too deep for anyone unable to swim. But there was no other way. He began to move forward again, and his companions did the same.

Fifteen or so yards closer, he stopped again to assess the shoreline, quietly emptying a mouthful of salt water down his chin. He could see a single torch burning, keeping the centre of the town somewhat illuminated. Other than the flicker of the torchlight, everything else seemed still. But only for an instant.

The torch's glow was blocked for a moment and, as Gunnarr adjusted his eyes, he realised that a man had been standing beside it and had just stepped across its path, very much awake. At the same time, Gunnarr was dismayed to hear voices from up on the shore just beside his head, muffled by the walls of the longhall through which they came. Gunnarr held his breath and listened for a moment, hoping that whoever it was was preparing for sleep. They would make their escape past this same point, and were unlikely to be as discreet on the return journey.

With their pace now dramatically slowed, Gunnarr led his band forward again until the sea floor was close enough to carry their weight, and his friends moved up alongside him. Together they drifted like jetsam towards the shore, keeping to the shadows of the bank to their left, and stopping just far enough away for any whisper passed between them to disintegrate in the breeze. Now all ten eyes examined the scene. Tyr raised a dripping arm carefully and pointed directly ahead of them to the area beyond the burning lantern, but they were too low down to see anything beyond the crest of the beach where the single sentry stood with his back to them. Ári started forward again, but Hilario held him back gently.

Taking his time to find secure handholds through numbing fingers, Gunnarr slithered out of the water until his upper body rested in the shadows of the overhead bank, causing a brief swirling noise to emanate from below, which tested all of their nerves. Immediately he felt a shiver pass through him as wet skin met the cold air. He shuffled a little higher, still hearing the voices from Egil's hall further behind. From this vantage point he could finally properly assess the terrain.

The first thing he noticed, to his surprise, was that the captives were directly in front of him. The outline of their group had been visible from the water, but mistakable as some formation of the landscape. They were clumped together like sheep against the cold. Most had rolled onto their sides to try to sleep. One moved her head and shuffled for position, dispelling any fear that they were corpses already. The man by the lamp was watching over them like a shepherd, and he was not the only one.

His eyes now trained, Gunnarr quickly analysed the task that lay before them. He could see what looked like four guards in total, one at each side of the prisoners, although the figure at the back was hazy and could have been two men, or not a person at all. To the right, he caught a glimpse of a fifth man moving away through the stumps of the houses. Gunnarr took a final image of the scene, making certain that he had not missed anything, but then, just as he had been about to slip back into the water, he was forced to freeze.

The nearest guard had looked aimlessly around and now was staring directly at Gunnarr over his shoulder. Gunnarr held his breath, too late to risk the movement of dropping back under the surface. The man looked for a few moments longer, while Gunnarr's heartbeat thudded out through his mouth, and then turned back to the women. Resisting the urge to slide gratefully back into the sea, Gunnarr shuddered with relief at his decision as the man looked quickly back again a final time, before returning seemingly contented to his watch. Without a splash, Gunnarr re-submerged and hurriedly whispered his findings to his companions.

It took only a few words and then they were ready. Part of Gunnarr wanted to wait to see if the fifth man came back, rather than risk him returning halfway through the job, but the water's chill was beginning to bite deep into their bones, and the night would not last forever. Gunnarr nodded grimly to his party. They slithered forward on their bellies until they were at the shore and the nearest guard was lost over the crest of the beach above their eye line.

'Not until you see mine fall,' Gunnarr breathed a final time, and then he watched with Tyr from the water as his three other companions rose up out of the sea and scurried on hands and toes across the exposed ground in front of them. Hilario arched left, along with Volundr who would circle to the back of the group, and Ári curved away through cover to come in on the right. So close were they now that Ári had not even dared whisper farewell to his son.

Gunnarr waited until the others had had time to reach their positions, alert to any sound they might make. He heard none. They had moved like ghosts. Now he started to crawl up the beach on his forearms, feeling the coarse sand and shale pebbles scratch at his bare skin. Tyr remained at the water's edge, where he had been instructed to stay in safety.

The closest that Gunnarr dared to go was the point at which he could just see the back of his target's head over the top of the bank. He was near enough to see the dirty blond colour of the man's hair, even the wrinkled lines down the sides of his thick-looking neck. Yet any further and the torchlight would have him, and there was no cover that he could use. Its handle still chilled from the water, he pressed the knife into his right palm, rose to his feet, and walked openly towards the soldier.

The guard glanced around casually upon hearing the sound of easy footsteps, impulsively returned Gunnarr's greeting smile, and almost turned away again before the strangeness of Gunnarr's appearance struck him. By then it was far too late. He spun back again straight into the point of Gunnarr's dagger waiting at his neck. Gunnarr thrust the blade in and across to tear away the windpipe, his other hand clamped across the victim's biting mouth, feeling the weight in his arms increase as the man began to slump away. As he went to lay the body down, he was shocked by a sudden movement no more than a yard in front of him.

There had been another man seated at the foot of the torch, whom Gunnarr had been unable to see. He turned now, still half in a dose, to seek out the source of the shuffling footsteps, and then his face suddenly jolted awake in horror. He opened his mouth to raise the alarm, but Gunnarr's hands were full, and though he cast the body he held aside and lunged forward, he was fractionally too slow.

Before the cry could leave the man's lips, Tyr sprang forward enthusiastically from Gunnarr's left and stabbed the man in the ribs beneath his right arm, moving so quickly that Gunnarr almost barrelled into him in his own attempts to cut off the shout. The soldier convulsed backwards, his face creased with pain, and Tyr yanked his blade free. Recovering from his shock, Gunnarr hurriedly knelt down and slit the man's throat as a precaution against the scream he would have likely let out after the initial agony of the wound passed. Tyr stared down at the dying man with fascination, and then looked to Gunnarr, panting, his face a mixture of emotions. Gunnarr shot him a reproving look, and patted him on the head. Then he remembered the others.

Glancing up from where he crouched in the middle of the lamplight, his eyes found all three of them hunched over and hurrying through the prisoners. He realised that they had done their jobs with such efficiency that he had not even noticed.

Some of the women were beginning to stir now, many exclaiming with relief, and Gunnarr held a pleading finger to his lips and begged for their cooperation. Ári, Hilario and Volundr had already begun cutting through the prisoners' ropes at the middle and back of the group and Gunnarr's heart began to convulse rapidly as he realised how close they were to success. To his side he saw Tyr bound across to extinguish the torch flame that gave away their presence, but Gunnarr snatched his arm and shook his head. Such action would surely alert their enemies, if anything. Besides, they could not work without its light.

Gunnarr hurried to the front of the captives now and began sawing through the rope that held them, instructing an eager Tyr to do the same. The women and children that had been freed already began to mill around him, many with nervous questions, and Gunnarr did his best to quiet them as their combined whispers seemed to reach a crescendo. Some wanted to scurry away into the darkness as soon as they were untied, meaning at intervals Gunnarr had to break off and reluctantly raise his voice to urge them to stay with the group. Others immediately began to untie their fellow prisoners, or asked for a weapon of some sort with steadfast resolve on their faces.

There was so much to worry about that Gunnarr barely noticed Bjǫrn and Eiric until he was about to set knife to their ropes. He hesitated upon seeing them, recalling their reaction to the death of Fafrir, and Eiric seemed to read what he was thinking.

'Hákon has betrayed us,' he said, not bothering to whisper. 'He killed Father. You were right, Gunnarr.'

Gunnarr felt a falling sensation in his chest, and his hands dropped down to his sides. Shamefully, he recalled the last he had seen of the old man's face, torn by his helpless love for his children. He remembered the words that had passed between them as they'd sat drinking ale together in the dimming longhall. 'I may be an old fool in many things,' Egil had said, with a smile, 'but I know I can trust my own son.'

'Where is Hákon now?' Gunnarr growled.

Eiric seemed to recognise his intentions. 'We do not know,' he said regretfully.

'Untie us, Gunnarr!' Bjǫrn cut in, holding his hands out impatiently. 'There will be plenty of time to hunt him down once we escape this place.'

Gunnarr looked around and found that most of the women and children were free, and the volume of their uncertain voices was beginning to grow to a perilous level. Gathering his composure, he swiftly released Bjǫrn and Eiric and the Anundersson brothers whom they were tied to.

'Start getting them down to the water. I must find my mother.'

He pushed his way to the back of the group, slashing through the ropes of the few that remained prisoner, until he realised that there were no more to release. Relieved, he began searching the faces of the crowding women for Frejya. After a few moments he reached the back of the prisoners without finding her, and realised that she must have already passed him in the confusion. The group was starting to make for the water now, their trampling footsteps deafening amidst what had been a perfectly still night, and Gunnarr circled at a tiptoed half jog back to the front to catch up with his mother, wishing he could afford to shout out and bring the noise under control.

But as he got there and began to watch the women file single-mindedly past him, he still could not see Frejya, and began to feel a bleed of concern. Confused, he cast a glance over his shoulder to see if any had reached the water already. It would even have been typical of her nature, he told himself, to strike out alone and lead the escape, but there were no figures ahead of him that he had not already seen pass.

His search became more desperate. He began clutching at women and pulling them out of his way, and still Frejya's precious face did not appear, until he forgot all about the importance of calm and silence and resorted to frantically asking each person that passed him for her whereabouts. They were all too hurried to even take in his words. A thought came to his head and he began looking for Tyra instead, but he had already studied most of the handful of faces that remained.

Someone whispered his name to his side, and although he did find familiar faces when he turned, it was only Ári and Tyr. Between them they supported Ári's heavily pregnant wife, Ingrid, her tired expression bolstered by sweet relief.

'Ári—' Gunnarr began to ask desperately, but his friend cut him off with regret.

'She's not here, Gunnarr,' he whispered. He gestured to his wife, and she answered Gunnarr's searching gaze.

'They took her away, Gunnarr, and the baby. I'm so sorry.'

Gunnarr fell silent and swallowed the words. 'Where to?' he blurted.

Ingrid shook her head and began to get upset. Ári stepped across her and placed a restraining hand on Gunnarr's shoulder.

'I'm sorry, Gunnarr, but we must away. The swim will take us longer than most.' He gave a last consoling look and then made for the water, he and his son supporting Ingrid over the slippery rocks.

They merged with the others and were swallowed into the waves, feet first, sinking before Gunnarr's eyes. He could not force himself to join them. He stood beside the solitary torch, its flame flapping as it neared exhaustion, and watched their escape.

When his gaze cleared, he was alone with the discarded rope at his feet, his pain forgotten by the rest in the selfishness of survival.

Chapter Nineteen

He could pour fear into the blood of even the wildest of men, but Olaf Gudrødsson had never had a temper. Tempers showed loss of control, and loss of control was weak. Instead, his expression in the crisp morning sunlight was closer to brooding intrigue than anger. He was quiet, seemingly absorbed in his thoughts. The gathering of men that now watched him in careful silence knew that that was when he was at his most dangerous.

He stood in the brown mud at the very centre of the empty north road, a position from which he should have looked down upon his newly acquired slaves, huddled up in orderly ranks. With his hands clasped loosely behind his back, he held his chin slightly elevated as he gazed at the new focal point of the deserted scene. In the eerie silence of dawn, the wind carried a shuffle of fallen leaves, a whistle of birdsong, and a creak of rope. The numbers in the watching crowd began steadily to increase. Many of their expressions were fearful.

A figure pushed through the assembly with flustered urgency, and Hákon drew up beside Olaf, escorted by the man that had been sent to fetch him. His hair, Olaf noted, was tufted up on one side. It was rare to find men with ambitions of greatness so accustomed to sleeping past sunrise. He looked quickly across at Olaf, swallowed, and then followed the leader's gaze, rolling his eyes upwards to study the pair of feet that dangled just in front of his face.

Beads of blood dripped steadily off the toe from a trail that followed the length of the right leg, adding to a drying pool at Hákon's feet. Those men with an eye for the dead had noted how the victim's arms were loose, his shoulders sagged and relaxed, his face showing no trace of gruesome contortions or purple bruising. Clearly the rope knotted tightly around his neck and hoisted over the lowest branch of the nearest tree had not been used to kill the guard, but to put him on display.

'What have they done to his head?' Hákon shuddered, looking back to Olaf.

Olaf remained grimly fixed on the hanging figure, twisting slightly with a slow creak in the gentle breeze. The killer had taken his time. Many small knots in the rope were visible from where he had patiently tied several pieces together to give him a noose long enough to throw over the branch and secure around the trunk of the tree. And then, strangest of all, he had somehow placed a coil of rope on top of the slaughtered man's head, so that it sat in a neat pile across the scalp.

Breaking his stare, Olaf turned slowly to Hákon and gave him a look of foreboding. 'Looks like a crown to me.'

While Hákon absorbed the significance of the words, Olaf glanced around at the faces of his clustered men as they comprehended the prisoners that had vanished into the air and the grisly relic that had been left behind for them. A hundred times must he have seen superstition render tough men feeble and childlike, even those that could laugh and sing through a battle. Flesh and blood held nothing to fear for them, nor anything else that could be lopped up with sword or with axe. But spirits and spells were something that speed or strength or skill with a spear could never contend against. Only submission brought leniency. Olaf beckoned Hákon's escort closer to receive a hushed instruction.

'Get him cut down and disposed of.' He turned to Hákon and jabbed him roughly on the shoulder. 'I need to discuss this with you. Inside.'

They walked down to the longhall in silence. Olaf sucked on his bottom lip and gazed around in contemplation. The day had turned out so bright and fresh that, to him, it seemed that nature itself was celebrating his difficulties. Blades of yellow grass swayed happily in the breeze. Seagulls glided on the gusts overhead, shrieking mocking laughter. On either side of his path, the waves crashed around, bright white and gleeful, as if goading that they'd never tell what they'd seen.

As soon as the two men were through the longhall's doorway and into the gloom beyond, the mood changed almost instantly, and Hákon could sense it. Prowling into the body of the hall, Olaf flung off his cloak and snapped out a hand, wordlessly directing Hákon to a bench. Hákon accepted the order without question and seated himself somewhat hurriedly. Olaf did not engage him initially. He paced restlessly, his face becoming dark and gnarled, and the space upon which his feet moved back and forth was marked at either end by the dirty bloodstains that still adorned the floor from the deaths the room had witnessed.

'So, do you know who did it?' Olaf began suddenly. His voice carried the strain of someone who had suffered immense embarrassment.

Hákon shook his head rapidly. 'No, Olaf.'

'But surely you recognise that they know you?' Olaf responded, almost before Hákon had finished his reply, and he followed his words with a hiss of irritation as he saw Hákon's confused response. 'That corpse hanging out there, with its crown, is a message for the person who would be ruler of this town.' Olaf shouted with frustration. 'That person, Hákon, is you!'

Flustered by Olaf's raised voice, Hákon stammered and struggled for a reply.

'Your brothers?' Olaf quizzed.

'It's possible,' Hákon spluttered. 'But—'

There came a sound from behind the partition to the master's chamber, and the conversation halted unexpectedly. Hákon saw Olaf hastily smother the growing aggression on his face in response. He nodded to Hákon, indicating that he had heard the noise, and then called out loudly to the back of the room.

'If you are going to listen then you may as well come out here where we can see you.'

Frowning slightly, Hákon swivelled his head to the back of the room. After a moment, the door to the chamber opened and Tyra leaned timidly out from inside. Her face was bowed low, apologetically.

'Come on, your friend too,' Olaf encouraged sharply, and he forced a quick non-threatening smile.

Gradually, Tyra revealed herself and stepped into the room, still dressed in the rags she'd worn before. She was not alone. In the cradle of her left arm she carried a baby, its legs kicking out from under the grey blanket it was wrapped in. Then, behind her, another figure appeared. Hákon recognised her immediately.

'What is she doing here?' he asked indignantly.

Olaf pointed impatiently for Tyra and Frejya to seat them-selves on the benches by the partition wall, and then answered Hákon with such self-assurance that it came across almost as defensive.

'I had them brought here last night, for Tyra's comfort.' His eyes flicked away from Hákon's more swiftly than usual, and he began to approach where the women had seated themselves against the back wall.

Hákon made an incredulous face and twisted on the bench so that he was facing them. 'You do realise that it's not her baby?' he spat pithily, and the glint in his eye as he spoke the words showed that he expected an enraged response.

Olaf merely looked back at him plainly from where he stood over the women. 'Yes, I do. Tyra told me everything yesterday.' He returned to face the females, with an attempted softened tone that sounded alien coming from his mouth. 'Did he take the milk?'

Tyra nodded uncomfortably, speaking with a muted voice. 'Some.'

'Good,' Olaf sighed, raising one cheek into a closed-lip smile. No army of his travelled anywhere without two goats being dragged along at the head of it. They were symbols of Tanngrisnir and Tanngnjóstr, the two noble beasts that propelled Thor's chariot. On this occasion, it also so happened that Tanngnjóstr was a female with a plentiful udder, and she'd probably saved the babe's life.

Olaf extended a grubby finger down towards the little boy.

'Don't you dare,' Frejya warned, with a fierce expression, and Olaf drew his hand away, smiling broadly at the old woman. She'd been nothing but trouble since the moment they'd ushered her, sopping wet, through the doors of the longhall just as darkness was falling. Ignoring Olaf as if he wasn't there, she'd set the baby down beside the fire and took off all her clothes to dry them, daring him to look upon the body of an old woman, and claiming he'd suffer more from it than she would. When Olaf offered her some food, she'd snatched two handfuls into her mouth and then hurled the plate at his head. He found her wonderfully entertaining.

Hákon's gloating voice cut in again, festering with sarcasm. 'Well, I hope you have thanked Tyra, Frejya,' he remarked, with a vindictive smile. 'If it were not for her, you'd probably be free at this moment.'

Both women appeared confused by the words. They turned, for once voluntarily, to the authority of Olaf for an explanation. Concealed behind his waist, Olaf's fingers clenched in reaction to the jovial tone with which Hákon spoke of his loss of a fortune, but he smoothed his anger away and enlightened the women in a composed voice.

'Last night the other prisoners escaped.'

He watched the women's faces fall. Tyra placed a hand to her mouth, and turned apologetically to Frejya, but her friend dismissed her own disappointed expression and stroked Tyra soothingly across the back.

'Do not feel too down,' Olaf continued, moving back now across the room. 'We'll be getting them back, won't we, Hákon? Just as soon as I find out who it is that could want you dead?'

Hákon flicked open his palm dismissively, missing the threat in Olaf's glare. He was buoyed still by some confidence he had gained from baiting Frejya. 'Like you said, my brothers,' he shrugged. He spoke like a man who had come to terms with his unpopularity.

Olaf growled with discontent at the answer. 'All of the guards had their throats slit,' he snapped. 'Apart from the one strung up by his neck, their bodies were lying in the exact positions I stationed them in. If your brothers somehow escaped their bonds, the guards would surely have seen them do so, and would at least have moved to intercept.' He glanced briefly at Tyra, before returning to Hákon with his conclusion. 'It seems to me that the killers were outsiders, enough of them to kill all the guards at once to avoid alerting the others. Or else the work of some phantom.'

'Perhaps your guards were sleeping,' Hákon ventured. 'One or two escaped prisoners could easily have done the job in that case, and my brothers did have two others with them.'

Olaf's lip curled angrily. 'My men are too scared of me to sleep easy in their beds, let alone at their posts. There are enough footprints leading down the beach for a blind man to follow. If they had a boat, they are gone. If they swam, they cannot be far.' Now he approached Hákon, very fast, until he was standing almost on top of him, causing the would-be ruler to recoil in his seat. 'Now,' he asked huskily, his tainted breath blowing across Hákon's uncomfortable face, 'do you know of anyone with a boat big enough to carry that many prisoners?'

'No,' Hákon insisted, 'other than the boat your own men have already taken.' His eyes bulged for a moment then, as if he'd given himself an idea, but Olaf cut him off before he opened his mouth.

'Save your tongue. They wouldn't steal from me either. Your answer is good,' he snapped decisively, taking a stride backwards. 'It means we can catch them. Especially,' he added with a jab of his finger, 'if you can tell me who it is that came for them and where they might be heading.'

Hákon's hands went up protectively. 'I don't know! Perhaps some of the men fled the battle, I don't know.'

'You do!' Olaf assured, leaning close again, but still Hákon shook his head and protested. Snarling, Olaf stepped forward and was about to become persuasive with a fist, when a voice stopped his movements.

'I know who it was.'

All faces turned to the source at the back of the room. Frejya was smiling, her entire face lit up. Her bright eyes were crinkled with pleasure, and they were focused on Hákon.

'I know a man who holds a grudge against you, Hákon. One that you will not escape from.'

Hákon smiled back and leapt to his feet. 'If you are about to say the name I think you are, then I assure you that you do not.'

Undeterred, Frejya turned to Olaf and continued, her voice purring with calm menace. 'Your friend here is responsible for the death of my son's wife,' she explained. 'Gunnarr will not rest until the both of you are feeding the gulls.' In her eyes there was absolute confidence.

Olaf found himself smiling at Frejya again. More interested than threatened, he looked across to Hákon for verification. To his surprise, he found him grinning broadly, savouring the words he was about to speak.

'I would have thought that even a deaf old woman would have heard the news by now,' Hákon sighed, moving closer so that he was near enough to see every bite of pain he was about to draw across Frejya's features. 'Gunnarr killed my brother, and in doing so broke the rule. My father had him executed even before Olaf's men attacked.'

Frejya faced him back without reaction, maintaining her steadfast expression. But Hákon saw something move behind her eyes, and he laughed aloud to himself in delight. Still Frejya did not look away, but her chin faltered slightly, and the colour began to withdraw from her wind-scorched cheeks as she remembered suddenly the desperate plea for forgiveness that Egil had made to her as he bled his life out on the floor. To her side she heard Tyra unsuccessfully try to stifle a sob, and then, for almost the first time, there was a choking sound, and the baby began to cry.

Without looking, Frejya held out her hands and Tyra passed her the child. The boy's wails almost immediately softened with the touch of his grandmother and he began to settle again, nuzzling his face against her chest. Frejya's expression changed.

'I don't believe you,' she replied solidly.

Hákon grinned and dropped down eagerly in front of her. 'Do you want to see proof?' he encouraged, inclining his head as if sympathetic to her doubts.

Again Frejya faltered only briefly. 'Yes.'

Hákon jumped up immediately and almost danced out of the doors.

For longer than expected, they waited. Frejya was staring unblinkingly at the floor, and her hands were trembling so much that she had to hand the baby back to Tyra, who had still not gained control of her tears. Olaf watched Tyra closely, troubled by her reaction.

When what seemed like a long while had passed, Hákon appeared again in the doorway. At first, as he strode energetically into the room, slightly out of breath, it seemed that he carried only a bundle of rope in his grasp. He even held out a length of it in one of his hands, to display it to them as he approached.

'This is the rope that Gunnarr was tied to as they took him away to have his throat cut,' he announced, unable to contain himself until he reached them. 'It was found still attached to the horse that led him.' He halted, exhaled, and tossed what he carried at Frejya's feet. 'Say a greeting to your precious son, old woman.'

Tyra screamed and jumped away as the weight of something within the coils of rope dragged the heap out of the air to land with a muted thud directly in front of where Frejya sat. The package rolled over and skidded, and two severed forearms slid forth from the bundle, coming to rest at right angles to each other. Again Tyra screamed, shielding her eyes with her arm.

Remaining where she sat, Frejya stared paralysed at the detached limbs. Clumps of dried mud were caked across them from where they had been dragged along by the horse. At the hands, the skin was a greying colour, the redundant fingers curled up like dead shoots. Of the open wounds, only one was visible, a rough, ripped cut that had torn a jagged path through the flesh. A yellowish, jelly-like glaze had formed over the stump, through which two cross-sections of splintered bone were visible, unclean breaks that looked like they had been smashed rather than sliced.

Frejya's eyes fell shut. She turned her face away from the body parts, letting her hair form a curtain across her features. Her throat pulsed as she swallowed heavily. Across from her, Olaf's face fell slightly with pity. He realised he'd been hoping she'd be spared, for her defiance, her cheek, her combative spirit. Beside him, Hákon began to nod with satisfaction.

They both grunted in surprise when Frejya suddenly leant forward again and took up one of the stumps in her hand. She held it up in front of Hákon with a look of contempt.

'This,' she stated, waving the arm, 'is not my son.' She dropped it again at her feet.

Tyra held her sobs with a strangled sound. Olaf again could not resist a smile of admiration. Hákon, though, merely laughed off her response.

'You're right, of course,' he replied, leaving a pause in which Tyra's eyes shot to him with hope. 'That is your son's arm. Your actual son will have bled out on the clifftops somewhere.' He cackled at his joke, and looked over to Olaf for approval, but the older man was watching only Frejya's reaction.

Her body language was transformed. Her shoulders were loose, her palms lying open in her lap. Her eyes were dancing like a maiden laughing at a jest. She rested her head back against the wall behind her, and smirked. 'It's not him, Hákon. You are not yet safe.'

The assuredness with which she spoke was such that Hákon could not help but be troubled. He thrust out his lower lip, colouring with humiliation. His tone switched from jovial to threatening.

'Perhaps you do not realise what you are doing?' he suggested, coming closer and kicking the coils of rope aside as he did. 'If, by some faintest chance, Gunnarr does live, I will ride out today and have him hunted down and ripped into pieces like a hare. Your stubbornness is such that you must insist that your son is alive. But in doing so, I can assure you this: you are hastening a death he might otherwise have escaped from.'

He paused, until Frejya gave a nod to signal her understanding. Then he fished with his hand until he retrieved one of the arms and held it up barely a wrist's width in front of Frejya's face.

'Now,' he said, 'this is the arm of Gunnarr Folkvarrsson. Are you telling me I am mistaken?'

Olaf stepped closer with intrigue.

'Frejya, don't!' Tyra begged, still shying away from the mutilated limb.

Frejya faced Hákon back, unflinching. Opening her palm wordlessly, she received the dismembered limb from Hákon and held it upright so that the lifeless hand and fingers were in the centre of his view.

'When Gunnarr was a boy,' she said, 'he was playing at sword fighting with one of his friends. In fact, you may know that friend rather well, Hákon,' she added darkly, and watched as his jaw tightened. 'Well,' she continued, 'that friend had always been somewhat jealous of my son and, unknown to Gunnarr, he'd taken to secretly sharpening his little wooden sword into a point. Are you beginning to remember?'

Hákon gave her a hating look, but she carried on, unfazed.

'Gunnarr came home that day with blood pouring from his hand and a great chunk of skin hanging off it. He carried a scar across the knuckles of his right fist ever since.'

She took the dead hand now, spat on it, and used her thumb to rub away the dried mud from across the knuckles with slow, deliberate movements. Then she drew her thumb away and revealed to Hákon the unbroken skin underneath.

'My son will be glad of the chance to see you again,' she said. 'And when he does, believe me, it will not be his blood spilled.'

Tyra let her chin drop sadly. Olaf shook his head slowly, in respect for the character of the woman, and in regret at the cost she would pay for it. Hákon kept her fixed in his glare, his upper lip curling above his quivering lower one, and then a thin smile slithered across his face.

'You're a proud old fool, aren't you?' he breathed, and when Frejya gave no reply but a bold stare, he continued. 'It may have just cost you your life.'

Chapter Twenty

The escaped prisoners had put as much distance as they could between Helvik and themselves while they still had the benefit of night's cover. Hilario had led them west, encouraging them to drag their tired legs as far as possible before daylight exposed them. They had kept to the shallows wherever available, using the sweeping motion of the waves to smooth away their tracks. Only when more and more banks of jagged rock began to disrupt the shoreline did they cut inland, climbing clumsily up the rolling stone trails where they would leave no print.

Despite their efforts, Gunnarr had been able to track them relatively easily, moving at the conservative jog of the hunter in the cold light of early dawn, and he masked any obvious spoor where he could. They had been hampered by the need to travel in darkness, and forced to move at the pace of the children and older women. Gunnarr followed them past Ymir's knuckle, where he had so nearly lost his life in the darkness two nights ago. When he eventually caught them, just as the sun's feet cleared the horizon, they were no more than five or six miles from Helvik town.

For a group freshly liberated, they were a dispirited bunch. Drenched by seawater up to their necks, their long woollen garments had all been rendered the same shade of overcast grey, and the chill that they felt from the wind on their backs ensured that the skin of their arms and faces did not much differ in colour. Of the children they carried or dragged by the arm, most looked to be younger than six. There'd been a bad spell of sickness some seven years ago, and most of the young ones at that time had perished. They stumbled along like a wearying herd, and a few of them looked prime for the wolves. Gunnarr hung back from the group as he reached them. All of their eyes at once would have been too much.

With the weaker ones fading and falling behind, the decision was made that it was best to find a secure place to hide out and rest rather than push on and risk being caught in the clear light of day. Once evening fell they would strike out again, either over the hills and on to the north, or westwards until they were lost. Anxiously, they drove half a mile further, glances over shoulders becoming increasingly frequent, until they reached the cover of a patch of woodland.

In another age, too distant to know, a stretch of bluff between two faces of cliff had given way in a rockslide, receding into a smooth sunken slope which led directly to a bay at the sea floor. While the walls of cliff at either side had remained rocky and impenetrable, the shaken earth at the centre had given way to soil, the whole surface of which was now littered with scraggy pine trees, leaning haphazardly against each other all the way up the slope. The townsfolk had various vulgar names for the patch of foliage in between two bare walls. In the summer, the hidden spaces were awash with amorous couples, for it was said to be a place of fertility.

It was also a good defensive position. A man could bind a dagger to a stave and defend a pass single-handedly, presented with each assailant one at a time as they were funnelled into the narrow alleys between the tree-trunks. The party traversed slowly down the hill and in amongst the trees, following the path cut by a small but determined waterfall from which they could drink. Sentries were sent back out onto the cliffs, three out of the nine men of the group. At age twelve, Tyr had been made part of that count. The escapees tried to settle themselves among the pine needles and fallen branches, lying down hungrily to rest. Nobody suggested a fire.

Gunnarr sat apart from the others, up near the summit of the hill. His father had hated woods like this. Vermin trees, he'd called them. They grew in such a greedy press that they deprived all others of the sun. So mulched was the ground that nothing else could live there, as if the pines were so possessive over their unlikely home that they would share not an inch of it, even with a single shoot of grass. Ants hurried about around him like fools. No one came to show concern for Frejya. Gunnarr supposed she had not been so popular. She was too bold of character, and while some had loved her for it, it was just as likely to alienate others. Boring women had many friends. And Frejya would never have dreamt of being boring.

Down the slope below him he could see Ári lying back while Ingrid slept gratefully across his chest. She was clinging to him like they were being tossed around by a storm. Gunnarr could not look at them for long, and rolled onto his side to put his back to them. The softness of the pine-rot bed he lay upon and the weight of his yearning heart seemed to drag him into the ground. Reflectively, he realised that he had not slept properly for many days, and that was his last thought before his eyelids collapsed and he fell into a deep, exhausted sleep amongst the smell of needle dust and resin.

He dreamed a memory. It must have been fighting to get into his mind when he was conscious, and had slipped through now that he was sleeping. The welcoming sound of the longhall full of laughter. Egil stood at the head of the table, declaring a celebration to warm them through the winter nights to come, and making the same joke he did every year about closing his eyes for a moment and missing the summer. His cheeks were red and his eyes were watery with mirth. Frejya boasted that she could drink as much as any man, and proceeded to get as drunk as one. The fire felt blazing hot on Gunnarr's neck. Kelda laughed and wriggled in his lap, scolding the men for the coarseness of their jokes. The lamps waned. After a valiant effort, Frejya fell asleep at the table, and Egil was forced to take her in his arms and carry her to one of the beds. Gunnarr told Kelda he could be happy seeing that sight every night. She smiled as if he'd tickled her, and whispered something in his ear, but the bench was tipping backwards, and as they hit the earth she was gone.

He awoke with Hilario's troubled face hanging directly above his own. His hands were placed across Gunnarr's tunic from where he had been shaking him hurriedly.

'Gunnarr,' he said again, seeing consciousness returning to his friend's eyes, 'you must come quickly.' He held out one of the swords that they had salvaged from the fighting on the clifftops. Gunnarr looked at him for a moment, and then took it in his hand.

The sun was already beginning to roll down from its midday peak. Hilario led them up the slope slightly, and then out over the clifftops, back in the direction from which they had come. They moved at a fast jog for longer than Gunnarr had expected, perhaps even reaching a mile. Eventually they came upon a sharp climb into a small rise on the coast, and Gunnarr saw people lying at the brow of the hill ahead of him. Following Hilario's lead, he slowed his pace back to a walk, and dropped down to crawl the last few yards up to them.

Ári was there, with Bjǫrn and Eiric, and Leofric Anundersson. Gunnarr crawled amongst them, breathing quickly through his open mouth, unsure of whether it was safe to speak. The others greeted him with serious expressions. Ári took Gunnarr by the shoulder and pulled him down beside him, before pointing ahead to what the rest were looking at. Gunnarr craned forward and observed the scene.

Down below them and back towards Helvik, on a lower point in the clifftop, a small group of men could be seen. Gunnarr immediately tensed and roved his searching eyes across them. He expected them to be hurrying, or at least casting about for the trail, but it did not take long to realise that they were no longer following. They were waiting.

The men had formed into a clumsy circle, seemingly so that they could see in all directions. Gunnarr counted them quickly. Eleven. His eye was drawn immediately to the one who was seated on a horse. As Gunnarr focused on him, the rider dismounted and moved into the middle of the circle. There was too much distance between them to see features, but the man looked reasonably short, nothing more.

Gunnarr could not understand what the men were doing. He almost turned to Ári to ask if they had been seen, or communicated with, when a last study of the group made him realise that it was not only men that he had counted. Not all of the people, it seemed, were stood in that circle by choice. At the top edge, nearest to the cliff face and the ocean expanse reverberating behind, someone was being held by one of the soldiers, and Gunnarr could even see the body language of their resistance. It was undeniably a woman prisoner, shorter than the others and clothed in pale skirts. She looked young and energetic, fighting relentlessly to get free.

Thoughts humming, Gunnarr began to ask himself how they could have let one fall behind when they had been so careful. He had even followed as a rearguard himself. Surely he had not missed anyone who might have been struggling at the back? Closing his eyes, he flicked his mind through the faces he had looked upon since sunrise, and it was at that moment that he remembered Tyra. He had not seen her when they had rescued the others, but he had been too concerned with finding his mother to even think of her.

Yet even as the thought of his mother flashed subordinately across his mind, he saw the man who had been on horseback approach the woman, saw the way that she swung out recklessly for his face as soon as he stepped within range, and he could not help but be reminded not of Tyra, but of her. The man stepped casually away from the attack, and then he turned so that he was almost directly facing them. They saw him shout first, his head thrown back and his hand cupped on one side of his mouth, and then the sound came bouncing off the hills and into their ears.

'Gunnarr!'

The other men lying around Gunnarr failed to react. Clearly it was not the first time that the man had made the call. As if to confirm it, Ári turned to his friend.

'He's been shouting for you since they arrived.'

Gunnarr looked back at him with shock on his face. 'I think they've got my mother.'

Ári nodded as if that much was plain.

'And that can only be my brother's voice,' Bjǫrn grunted from the other side.

Gunnarr jolted up onto his knees. 'You're sure?'

'Certain.'

Gunnarr was on his feet. 'Circle around behind them and cut off their escape,' he said, and then he took off back down the hill before they could even question him. The north wind roared in his ears. He drew his sword from its sheath and tossed the leather guard into the grass.

Chapter Twenty-One

From where he stood with his men on the open clifftop, Hákon had not seen any movement on the hills in front of him. He knew that they were there, though. They had been following traces of the trail intermittently and had moved at speed, so that the prisoners could not be far ahead. Now surely close, he had positioned his men where the ground was good, flat and open, so that they could not miss any approaching foe. The wind from the sea was reasonably strong. It would carry his shouts to them even if their pace had exceeded his expectations.

He looked around at his party while they stayed concentrated on their surroundings. Olaf's mood had been strange, hostile, all morning. He had offered Hákon only nine men, claiming that he wanted to retain the rest in case of another raid on the town. They were good men though, brainless and ever so slightly twisted. Hákon particularly liked Fraener, the one he had charged with holding his female hostage. He was a brute, cruel by nature and as tall as a spear, with a mouth full of black teeth and curses. Even now Hákon could hear him berating Frejya incessantly, and when she struck him he struck her back without restraint, chuckling in the manner of one who loved his work. Looking over his shoulder, Hákon smiled wickedly at Frejya, and then called out to his target once more.

'Gunnarr!'

Almost as soon as the sound of his echo had died upon the hills, there was a grunt from one of the men in Hákon's group and a bustle of excitement grew up around him. His heart jolting, Hákon bounded over to the commotion, and soon picked out the lone figure jogging down off the hilltops ahead of them.

He was moving quickly, with worry. A flash of sunlight revealed that his sword was already drawn. Hákon called to alert the rest of his men, who then broke positions and came to cluster together to watch the approach of the so-called phantom who had left them with five dead comrades to wake up to that morning.

The blond of Gunnarr's hair was visible now as he drew closer. He had not slowed, in spite of the fact that the waiting group had clearly spotted him. Hákon's men were shouting threats and yelping excitedly like a pack of hounds. Still flustered, Hákon glanced to his left to check on his captives. Frejya was still locked in Fraener's grip, watching her son's approach. Hákon thought she might scream out to him to stay away and save himself, but she was silent. Also mute was his second prisoner, but that was to be expected. The soldier standing to the side of Fraener was clearly not accustomed to handling babies. He held Gunnarr's child with one arm around its chest, so that the little boy's naked legs were hanging out underneath his grip and kicking weakly.

Some ten yards away, Gunnarr drew to a halt. He watched the group cautiously, still slightly elevated by the levelling slope of the hill, and thrust his sword into the ground. His eyes sought out his mother behind the crowd of restless men that cajoled him and brandished their weapons. He nodded to her reassuringly, to which she replied with a brave, supportive smile. Unseen by the others, Gunnarr's eyes quickly scanned the empty landscape behind the group. Then he swept his wind-wisped hair back over his head, and waited for someone to speak.

With more effort than he would have hoped for, Hákon bade his battle-charged party to stand aside and let him through. The instant he made himself apparent, Gunnarr's eyes locked onto him like a buzzard. The intensity of the stare almost pushed Hákon off balance. He saw Gunnarr's hand drop to the hilt of his sword.

'I've brought you some visitors,' he managed to call across the wind, in response to which Fraener, a natural, snarled and enthusiastically kicked Frejya down onto her knees. Following his lead, the other soldier held the baby clumsily aloft.

'What do you want?' Gunnarr snapped, disguising his surprise at seeing the child a prisoner also. He'd barely even remembered he had a son.

Hákon wanted to respond with some stinging remark, but his wit failed him. He could not tie down his nerves. 'These men—' he started. 'You will lead these men to where you are hiding Olaf's prisoners.' He paused for a moment to gather his thoughts, and it allowed Gunnarr to cut in.

'I thought you wanted to be a ruler, Hákon? You sound more like a ruler's child now than ever.' He was bartering for time, continuously monitoring the horizon out of the sides of his eyes. Now he picked up some movement in the distance, and quickly ignored it.

'You will lead them to where you are hiding the prisoners,' Hákon repeated in a strained voice, 'or I will have your

220

mother and child killed.' He fixed Gunnarr with an intense stare of his own. 'When you return with the prisoners, your family will be returned to the slaves, and I will have you killed in their place.'

'Me killed, and my mother and child sold as slaves? You give me little incentive.'

Hákon spat with anger, and impulsively he whipped around and approached the hostages. Without breaking stride, he snatched up Gunnarr's son by one of his ankles, causing the child to yelp with shock, and hoisted him upside down into the air.

'This is your incentive!' he snarled, and took the remaining two steps to the cliff edge, holding his arm aloft and dangling the child over the abyss like a bird ready to be plucked. Gunnarr's ribcage shuddered at the sight. Frejya made a horrified sound and fought to free her hands. The baby began to cry out and wriggle its thick little arms and legs in a frenzied attempt to break free. Fear sprang to Gunnarr's face for the first time and, seeing it there, Hákon jerked the child back to safety and stuffed it back into the soldier's hands, a look of satisfaction on his face.

Screaming with outrage, Frejya lunged at Hákon with feet and fists, only for Fraener to restrain her easily and cuff her with the flat of his forearm.

'And I will take pleasure in killing this bitch mother of yours with my hands alone,' he shouted to Gunnarr as he wrenched Frejya back into a kneeling position, prompting Hákon to turn to Gunnarr with eyes gleaming in support of the suggestion.

Gunnarr was not really hearing the words. Through the turmoil of his emotions, he was secretly watching his comrades closing in on their prey. They were out in the open now, only fifty yards away, five clear shapes against the barren terrain, running as quietly as they could. If a single one of Hákon's men was to turn his head he would not have been able to miss them. Gunnarr swung up his arm, and pointed it to the man who held his mother.

'What is your name?' he asked loudly, seeing the man's face break into a smile as he picked up Gunnarr's mood.

'Fraener,' he sneered, and took himself a fistful of Frejya's hair to shove her back down again as she tried to regain her feet.

An arc of soil showered through the air as Gunnarr snatched his sword out of the ground. 'You will be the second that I kill,' he said.

The watching soldiers tensed, bunching together and bristling towards his threat. Every single one of them was focused on Gunnarr and his sword, but Hákon was thinking of his horse. He whipped his head around to check that his steed was still within easy reach, and immediately came face to face with five swordsmen bearing down upon his men. Two were charging straight for him, and he knew his brothers' faces well enough to tell when they were in a murderous mood.

A strangled shout burst through his lips. He stumbled backwards and down onto his back, and immediately felt knees bashing past his head as his alerted men hurdled him and went to defend the ambush. The attackers did not slow. Someone shouted a battle cry. Olaf's men braced their legs for impact. Then another shout splintered through the air.

'Stop!'

Gunnarr had rushed forward only five yards, but now he stood frozen in his tracks. Somehow his friends heard his call, picked up the desperation in his voice, and they skidded to a halt, themselves only five yards from the wall of seven men poised to meet them. One of Hákon's soldiers took the chance to spring forward into an attack, prompting Hilario to clatter the sword away with his own blade, and then a different voice screamed out.

'Hold your blades, all of you!'

Olaf's men recognised Hákon's voice and they stilled their feet, the man who had attacked breaking off just before his second strike and retreating reluctantly back into the group. The two bands of men faced each other down, chests heaving, blowing hot breath into the wind. Their faces itched for action, bodies primed for any movement.

Gunnarr's features were tight as if with pain, and his eyes were locked on where the tip of Hákon's blade rested just underneath Frejya's chin. Her head was forced backwards, leaving her unable to speak, pushing her back against the barrel chest of Fraener as he gripped both of her arms.

Warily, Gunnarr began to creep forward. Closest to him was the guard holding his son, who had managed to draw his sword but was now looking uncertain as to his place in the stand-off.

'Not a step closer, Gunnarr!' Hákon warned, his voice shrill and reckless. 'You know I'll cut her throat if anyone so much as moves!' He readjusted his grip on the weapon, renewing its clutch on Frejya's neck, while she remained quiet and kept her eyes on her son, seemingly calm.

'One of you,' Hákon snapped over his shoulder, 'bring me my horse.'

After a moment of hesitation, one of the soldiers at the edge of the group carefully detached himself and stepped sideways to reach for the creature's reins, leading it over to Hákon while the others stayed locked in their uneasy suspension. As soon as he felt the leather between his fingertips,

Hákon snatched away his blade and mounted in a rush of movement, switching his sword to Gunnarr as soon as he was upright in the saddle.

No one had reacted. Hákon took a quick nervous look across all sides, and then allowed himself a tentative smile.

'You're a coward, Hákon,' one of his men muttered from where he stood facing Eiric's blade.

Hákon ignored him. He backed the horse up slightly, putting distance between himself and Gunnarr, as well as his brothers, and Gunnarr immediately took a few steps inland to where Hákon had stood, so that his child and mother were now equidistant from him and Hákon was almost behind him on the left side. Still Hákon did not complete his escape. He kept his eyes wide and wary, but a look of triumph was beginning to form on his face.

'Any man who returns to me with the bodies of my brothers will be rewarded,' he said loudly, pointing them out and giving Bjǫrn and Eiric each a vengeful stare. 'As for you, Gunnarr, it looks like you will have to make the choice between your child or your mother. You will only have the chance to save one of them.'

With a kick of his legs, he made to ride away, but immediately he tugged sharply on the reins and brought the horse back to a skidding standstill. An idea had formed across his face. Staying mounted, he carefully returned to the hostages, and then slid from the saddle again, keeping one hand on the reins.

'In fact,' he suggested delicately, 'why don't you choose now?' He held his sword up against Frejya again, and then stepped across and brandished it at the baby. 'Tell me which one I may kill, Gunnarr.'

Gunnarr's throat quivered. 'You make good your escape while you still can,' he advised.

'No no,' Hákon replied, raising his voice into a challenging shout, 'I want you to choose! Either that or I kill them both.' His face was ugly with rage long stored inside. There was something unhinged in his eyes.

Gunnarr screwed up his face and shook his head. Rapid combinations of movement flashed across his mind, paths for his blade, but there was no way he could save one without surely sacrificing the other. He let his sword fall by an inch.

'If you wish for my death, you may have it. Do what you will with me, and leave them be.'

'I will have your death anyway, you fool,' Hákon spat. 'But first you will answer my question.'

'Why are you doing this?'

Hákon began to reposition his feet, preparing for action. 'Wait!' Gunnarr begged, suddenly weak, and he almost succumbed to pleading with Hákon, who watched with a look of elation. The smile on his face was becoming more manic. His sword remained poised, excitedly.

'Gunnarr.' It was his mother's voice. She was making sure that she spoke evenly, trying to give him strength. 'Look at me, boy.'

He turned to focus on her, and was almost doubled over by the agony of seeing her in such peril. Hákon had his sword at her throat again, bidding her to mind her tongue. Her chin was pointed skywards, so that she could only look at Gunnarr from the bottom corner of her eye. Her throat pulsed as she swallowed. To escape the press of the blade she had risen up onto her toes, but could not hold her balance in such a position, and had been forced to lie back into Fraener's arms. He could hear her quick breaths whistling in and out of her nose.

'Tyra is prisoner still in Egil's hall,' Frejya continued, ignoring Hákon as he turned towards her with a quizzical expression. 'She is such a lovely girl. You must not leave her there, do you hear me?'

After a pause, Gunnarr nodded distractedly. The sound of her voice was like a key to his memory. It was more than a sound. It was the sound he'd been hearing since the day he was born, the sound he'd heard more than any other. The one thing his life had always had was her. What would his life be without her?

As he looked across then at the wriggling infant, he found he felt no such connection. The boy barely knew of the things he had lived through, like a seed that had not taken root. He was just a shadow from a life that might have been, but no longer was, and never could be. Gunnarr's hand went out.

'Ma, come to me.'

Hákon stretched his mouth ajar with intrigue and angled the sword towards the child. Frejya did not move. Every eye and ear waited for her response.

'Gunnarr,' she said, her tone bordering on stern, 'the child was not yet born when Álfr attacked us. Kelda pushed and pushed afterwards, knowing that someone would come for her soon. I watched her bear that child for you, despite her fear and her pain. She did it because, even in her dying moments, she was desperate for you to have your son.'

'Mother, please!' Gunnarr begged, fighting to close off his mind against the flood of barbed memories that came rushing back to him. He thrust out his hand again, and did not look back to his son.

'Come to me, Ma.'

All faces turned immediately to Frejya. She gave Gunnarr a simple, fulfilled smile and let her tears flow down her cheeks.

'I have been the happiest woman in the world having you as my son, Gunnarr,' she told him gratefully. Then she jumped.

Unknown to anyone but herself, Frejya's struggles with Fraener had been taking her closer to the cliff edge with every movement. Through the pain of Fraener's beatings, she had calmly manoeuvred him towards the great open space. As her lips fell shut on her final words, and the first tear rolled off the wrinkled bulge of her smiling cheek, she planted her heels into the earth and drove the weight of her aged body triumphantly backwards.

The force that she generated lifted Fraener clean off his feet. His brutish, sadistic grin was replaced momentarily by whimpering fear, and then he disappeared over the edge. Gunnarr was given a last glimpse of his mother's shining face, her eyes sparkling above her victorious smile. She seemed to hover for a moment as her skirts took up the wind behind her, and then she too was gone.

Everything was stunned into stillness. The air in Gunnarr's lungs choked him. His nerves momentarily deadened. Dumbly, Hákon watched the two that had just stood inches in front of him now plunging away below. Both men suddenly looked at each other, their faces aghast with shock, and then there was a ringing crash of noise as the soldiers to the side of them broke free of the uneasy stand-off and crashed together like waves in an ocean swell.

The noise jolted Hákon and Gunnarr into action. Hákon reacted first, scrambling clumsily onto his horse. Gunnarr's anguished, crying strike was fractionally too slow, and his sword flashed past Hákon's shoulder as the fleeing traitor kicked hard against the horse and sent it lurching wildly away. Before Gunnarr had even chased two footsteps Hákon was already bringing the beast around in a half circle and speeding at a gallop back towards Helvik, and though Bjǫrn broke off the main group and tried to close his brother down he could not cut off the escape.

Letting him go, Gunnarr turned immediately to the last man standing before him, the soldier holding his son. Upon meeting Gunnarr's eyes, the man dropped the baby like a bundle of sticks and threw up his hands for mercy, but before he could even open his mouth to plead his face was dropped into a nerveless stare as he met instead the fury of Gunnarr's sword, and was cleaved almost clean in two with the ferocity of his swing.

Leaving the child where it lay screaming, Gunnarr charged recklessly into the back of the group of Hákon's remaining men. He dealt out death left and right through eyes that were barely open, oblivious to any opposing blade, swinging with two hands and awaiting the jolt through his arms of sword meeting bone, until finally Ári had to tackle him to the ground when there were no more left to fell. He lay down on top of his friend amidst the warmth of the corpses until Gunnarr's muscles went limp and his wrath collapsed into howling tears.

For some time he lay there in Ári's grip, his sword gone from his grasp, crying with the fervour of a child, while his other friends stood over him with heads bowed in discomfort. When the sounds finally faded from him, he picked himself up with abruptness, without speaking, without even looking his friends in the eye, and walked over to take up with bloodied hands his son from where his comrades had left the child lying whimpering in the grass. Still without speaking, he handed the baby to Hilario, and then wandered away across the clifftops.

Before sunset, he climbed down to the grey beach and retrieved her broken body from where it had been washed up among the rocks, carrying her safely across both arms, as she had done to him as a sleeping child. The sun sank below the horizon amidst a wounded red glow. He walked with her beneath the stars.

Chapter Twenty-Two

That night, as the moon glided skyward and the waves whispered placid farewells and withdrew for the evening, Tyra lay down in the master's chamber of the longhall and wept.

Beyond the walls, the atmosphere was all still and remote. No distant voices drifted down to her from the town, nor any squawk from the nesting gulls, who, it seemed, had disappeared again almost as soon as they had arrived. Even the constant sweep of the surrounding ocean sounded muted. The silence was so dense that the air felt heavy with it. Every now and then Tyra held her sobs and listened to the empty sound, and it made her feel even surer that she was utterly alone in the world.

Sombre as she was, her thoughts were wild with emotion. At intervals she would sit up swiftly, with evident purpose, and drag an arm across her face to smear away her tears, but each time her body tensed as if to move she realised that she did not know what she was intending to do, and would flop down again in despair. Her crying alternated between passionate wailing and gentle sobbing, but neither volume made any difference. No one came to bring her comfort.

The night drew on, and still she did not leave the gloom of the chamber, though the whole hall was empty but for her.

For long periods she kept her face pressed down amongst the coarse furs that she lay upon, but they carried the warm reek of the men that had been sleeping within them, a scent that made her recoil with repulsion. Now that she had become aware of it, the odour seemed to fill the entire room. She wanted to go outside into the crisp night air, but she could not bring herself to do so. Instead she bowed her face into the crook of her elbow and sat there in a doubled-up hunch, inhaling her own skin, feeling for all the world that, just as there were insects that seemed to exist only so that the spiders had something to catch in their webs, so too she had been made. Her role was to suffer so that the rest of the world could see why they were happy.

Later, after she had succumbed and lain down on her front on the cold wooden bench and struggled through many periods of fitful sleep, Olaf returned. She awoke to his presence lingering in the shadow of the partition doorway.

He had been drinking, she could smell, some fierce liquid stronger than ale, but he never seemed to be drunk. He waited a moment longer and then came into the room, sitting on the bench beside Tyra with his back in line with her waist and giving a tired groan as he lifted each leg and tugged off his boots. He turned to face her and paused again with an air of expectancy, and when she did not react, lying still in the position that she had slept in, he leant across and placed a hand on the back of her thigh.

Tyra felt his touch and thought that she would scream or thrash out, but found instead that she was suddenly overcome with a feeling of deepest exhaustion. The buzzing of the silent atmosphere was louder than ever. She could muster no fire in her blood. She felt too weary for another fruitless battle in which she would inevitably fail to prevail. Something was changing within her, as if she was drawing away from herself, hardening up like a brown leaf in the frost.

'Are you awake?' Olaf whispered. His fingers inched forward across her skin.

'Yes,' Tyra replied, not bothering to lift her cheek from the bench. She felt the weight of Olaf's hand instantly snatched away.

'Then you are not yourself,' he judged, and climbed swiftly back to his feet.

She heard his footsteps disappear out of the room again. For a moment longer she remained without reaction. Then, as she rolled over and came to sit upright, she saw through the partition doorway a wayward white wave roving along the wall towards her, and realised that he had gone to fetch some light. He re-entered the chamber with a long log from the fire, blazing orange at one end, and set it down on the floor away from the furs.

'You must feel sad and alone at the moment,' he said, lowering himself back down to the bench so that he sat adjacent to her, about an arm's length away. Only one of his eyes was visible in the weak light and it was not looking at her, but staring into the crackling log.

Tyra remained in silence. The smell of woodsmoke began to fill the air.

'You must know already that I admired your friend,' Olaf went on reflectively. 'She was old, though. She will have been grateful that her life lasted for as long as it did.'

'She did not deserve to spend her last days enslaved and then killed,' Tyra muttered, feeling her anger awaken a little.

Olaf shrugged. 'My mother choked on her food and died when she was barely a woman. I'm sure Frejya would have chosen her own life over that one.'

Tyra fell silent again. Olaf turned the log over and tried to spread the flames a little.

'Anyway,' he finished, 'I wanted you to know that I have thought of her tonight, and drank to her while I drank to the men that were killed.' He smirked with a little embarrassment and looked at Tyra for the first time. 'Did you hear that I lost every one of the men I sent? He must be some fighter, this man that you love.'

'I love nothing and no one!' Tyra snapped with sudden vehemence.

Olaf smiled again to himself and seemed content enough not to press the point. He stared upwards and watched the firelight play across the ceiling.

'When we catch them, your life will not be like the others',' he said in a plain tone. 'As of this moment I am second to but one man in this entire land. You will have a pleasant life, with many nice things, and I will not be around so often that you must put up with looking upon this grizzled old face every day.' He looked across at her with a twinkle in his eye, as if to give her some encouragement, but when he saw that she remained unmoved his expression hardened, and he shifted his position. 'Well then, you are tired and perhaps now is not the best time to speak of such things. You may remain here to sleep, if you are comfortable, and I will sleep in the next room.'

Tyra rose briskly to take herself off to the main hall, but Olaf stretched a hand out and restrained her by the wrist.

'Or, I can stay with you here, if it will be difficult for you to be alone?'

Tyra stopped. Her chin dropped slightly. She shook Olaf's hand from her and stood numbly with her hands pressed firmly down by her sides.

'You will do as you please,' she said bitterly.

There was a rush of movement, and Olaf shoved her roughly down onto the furs with the back of his forearm. Tyra landed clumsily before she was even aware of what had happened. She deadened her body and scrunched up her eyes. When nothing happened, she opened them again, and again she found Olaf standing in the doorway. He carried the smouldering log down low at his side.

'You are not yourself,' he repeated. 'It would not please me any other way.'

He turned, sweeping the log through the dark, causing a flame to flare up with the rush of air, and went out to sleep by the low night fire in the main hall.

Tyra lay down in the darkness once again, listening to the spiders spinning and weaving in the rafters above her head.

Chapter Twenty-Three

Those that had witnessed the scene on the clifftops feared that Gunnarr would never return. They worried that he too might give his life away to the ocean, or wander until he found a place to fall upon his sword. Hilario and Ári had waited loyally beneath the first line of trees that screened their camp, expecting only to meet defeat by darkness, until the then peaceful sea had reflected enough starlight upon the rolling coast to reveal his silhouette stumbling back beneath the weight of her body.

The women were awake and well rested, but overhead the distant moon served no purpose other than to make the few stars bright by its dimness, and a fog had rolled down off the hills. Any attempt at a march would be treacherous, yet they might still have taken their chances and gained a few arduous miles. Why bother, though? Who were they hiding from? They knew they'd already been found. It was suggested by Bjǫrn and a handful of others that all routes would already be blocked. Better to stay in the position they had than in all likelihood come upon worse. The women had nodded to each other in agreement, a heaviness to their manner, as if they knew that they were assenting to more than simply an extra night of rest. They had settled down in the depths of their meagre woodland, and prepared for a long night.

Gunnarr could have chosen to stay apart from the careful company of the others and spend the night alone. Maybe he would have been carried away in the darkness and never seen again. He might have given in to any of the dark thoughts that roamed his head, had it not been for the wide-eyed infant that Hilario had thrust into his arms just as soon as Gunnarr had laid Frejya down among the moss and fir needles.

At first Gunnarr was numb to the weight in his arms, the smell of freshest skin, the warmth emanating from the little heart that beat against his own. Yet, unknown to him, the roots of a bond were interweaving. He watched the infant's face staring up at his own through vast, absorbing eyes, as if the child's body and mind were a hollow space into which he was trying to replicate and become everything he saw in his father before him at that moment. For the first time since his torment had begun, Gunnarr did not feel alone with his loss.

Instead of keeping his grief to himself, something made Gunnarr allow himself the company of his friends and their families. As the night hemmed in around them, they sat together around a spitting fire, concealed by a hollow in the ground, watching the boy as he stared in constant wonderment at anything Gunnarr turned him to: the sparks that puffed out from the burning logs and rose gently up towards the looming tree tops; the steady motion with which some of the women dragged a comb through their hair; the men coming and going at intervals to drink handfuls of water from the stream, or to take a turn as sentry.

All spirits seemed to be lifted by the sight of the child, and the infant could not have known how much the group had need of it. A sorrow lurked in their smiles. The reason they'd allowed themselves a peaceful evening, the careless luxury of a warming fire, was because many of them sensed that it would be their last. Tonight they enjoyed their concluding moments, for tomorrow would be a day to forget. Even tomorrow seemed, for some, to be too much to hope for. Ári blackened a wooden spear tip at the edge of the sputtering fire. He kept flicking his eyes out into the distance, and turning his ears towards the blackness.

The women had been rescued in the instinct of duty, but no one had thought much beyond that. What now lay before them, to north and west, were miles of bleak open country. It was leached and infertile, wind-parched and grey, and their pursuers would hardly be able to miss them. If they doubled back sharply and headed north-east, they might yet surprise and evade. But then they'd be marching a more treacherous course, to the heartland of Hálfdanr Svarti.

It was foolish to flee but a few token miles and then sit like an elk in a mud sink. Yet many of them felt safer huddled together in their little group amongst the trees. They knew they were hunted. If danger was coming let it come to them there, where they could watch its deliberate approach, not fall upon them in the wide, open darkness where they could barely see their own footsteps. Here there were enough knives to go around. And they would have the time to use them.

It grew steadily later. Eiric began to explain what had happened on the night of the attack on Helvik, their plan to escape until Hákon's treachery, but his wife soon suggested he stop. Instead, the group talked nostalgically of events from the past, and made observations about the child. Even Gunnarr found himself smiling sadly at some points, as a feature of his young son drew a memory of Kelda into his thoughts, and he would unconsciously tuck the boy a little closer then. He still did not know if he wanted the babe, at least not for himself. What use was the child without the woman he had made it with? But Kelda had died thinking she had succeeded for him, and he could not just make worthless her efforts. He remembered Frejya's words on the day that she had first placed the boy into his arms. The son that they had made together was Gunnarr's last treasured piece of the wife that he should not have been living without.

At one point the boy started to fidget and let out quiet little bleats. Gunnarr tried rocking him and shifting his position, but he would not quieten. Someone stepped across, and a set of hands reached down to take him.

Gunnarr looked up. It was Nanna, the wife of Steinthor Anundersson. Gunnarr knew from his mother that she had lost her own baby to sickness only days before the invaders arrived.

'You don't have to,' he told her. He knew from her face what she intended.

'Please,' she replied. 'I want to.'

She went back across the fire and looked down with a sad smile as the child began to feed from her breast. Steinthor rubbed on her back and murmured at her not to get silly. Gunnarr wanted to thank her, but he saw that it would only bring her to tears.

As the fire embers dulled and the sky gradually brightened, Gunnarr politely declined other offers and volunteered himself to take the last watch. Taking his son, he climbed to the highest point of the immediate landscape and found a flat place where they could lie down among the crunchy blades of grass and overlook the broad expanse of sea and shore that fell away beneath them.

The fog had cleared and the stars up above him seemed to twinkle like dwindling lamps. His belly now full, the baby slept, tucked gently against the warmth of his father's chest in a coarse woollen blanket that Gunnarr pulled up and around his head to keep off the biting insects now there was no longer the fire smoke to deter them. Lying there in the perfect stillness of the night, tasting the fresh sea air being carried to his cheeks, Gunnarr again allowed himself to cry, a brief, nostalgic passage where he silently released his tears and begged one last time for his wife and mother to be returned to him, if only until the dawn.

Then he turned to his son, whose tiny face was sinking deeper and deeper into his puffed-out cheeks, a masculine little frown denting his forehead. He slept as if he were in the safest place in all the nine realms. It was tempting to think him oblivious to what he had suffered, but Gunnarr began to feel as if the boy had understood his loss, and was now summoning the strength to overcome. He watched his son sleep, and drew heart from his example, telling himself that the two of them could learn to defeat their pain together.

When the crest of the sun finally began to appear, Hilario climbed up to fetch Gunnarr and they went down to meet the rest of the group. Ári and the women were already on their feet and ready to move.

'We must make haste,' Ári suggested, retying his cloak around his shoulders.

Gunnarr studied the bustling group. 'Where do we go to?'

Ári looked to Eiric, who responded with a shrug. 'West, if we can.'

'We must at least try, Gunnarr,' Ári entreated. 'The Gods might be giving us a chance. We cannot just sit here and waste it.' His eyes loitered on Gunnarr, and he read his friend's expression. He turned to his wife, and then back to

Gunnarr. 'Give the boy to Ingrid,' he said, with a nod of resolve. 'I will help you bury her.'

Hilario grunted and stepped forward. 'I'll come too.'

While the rest of the group made their final preparations, Gunnarr, Ári and Hilario climbed back up the hill away from the ocean. Gunnarr retrieved Frejya's body from its moss bed and carried her alone, hugging her close so that he was unable to look upon her face. She was light, like a child rather than a mother.

They were forced to go inland some distance, onto ground that was neither tangled with the grappling roots of the pine trees nor cold and boggy from the nearby watercourse. Gunnarr would have liked to search further afield but, though they said not a word, he could see that his friends were growing anxious. In the end, he settled for an ordinary piece of ground out on the open clifftops, where the land was slightly raised to give it some prominence. The sea wind had scorched away any young shoots with its salted breath. It left a landscape that felt barren and lonely, not the sheltered, peaceful spot that Frejya would have liked to lie down upon and rest in life.

With no spades, they used their swords to score and lift out chunks of turf. Soon after they had started, Bjǫrn and Eiric came up to join them, as a token of respect or some penance towards the damage that had been done by a member of their family. Tyr too arrived at one point and lingered uncertainly at a distance, evidently sent up as a gentle reminder by some of the more agitated women.

With the turf stripped and stacked up, the topsoil beneath was dark and crumbly, so that the five men were unable to cut it out in squares and instead had to lift it with their hands. It was but a thin layer though, and immediately below it the ground became coarse and sandy, a drab grey colour, held loosely together by tiny white burrowing roots.

Frejya had always wanted to go with a pyre, a swift, white-hot passage. 'You burn me, boy,' she had announced unexpectedly one night. 'Don't leave me lying around in the ground waiting to rot.' But he was unable to grant her that wish. They could have gathered the wood and set the blaze in a reasonably short time, but he would have wanted to stand by her and watch until the end and then gather up her ashes, not leave her unattended only for the fire to fizzle out with just half its work done, or to act as a beacon for Hákon's soldiers, who would cruelly drag her off her resting place and leave her in a heap on the ground.

He worked on through his thoughts, digging with his sword again, but now that they were getting deeper the soil was becoming claggy and greasy, with beige streaks of clay smeared through it. Gunnarr thought about the airless smother of such a berth. Stones began to be thrown up, more and more of them, and the team's progress stalled.

Eventually, when the grave was barely knee deep, hardly enough to keep the foxes out even for a day, Gunnarr began to notice his friends slowing their pace. Their cutting strokes turned into measured alterations, squaring up the hole and evening out its base. They straightened their backs more frequently and he could feel them watching him carefully while he worked on. His next stroke crunched against a chunk of stone that almost caused him to lose grip of his blade. He found that his heart was pounding in his head, and he threw down his sword.

'You go on without me. I cannot bury her here.'

The others looked at each other dubiously. Ári sighed and then leant forward to pick up Gunnarr's sword, nodding to the others to continue digging. He held out the sword to Gunnarr and spoke in a soft voice.

'Alright, we'll make it a bit deeper, but then, I'm sorry, we must get moving.'

Gunnarr took the sword but he did not resume digging like the others. 'What lies to the west, Ári?' he asked. There was something new to his voice, a weariness.

Ári stirred a little. 'Land,' he answered, as if it was obvious. 'Distance from Helvik and Hákon's soldiers.'

Gunnarr's face was bleak. Turning, he climbed up out of the grave and, seeing his movement, the others left off digging and looked to Ári with concern. Gunnarr spoke with his back to them.

'There is no place to go. This land has no place left for us.'

Ári became very still at the words, bristling with quiet anger. Hilario looked across at him and then stepped out of the hole, moving alongside Gunnarr.

'Gunnarr,' Hilario said delicately, 'even one with no family such as myself can see that we must help lead our friends and their loved ones to safety.'

'There is nowhere to lead them to!' Gunnarr snapped. 'This starving land has given us all it had to offer, and there is nothing left.'

'Father.' From where he still waited some ten yards away, Tyr called across to the group, but Ári's anger had risen, and he ignored his son. He leapt out of the hole and started striding back down towards the camp, shouting across as he passed where Gunnarr and Hilario stood.

'I'm sorry for your loss, but I'll not waste another moment helping your family when you care so little for mine.' He called Tyr with a bark, and went on walking, sword slung sheathless over his shoulder.

'Go then,' Gunnarr shouted after him. 'The next inhabitable place you find will have a town there already, suffering just as Helvik was, and the people there will drive you off as competition rather than welcome you in.'

Ári turned and came back up the hill a few paces. 'Your wife and mother are dead, and you probably wish you were too. Mine are alive, and I have to try and keep them that way.' He turned back to the sea, shouting over his shoulder as he continued walking. 'I'll tell Ingrid to leave your son on a log. Come on, Tyr!' he added angrily, for his son had still not moved, and the boy even started to protest, but his childish voice was drowned out by Eiric's, who now also entered the argument.

'Gunnarr is wrong, Ári,' he called after him, from where he stood beside his brother as the only two remaining in the half-dug grave. 'There are green and empty lands just across the sea from us. We've seen them.'

'Then we need a boat!'

It was Tyr's voice, and he sounded exasperated. He might have been ignored again, had they not realised that he was pointing out to sea.

Chapter Twenty-Four

Dagr Dagrsson, Olaf Gudrødsson's most trusted man, stood bleary-eyed at the helm of what he had begun to call his ship, as it cut through the waves and sent spray whistling past either cheek. A persistent westerly headwind blew in his face, and rather than waste the time and effort of laboriously tacking to meander through it, the sail had been furled up and wrapped away and the men at either side of Dagr were bending their spines as they drove directly up the coast under the power of their oar strokes alone.

They made good pace, in spite of the load that dragged them low through the water. Cluttering the foot-wells of those that heaved against the oars lay a vast collection of plundered objects. Dagr turned to survey them at intervals, always with the same hint of a smile dancing in his eyes. He had never been a lucky man, until this voyage.

Their cargo was as rich in variety as it was in value. Weapons were always popular, as were all items of warfare, and there were various pieces scattered across the deck: fine hunting knives, a gracefully shaped axe with a smooth oak handle, some reasonably ordinary swords. Other men, perhaps with more of an eye for trading, had gathered up items of necessity: sacks full of beeswax candles, bundles of felted wool or tanned hide, lamp oil and barrels of salt. Some had been thinking in terms of even more immediate need and, perhaps with bleak and barren Helvik in mind, had taken all the food that they could find: cured joints of meat, barrels of apples, the odd cask of cider or ale, though most of that had been drunk by now. There had even been a fully grown horse on board at one point, Dagr recalled with a smile. It had been his own idea for a token to sweeten Olaf, but the beast had become maddened by fear and leapt clumsily overboard when they were at least half a mile out from shore. They had back-paddled and watched to see how long it would last before it sank, and then threw spears into it when it became clear that it might actually make it.

Those items aside, by far the most numerous things they had claimed were the precious metals, with the alluring warmth of their glow. Broaches, plates, ornamental figurines to simple dining cups, they had snapped necklaces from carcasses, stripped plating from woodwork. That which would not fit in the sea trunks lay stuffed hurriedly in slouched barley bags, while the rest was scattered without care across the ship's floor, coated in seawater. Dagr could not tire of hearing the clanging of his treasures as the rowers extended their legs with every oar stroke. He closed his eyes and patted briefly across his person, feeling for the reassurance of the few select pieces that he had elected to keep for himself. In a single day, he'd become a wealthy man. And the best thing about it was that someone else had stolen it all for him.

Dagr's orders had been to follow the coast west until it began to curve north and then strike out across the open sea, but Dagr had soon come to realise that his navigational skills were about as rusty as the blade he'd been carrying since he was a boy, and, in truth, he'd been intimidated by the sight of the great stretch of featureless water. He'd ordered that they carry on trailing the shore. As darkness fell and his men became mutinous, they'd pulled into a cove for the night. Come morning they found that it was in fact an estuary and, further up the fjord, discovered a settlement, a poor-looking town consisting of a clutch of drab buildings with turf on the roofs. It was the richest place they had ever found in their lives.

The men of the town, it seemed, had also been trying their luck at raiding. By the length of the weeds in the paddocks and patches, it was clear that they'd never returned to their previous professions, and now the town that once they had lived in had become no more than a storehouse. Many of the wares looked untouched since the moment they had been dumped off the ship, and the menfolk, presumably maddened by greed, appeared to have packed themselves back into the boat and gone straight out to bring home more. As Dagr strode through the near-empty village, kicking in doors on a whim, he found dank little huts that were brimming with silver, and stables more wealthy than fortresses.

It had truly been a blessed voyage. Only one man of their band had lost his life, and even that was due only to a rogue wave that had lifted him clean from his seat. Unable to swim, he had disappeared almost immediately, and they had not even broken oar stroke.

Now, almost back to their temporary home, and days early at that, Dagr returned to facing out like the eyes of the ship, and gave his rowers another shout of encouragement to speed their passage. He began to focus his thoughts on a warm fire, and a bed that did not lurch with every wave. He went off to the rear of the ship and pissed over the side, and as he returned to the fore and they rounded a slight headland in the coast, something new snatched his attention. More treasure for the taking.

The town that they'd pillaged, so heaving with riches, had been strangely lacking in one. Perhaps the menfolk had decided that it was not only wealth that they could take their fill of across the seas, for Dagr and his men had found only one woman amongst the dismal band of old and sick that remained, and some blundering idiot had killed her before anyone could think of a better idea. There had been no trophies with which Dagr's soldiers could celebrate their victory, and they had built up a thirst that had not been slaked. For that reason, the sight of three females bathing themselves by the water's edge just ahead caused the oar strokes to fall out of time and excitable shouts to spread like fire across the boat. The vessel began to list to and fro as the men stood to catch a view, like hounds sniffing the air.

Dagr swallowed and studied them quickly, ignoring momentarily the shouted suggestions that began to come forward from his eager comrades. He was amazed that they had not noticed the ship, although they had probably not expected one to appear around the coastline in the early part of dawn. Waist deep in the water, they stood with faces to the shoreline in a quiet pool at the foot of a wooded hill, with a canopy of branches hanging overhead to frame them. Each was unmistakeably feminine, hair almost down to the waist, clothed either in pale skirts clinging wet against the skin or perhaps even undressed completely, and washing their bodies with an oblivious grace that drained the moisture from Dagr's tongue.

'Let's take them!' one of his men hissed excitedly, alarmingly close to Dagr's ear, and he realised that some of them had gathered up thirstily behind him.

He was in need of little encouragement. To be here in such an odd location, so close to Helvik, they must have been women of the town anyway. By rights they belonged to the conquering army. Sniffing in a noseful of air, Dagr turned back to his watching men, pointed to the oars, and then jabbed the same finger three times at the figures in the water. The men scrambled back to their seats and soon fell back into a clumsy rowing rhythm, picking up speed. Grinning like mad things, they came up behind their victims with pace and stealth, driving their boat headlong towards the beach.

The three women held their positions admirably. They fought the desperate urge to turn around, and forced themselves to trust the voices that instructed them from somewhere hidden among the trees. Soon they could hear the splashes of the oars as they ploughed into the water, the sound of the prow carving apart the surface, even the garbled words that the excitable attackers thought that they had whispered. It seemed that the boat must be nearly upon them, yet still they obeyed the words from the woods, bravely going through the motions of rinsing their goose-pimpled skin.

Only when she began to feel the motion of the boat's fore-running waves against her lower back did one of the women's resolve finally snap. She turned in horror to find the leering serpent head looking down at her only yards away. Hungry faces protruded restlessly over its sides. She screamed and began to stumble for the beach, and the other two women needed no further persuasion. They lunged to follow her, deaf in their panic to the redundant call that now finally came out of the trees.

'Run!'

*

247

Dagr had been leaning perilously over the bow as the women scattered like spooked deer, and he was almost thrown into the water as the boat crunched its nose against the rising sea floor.

'Five of you, after them!' he ordered, pointing needlessly into the space between the trees through which the women had disappeared, and at least ten of his men leapt wildly into the shallows and gave chase, racing off into the woods.

Bursting with anticipation, the remaining men clumsily shipped oars and crowded against the rail. They heard the first few sticks snapping under the feet of the chasing pack, caught brief glimpses of them flashing through the trees and heading up the slope of the hill, before they were lost from sight and sound.

A cloud of animated noise swamped the ship, as the men shouted encouragement and laughed excitedly among themselves. Already they were pushing and bustling, forming a rough queue that no one wanted to be at the back of. It was only after a curiously long time had passed, and the amusement started to ebb, that they began to fall quiet again.

'They're taking all the fun for themselves!' one of them accused, and a chorus joined in with his indignation, several men beginning to climb the sides to go after the first group. Dagr was almost forced to go amongst them and settle them down, but then they finally did hear a sign of their fellow soldiers, and it was one that threw a damp blanket of silence across them all.

From out of the woods, the sound of wailing agony corrupted the still morning air. Unmistakeably, it was the call of a horrified man begging for his life. The man cried again, but this time his voice was abruptly cut short. In its place came a high-pitched cackle that echoed in the trees.

Frightened faces turned to Dagr. Faces wracked with the superstition that formed from too many nights spent around the stories of the campfire.

'Witches!' one of the men whispered, and his suggestion took the grit from many of the other soldiers' expressions. The boat creaked ominously from where it lay beached in the pebble bed, shackled to the unwelcoming forest.

Dagr saw the sense falling out of his men. Picking up his shield and drawing his sword, he made a show of leaving the safety of the ship and splashed down into the shallows.

'Half of you with me,' he ordered in an uncompromising tone, and gestured to the men on his left. 'The rest of you guard the boat.'

After a brief commotion, the required men dropped over the side. Dagr led them at a cautious creep onto the shore and amongst the eerie trees, while the waves licked up after their footsteps behind.

From higher up the slope inland, Gunnarr peered through a gap between two crossing trees and saw them entering the gloom of the woods. His first response was to peer up over his left shoulder, where he found the three women now almost at the top of the hill and safe.

Next Gunnarr sought out the positions of his comrades. Bjǫrn was behind another tree about ten yards to the left, already watching the raiders beginning to climb the bank. Volundr was crouched down circling in a wide arc to Gunnarr's right. The rest were hidden, but close by.

Gunnarr slowed his breathing and let them come on. By his knees lay the corpse of one of the ship's original chasing pack, which Gunnarr had dragged with him into cover. The man's blood glugged out into the earth, drawing a strong smell from the pine needles. His arms were shifting gently, even now.

Still moving with exaggerated stealth, the soldiers below had reached the first of the bodies that Gunnarr and his party had failed to conceal. Gunnarr could see one of them bending down to study it, while the others nervously scanned the rustling tree tops. They were coming in relatively small groups, playing to the advantage of Gunnarr's short-handed force, but they needed to be drawn deeper, far enough for the trap to be closed behind them and for them to be dead before the ship's reinforcements could come to their aid.

Instead, they had frozen. They were spooked, bewildered. Their leader had ceased to step forward, and was looking back towards the ship. If they fled, it was over. Gunnarr realised that he would have to come to them.

Catching Bjǫrn's eye for long enough to demonstrate a shake of his head, he hefted his sword and rolled around the tree, flitting to the cover of the next one within three bounding strides. He had not meant to step on a stick, but when he did the sharp snapping noise had the desired effect. The boat crew's ears pricked up at the sound, and Gunnarr almost felt the warmth of their eyeballs through the thick trunk of wood that shielded him from view.

From his new angle Gunnarr could now see Hilario and Steinthor Anundersson crouched on all fours below him. They too were creeping cautiously towards the landed party, like foxes in the long grass. He felt four brief vibrations through the earth as Bjǫrn too moved up. They were closing in like a wolf pack, without even having to discuss it.

Some of Olaf's men must have spotted the movement, for there was a commotion within the group below. One of them shouted a challenge, and their ranks tightened a little at the wind's empty reply. They came forward again.

Moving faster now, they came directly for the tree that Gunnarr crouched behind with his pounding heart. He knew that he would have to move again to have any chance of a surprise attack, and so he waited until the raiders reached the foot of the steepest part of the climb and, while they were momentarily concealed by the slope, he dropped to his front and scrambled one or two trees further forward, uncaring now as to the sounds he made through the sticks and pine needles. They began to take the slope, and were too close now for Gunnarr to risk revealing his head to watch for them, so he relied on his hearing alone, gripping his sword as he began to feel the ground shake with each of their footsteps.

They seemed to come on and on, and Gunnarr began to think that soon they would surely be past him. Then a thrash of movement from somewhere below scratched at his ears. There was a grunt and the sound of contact, and he heard a man scream a dying cry. Immediately he was up and charging down the hill, knowing that his fellow ambushers could not afford to be unsupported for even a moment.

As he stumbled out of cover, he found the raiders bunched only ten or so yards away. It must have been Eiric that had made his assault from his position furthest down the slope, for the raiders were turned to meet an attack from the rear, and Gunnarr could see the most distant men's arms rising and falling as they hacked at someone lost from view down the hill behind them.

Gunnarr lifted his sword high. From the left he saw another of his comrades spring from out of the trees, but his vision was too shaky to see who it was. Olaf's men were roaring in defiance and flailing with their weapons. Another two pounding steps and Gunnarr saw Ári too appear like a flash across his vision and cannon into the side of the massed enemy soldiers. In the time it took to inhale one breath, Gunnarr too was amongst them.

Dagr, still at the head of the group, did not see Gunnarr until the last moment, but he reacted with practised composure, throwing up his shield, and Gunnarr's savage blow bit through the rim and almost halfway down to the centre with a snap, rocking both men with its force. Without giving ground, Dagr twisted the shield with a flick of his wrist so that it almost ripped Gunnarr's wedged sword from his grip, and as Gunnarr's weight was pulled off balance Dagr stepped forward into a thrusting counter-strike at Gunnarr's exposed stomach.

Gasping, Gunnarr barely managed to react in time, somehow finding the momentum to jump backwards up the hill, so that the full extension of Dagr's arm thumped the very tip of his sword into Gunnarr's waist. Pain flared and then disappeared. With a crack of breaking wood, Gunnar managed to drag his sword free from Dagr's shield, and stumbled backwards, reeling.

Now the man beside Dagr also stepped in to help repel Gunnarr's attack, aiming a swipe at Gunnarr's face while he was still stumbling backwards. Gunnarr managed to block awkwardly, but without the force to repel the blow completely, and the weight of his own sword cracked against his head like a blow from a club. Again he stumbled, almost going over, but as the attacker moved hungrily towards him Bjǫrn shoved past Gunnarr's shoulder and arrived roaring into the scene, barrelling the man backwards into those crowded behind him with a slam of impact.

Immediately Gunnarr found himself back facing Dagr, who stood in a contained position behind his shield, chin low, sword tip measuring the next attack. He pushed forward, but Gunnarr used his natural speed to beat him to the strike, forcing Dagr to readjust his blow at the last moment to switch it into a defensive one. Their swords clanged shatteringly, metal denting metal. Dagr rocked back to re-measure his opponent. Their eyes briefly met. Then Bjǫrn, fresh from dispatching his first opponent, stepped across without pausing and felled the ship's captain with a single swipe to the back.

Dagr cursed and fell away. Bjǫrn barely acknowledged the kill and was already clashing blades with another. Momentarily, Gunnarr stared down at his toppled opponent. His legs were trembling. He found himself suddenly fatigued, so that he could barely lift his sword.

Few enemies remained. It had been enough that each ambusher's initial surprise attack had found at least one victim. Gunnarr saw Hilario puncture the chest of one of those still standing, and thought that he might fall back to rest, but a shout from Ári snapped him back to his senses. His friend was some yards to the right, inhibited from moving by the sprawl of the dead and dying around him, but he was screaming at Gunnarr and pointing desperately to the other side of the battleground. Still rattled, Gunnarr turned to follow Ári's finger, and to his horror found Tyr just to his left, unguarded and unsupported, being overpowered and thrown to the ground by two of the raiders.

Frantically, Gunnarr tried to lunge across to fend off the attack, but his feet slipped on the muddy bank and he stumbled to all fours. If they had meant to kill Tyr he would have been too late, but instead they merely battered him aside and hurdled over him, and now they were sprinting back down the hill to alert their reinforcements.

Leaping Dagr's carcass, Gunnarr gave chase down the beaten slope. Already the lead runner was shouting madly for support, screaming out that it was only men they faced. The second man was injured, his arm half severed near the shoulder, but though he was slower, their lead was too great. Gunnarr tripped onto the bottom of the slope as the leader reached the fringes of the beach, and in a last act of desperation he hurled his sword through the air at the second man. The blade spiralled clumsily and bounced harmlessly off the man's back, causing him to stumble and cry out in shock, but not slowing his legs.

Gunnarr could only skid gratefully to the earth to retrieve his weapon and look on at the men escaping around a bend and to the ship. Moments later he felt arms feed under his shoulders as Ári dragged him roughly to his feet. The rest of his party formed up around him, blowing hard, and together they watched the path ahead of them with pained expressions.

They did not have long to snatch back some breath. A communal roar erupted from behind the trees, and the remaining boatload came surging around the corner like a murderous flood. Their feet tore up the ground. The air hissed with the sound of rattling ringmail. They had halved the distance before Gunnarr had even raised his sword. Instinctively, the men of Helvik hunched closer together, trying to form some sort of barrier for the onrushing wave of fur and iron to break itself against. Gunnarr had just time to select a screaming face from the stampeding crowd, before the air rushed between them and the two forces clashed with a thunderous impact.

Gunnarr angled his sword upwards and planted the heels of his feet, stiffening himself against the hit. The man opposite him came steaming in with his searching blade thrust forward.

It found the space just past Gunnarr's side as the soldier was smashed against him by the weight of the bodies piling in behind. The shattering force of the impact closed Gunnarr's eyes, and he felt himself lifted off the ground slightly as the attacker's shield cannoned against his ribs. He was driven back almost five paces, in unison with Ári and Bjǫrn at either side of him, and when his eyelids opened a fraction of time later he found a red-headed stranger's open-mouthed face barely an inch from his own, so close that Gunnarr instinctively butted his head forward and felt his eyebrow connect with his enemy's nose. He and the soldier were crushed chest to chest, too close to swing their blades at each other, and instead it was blows from the raiders pushing up behind the first wave that now began to rain down at Gunnarr's head.

He avoided them by giving more ground, shrinking out of range and feeling the thump of Bjǫrn's shoulder as he did likewise. At the same time Gunnarr used his left arm to lock the red-head's blade against the waist it had just missed, wrenching it backwards and trying to free it from its owner's grip. The red-head growled with determination and kept hold, buffeting Gunnarr again with his shield. With the red-head locked against his chest, Gunnarr now freed his own blade and used it to attack the space he had created behind, swinging it around and sending it clanging off the helmet of the man next in line, opening a thick welt down the victim's cheek as his cheekbone was snapped in two. The wounded man stumbled at the impact, propped up by those pushing and snarling behind him, and Gunnarr followed it up with an identical lightning-quick hack to almost exactly the same point, but this time he cracked the skull open and the man threw his hand across his face and went to ground.

With a grunt of effort, Gunnarr let the red-head free and shoved him backwards to where his retreating heels were blocked by the writhing body of the soldier that Gunnarr had just felled. The red-head went tripping backwards into those behind him, and that was all the space that Gunnarr needed. He slashed his sword forward in a punishing vertical strike, cleaving straight through the man's hastily thrown-up shield and down to do the same to the top of his head.

The force of the initial charge was broken, the fighting becoming looser. Gunnarr could hear Ári's rasping breaths as he hacked away at a shield somewhere to the left, beating a sound that thudded and thudded then cracked. With two corpses forming a breaker before him, Gunnarr took back the ground that he had given earlier, trampling over the dead and dying as he pressed forward. He felt a rush of movement just at the edge of his vision and found himself parrying a high blow from a cringing warrior with a smear of blood all across one side of his face. Gunnarr held the strike, and then twisted his defensive blade into a point, thrusting the tip forward into the man's chest with a shrill scratching sound as the blades ran against each other. It was not a killing strike, and before finishing the man Gunnarr was forced to throw him sideways to knock aside another soldier who was seeking to punish him while he was distracted. Bjǫrn stepped in from somewhere and finished the first with a sideways hack across the chest, and Ári sheared through the neck of the other as soon as the man stumbled into his destructive path.

The raiders were tough, experienced men. They would not flee, nor surrender. But they had not the pain in their hearts of the men of Helvik, the anger in their blood, the desperation in their guts. Gunnarr's band were fewer, they were poorer equipped, but their strikes were faster, their blows stronger, their blades more venomous. Cuts did not slow them, fatigue did not deaden their arms. No enemy sword, however skilled, could withstand their hunger.

The last two fought hard and well, but one of them was bemoaning aloud his misfortune even while he yet lived on, and they did not last long once they were surrounded. The last gave up when he saw his comrade felled, lowering his sword and facing his attackers with a wry expression that seemed to accept the futility of resisting. No one of Gunnarr's party was eager to cut him down in such a manner, but after a moment's hesitation Eiric gave the man a reluctant nod and stepped in to finish it with a clean strike. When the man fell numb down on top of the rest, the eight men of Helvik remained standing, beaten but victorious.

The air was suddenly quiet, like the moments just after a rainstorm. They propped each other upright beneath the trees, and had not even the strength for an exhausted cheer. There was a soft ringing thud as Bjǫrn let his sword slip from his fingers and fall down amongst the pine needles, and some of the others followed his example. Tyr came forward from somewhere behind them, weeping with shame, but Ári hugged him tightly and showed him the blood on his blade. Volundr turned his back and vomited.

As soon as their legs were able they stumbled and limped towards the shore to claim their prize. With the movement of walking Gunnarr felt a stinging pain in his side, and found a mess of broken skin just above his left hip bone. A steady flow of blood was creeping down his thigh. He dropped his clothing again and thought no more about it.

The sun was high by then, and for once not shrouded in cloud. As they rounded that last clump of trees, some of the men let out a burst of incredulous laughter. Beached in the shallows of the tiny inlet, the hissing serpent's head reared up over them. Bjǫrn approached the great beast with his arms wide apart and fell gratefully against its strakes, his eyes closed with relief.

'Greetings, old friend,' he whispered.

Eiric went further and collapsed fully clothed into the water, feeling the cold chill rinse away his exertions and the cleansing bite of salt tend to his wounds. He lay back and roared with laughter, splashing in the water with outstretched arms, and, as if it signalled some invitation, some of the others rushed forward to join him, piling on top of each other in the water and hooting with joy. Hope had returned to the last survivors of Helvik, for they could finally escape from its boundaries.

There was more elation when somebody finally climbed aboard. Hilario tripped and fell backwards against one of the trunks, and his surroundings crashed metallically with the impact as he found himself half-submerged in a sea of treasures. He swore and swore, and his friends could not come running fast enough.

Tyr danced around the ship like an excitable child again. From high on the hilltop the women heard their happy sounds, and began to climb hurriedly down to them. Only Gunnarr did not stay aboard the boat and enjoy the euphoria. He took a sack of plunder and carried it back down to the beach, and then set off into the trees.

He had gone no more than twenty yards when he heard footsteps following him. He turned around and waited, and after a moment Hilario appeared. He stopped against a trunk a few yards away, and shook his head sadly.

'Where are you going, Gunnarr?'

Gunnarr's chin was firm. 'There is one more thing I must do.'

'Forget him, Gunnarr,' Hilario urged, taking a gentle step forward. 'You will never cross paths with him again.'

'Which is why I must go!' Gunnarr cried.

Hilario looked at him carefully, his bloodied face soft with compassion. 'You know that we cannot delay,' he said quietly. 'Soldiers could be on their way here as we speak.'

Gunnarr glanced over his shoulder, and saw the women coming down through the trees. They were laughing like girls, clutching at each other excitedly. Gunnarr felt a bite at his conscience. But then he thought of Egil's sad features, watching him proudly. And then of his mother's devoted face before she jumped bravely from his life. And then of Kelda's honest smile, whispering happily her love for him.

'Give me just one day,' he said, beginning to turn away. 'Please wrap my mother in something and put her aboard, and take care of my son.'

'Gunnarr—' Hilario protested, but Gunnarr looked back and cut him off.

'If I am not back here by dawn tomorrow, you may sail without me.'

'Dawn tomorrow?' Hilario gasped.

'Please, Hilario.'

A heaviness slumped Hilario's shoulders. He fixed Gunnarr with a look of regret, and then rolled his head skyward and sighed.

'I'm sorry,' Gunnarr added, genuinely, and then he lifted the sack and disappeared into the trees, before the women could see him, and before he could be stopped from embarking on his helplessly selfish task.

Chapter Twenty-Five

One of Olaf's soldiers picked out the approaching figure from a distance. A fair man walking alone along the shore-line towards Helvik, making no attempt to avoid exposing himself in the glare of the afternoon sun. Immediately the soldier sent someone to fetch Olaf, and the leader came out of the longhall chewing on a mouthful of horse meat and stood on the point of the bay with an arm across his brow, fixing his eyes on the solitary figure moving unhurriedly across the shingle.

After a moment Hákon rushed after Olaf. He recognised Gunnarr even before he could properly see him.

'That's him!' he hissed with agitation. 'Send out a pack to kill him!'

Olaf chewed a few more times, swallowed his mouthful, and shook his head, continuing to watch the man's approach with an expression of intrigue. 'Let's see what he wants.'

At the charred west gate of the town, Gunnarr was met by a large group of men and swiftly disarmed of both sword and dagger. They also insisted on relieving him of the sack that he carried over his shoulder, and for a moment the men crowded around to gawp at its contents. Then he was enveloped into their hostile fold and escorted directly towards what he knew still as Egil's hall. Glancing over his shoulder, Gunnarr caught the man who carried the sack at the back of the group rummaging hurriedly in his trousers and then smoothing them flat again. He said nothing. He went calmly, and made no attempt to resist.

It had been but a matter of days since Helvik was lost, but the exterior of the longhall made it look as if it had been derelict for years. At the entrance, the two torches that framed the doorway had burnt out and no one had bothered to see them replenished. They spilt grey ash down the walls and into two small piles at their base. An iron handle appeared to have snapped off one of the doors, leaving a bright angular splinter in the wood. Gunnarr paused at the entrance, and with a shove was bundled through the doorway.

A room full of men awaited him. Their eyes were heavy on his shoulders. Already they were hushed in preparation, having heard his arrival into the antechamber. Standing shoulder to shoulder along the benches, they crowded the peripherals of Gunnarr's vision like ghouls in a suppressed nightmare. They blocked out the lamps, giving the room a gloomy light more suited to dusk. Gunnarr made no eye contact with any of them, but he could see the way they looked at him. Their bearded chins were thrust forward and their jaws clenched, and some sought to show him what their knives would do to his guts, talking at him quietly or glaring with manic eyes. As Gunnarr passed through into the coolness of the interior, he brought back to himself the times when the room had felt warm, friendly. Now the vapours tasted stale, the floors and walls looked grubby, and an odour of hostility fused with the smell of male sweat in the damp air.

Olaf was seated at where the head of the table would have been, directly before Gunnarr's eyes. He was slumped back against his chair in a relaxed fashion, head tilted slightly as he watched with all the curiosity of the others. It was not he that caught Gunnarr's attention, though. His eyes immediately fell on the two places at either side of Olaf's seat: to the left, where Hákon was lingering, almost cowering, watching Gunnarr through a series of glances, his face curdled with hate; and to the right, where Tyra had jolted upright where she stood, her expression scarcely credulous, as if she dared not to hope. Her femininity looked so alien in the sea of surrounding males. She seemed to tense, as if recklessly ready to bolt the moment that Gunnarr ordered it.

The room remained hushed and rigid. All eyes were pinned on the newcomer, who now drew to a halt as his escorts found places behind and to the side of him. Olaf waited for a moment longer, enjoying the significant quality of the atmosphere. Then he opened a hand, and invited Gunnarr to speak.

'Your ship returned this morning,' Gunnarr said, without introduction. His voice was clear and bland.

Olaf sighed and let his eyes fall closed, knowing already what had happened. The stranger was dressed in a fighting tunic. He looked weary, his hair in greased knots, and his forearms and trousers were daubed with dried blood. Olaf re-settled himself in his chair, now slumped a little at the shoulder, and flicked a hand to gesture for Gunnarr to proceed.

Gunnarr turned to study the spectators briefly until he identified the man carrying his bag, and held out his hand for it. The man eyed him with mistrust for a moment or two and then handed it over. Gunnarr tossed the bag to the ground, causing a loud clang as it fell open at the mouth and spilled forth a stream of its contents.

'I believe this is yours,' Gunnarr said.

Olaf leant forward in his chair and looked down at the polished metals now decorating the floor. Bronze plates, small sculptures, dented beakers. He pursed his lips questioningly. 'Is this all there was?'

'No,' Gunnarr answered, 'but it is all I could carry.' He held out a finger towards the man who had passed him the sack. 'This one has the rest of it hidden between his arse cheeks.'

The room stirred a little. Cursing under his breath, the guilty soldier fished bitterly in his trousers and tossed a couple of extra items onto the pile with a clunk. Olaf glared at him with loathing, and then returned his eyes to Gunnarr.

'Very well,' he accepted quietly. 'My guess is you wouldn't have bothered lugging it all this way if that was all you had to say?'

Gunnarr kicked his bag of offerings aside and shook his head. 'I have given you what is yours. Now I ask you to let me take what is mine.'

A shiver of anticipation swept over the room. Through his chair, Olaf felt Tyra jolt helplessly with excitement, and his face darkened. 'And what might that be?'

Gunnarr sniffed in a breath and did not hesitate. He pointed to the left of Olaf's seat.

'The life of that man, Hákon Egilsson.'

Tyra's face fell. Her knees wavered to the point where she almost dropped. To her right, Hákon burst out with hearty laughter, glancing around and expecting the others to join him.

'Fine,' Olaf answered, and his face did not even quiver.

Hákon continued to smile at the preposterousness of Gunnarr's suggestion. But then he saw the way that Gunnarr's eyes flashed, and the startled reaction of the watching men, and he clasped at Olaf's shoulder.

'What are you doing?' he gasped.

Olaf scowled with irritation. 'You have slain the man's wife and mother. He deserves the chance to fight you.'

Hákon cut a fearful glance at where Gunnarr stood watching him carefully, and then he suddenly shouted, shaking Olaf's shoulder with distress. 'What about our agreement?'

Olaf jumped to his feet in a burst of anger.

'You embarrass me!' he roared, full into Hákon's face, with a power that brought dust from the rafters and would have made Tyra jump backwards had she not been so numb. 'You want me to endorse you as a ruler, but you have done nothing to act like one. All you have done is betray your family and slay women and children. Yesterday you left ten of my men to die while you rode away to safety. You are not a man, Hákon!' Olaf watched Hákon shrivel before his onslaught, while his own breath hissed furiously in and out of his nose, and then he slung himself back down bad-temperedly on his chair. 'Fight this man now and prove to us that you are a worthy of the title you claim,' he finished in a quieter voice.

The shaken room began gradually to resettle. Hákon straightened from where he had shrunk away backwards, and swallowed his embarrassment, turning reflectively to look at Gunnarr.

'In fact,' Olaf spoke again, 'let us do this outside in the air. Give that man back his sword.' He waved his arms to usher the soldiers outside, and then turned to order Tyra to stay in the hall, before following them. The room had barely emptied before she sank down onto the floor and began to weep.

*

Olaf directed them down to the grey beach, where they could use the wide, flat space. The sun was heading seaward, its light more cutting with the shallower angle, and the last heat was seeping from the air. Gunnarr walked at the front next to Olaf, lost in his thoughts. Hákon followed reluctantly at the back, almost forgotten, his eyes flitting about amongst his curled and troubled features. As they moved over the bigger stones and down to the finer shale of the beach, Olaf leant across to Gunnarr and patted him stoutly on the waist, seeing him grunt with pain as he did so.

'I'd keep that quiet if I were you,' Olaf remarked, holding up his hand and looking across at the smudge of blood that had been left on his palm. Gunnarr gave no reply.

Before their feet touched the finer pebbles of the beach itself, the spectators drew up and left the two opponents to walk out into what was to be their arena, so that a line of men formed a wall on one side to match the role played by the sea on the other. The waves were green and high, crashing in towards the shore like an excitable audience. Hákon pushed through the line of onlookers, their numbers growing every moment, and stamped towards where Gunnarr waited for him. He wore still the bitter, sulking expression of one forced to act against his wishes. Scowling, he hastily ripped out his sword, and wasted no time waiting for Olaf's command. Gunnarr read Hákon's intentions and tossed his scabbard away to the side, bringing his sword into both hands and taking up a low guard.

No son of Egil grew up not knowing how to fight. Hákon darted with quick, balanced footsteps across the shingle and drove at Gunnarr with a flashing combination of swings that beat the air like the wings of a launching eagle. Normally Gunnarr would have retreated backwards and simply evaded the lashes, but for this battle he would give no ground. Oblivious to Hákon's blade, he launched his own strike straight for his opponent's contorted face. Both reckless swings missed, slashing the air beside each other's heads, and instead the men collided shoulder to shoulder and stumbled apart from each other. The watching crowd murmured with anticipation.

Without hesitating, Hákon growled and charged forward again, sword held in both hands above his head. Again, in any other fight Gunnarr would have waited for the miss and then punished the open defence, but he was utterly detached from his senses. He could not hear the emotions of the crowd, nor the crashing of the waves. He could not see the defence stroke, or the counter-strike. All that he saw he saw through a shroud of tormented memories, manifested into the icon of hatred now finally within grasp before him, and he sent another swing flashing towards Hákon's face.

The relentlessness of Hákon's attack was the only effective defence against Gunnarr's single-minded style, and Hákon was rewarded as the tip of his blade slashed across Gunnarr's shoulder, popping open the leather of his fighting garb. The impact knocked Gunnarr a step backwards. A collective gasp was released by the audience of soldiers. Olaf sighed and shook his head, disappointed by a promised spectacle in which he had drastically overestimated one of the parties.

The pain bit through into Gunnarr's consciousness. The blow had dented across the bone, battering the nerve that ran down over it, leaving the entire arm numb and humming with pain. Gunnarr tried to ignore it and prepare for Hákon's next attack, but his opponent was circling now, growing in confidence. Hákon's lips were slightly parted, his cheeks elevated into a half-smirking grin, and his eyes were ablaze with a malign sense of power. It was the same face he had worn on the clifftop as he held his blade against the throats of an old woman and a child, and it was exactly the face that Gunnarr needed to see at that moment.

With a scatter of flying stones, it was Gunnarr's turn to come charging forward, and he did so with such speed that Hákon's eyes rolled back with shock. Somehow Hákon managed to get his sword up to block with a bone-breaking clash, but Gunnarr kept coming, his face barely recognisable in its fury, raining blows down at Hákon as if he were trying to shear straight through the defensive blade rather than avoid it. The battering onslaught rang out like a metalsmith hammering away in the forge, and Hákon was driven stumbling down the beach, gasping with every blow. Cheering with excitement, the watching masses surged forward to stay close to the action.

Hákon had not even realised how far he had retreated until the first wave crashed against the back of his knees and almost swept his feet from under him. Gunnarr was forced to correct his aim as Hákon stumbled and, in the fraction of time it took him to do so, Hákon flicked a handful of grainy seawater into Gunnarr's face. The burn of salt closed Gunnarr's eyes, giving Hákon finally the chance to offer a strike back, and Gunnarr forced one eye half open for long enough to block the horizontal swing inches before it met his ribcage, almost hearing the whistle of the blade rather than seeing it coming. Reeling, he staggered away deeper into the water, trying to create enough space to throw a forearm across his brow and clear his vision.

As Hákon lumbered hungrily after him into the waist-deep waves, Gunnarr whirled a half-blind strike to keep him at a distance, and the flat of his blade bounced across the surface of the water, carving out a shower of spray of its own that smattered across Hákon's chest and caused him to shield his eyes. Through obscured vision, Gunnarr saw his chance.

Lunging a step forward, Gunnarr swung his right foot through the water and felt the base of his shin connect bruisingly with both of Hákon's legs, whose balance had been thrown upwards to jump clear of the blinding shower of water. The trip swept Hákon's feet clean away and he dropped heavily onto his back, just as a wave came crashing over him and submerged his head. Instantly, Gunnarr whipped his earlier missed strike back around into a plummeting backhand and his sword smashed through the surface of the water that momentarily concealed Hákon, throwing up two splashes of impact that soared high over Gunnarr's head and rained back down upon him. The pressing crowd, stood now almost in the water with the fighters, exclaimed painfully at what was surely the finishing blow, but Gunnarr felt the muscles at the back of his neck stretched as his blade carried through right down into the sand and almost dragged him under with it.

There was a shoot of water and Hákon emerged just to the right, gasping, hair across his eyes. He stumbled backwards towards the shore, but Gunnarr went after him and punched him full in the centre of his blinded face, knocking him down to slap onto his back against the wet black sand at the very edge of the water. The audience jumped back to clear the space at their feet. Hákon's blade went up tamely to block any strike that Gunnarr was about to rain down upon him, but Gunnarr instead hurled his sword sideways against the flat of Hákon's blade with such force that it sheared straight through the shaft just above the handle, and a clump of the watching men were forced to duck as the fractured piece came spiralling wildly through the air and battered one of them across the shoulder.

Hákon felt the weight go out of his blade and let his arm flop defeated against the shore, still clasping the severed handle. Every watching face fell silent in anticipation of the final blow.

Opening one eye, Hákon looked up at Gunnarr standing over him with his sword poised. It looked as if he was at the point where men give up on any hope of living, but then, in a final act of cowardice, his face charged with fear, and he spoke through racing breaths.

'We were friends once, you and I. It was not I that killed Kelda, or your mother. Would you really break your precious rule to see me suffer?'

Gunnarr did not flinch, and he kept the sword high above his heaving chest. 'Perhaps you don't remember me breaking the rule whilst slaying your coward brother?' He gave an unforgiving look. 'If such a place as Helvik still exists, I am no longer one of its people, and I no longer abide by its rules.'

A rushing wave drew up past Hákon's ears and ran away again. He spat out a mouthful of seawater down one cheek and coughed a little. 'You said yourself that Kelda was innocent. It should not have been a breach of the rule to avenge her. You are still a person of Helvik, Gunnarr. You would lose that. You'd be no better than the men that killed your father.'

Gunnarr ground his chin left and then right, unmoved. He flexed his fingers around his sword handle.

'You killed my father,' he said bluntly. 'You killed Egil, the man who was father to us both. And if the new ruler of Helvik says that I am still a member of this town, then let my first act be to say this: you have broken the rule, Hákon Egilsson.' He angled his head, and focused on Hákon's now startled eyes. 'And I do this to punish you for it.'

Before Hákon could even wince, Gunnarr's vengeful blade thundered down and carved vertically along the centre of his chest. With a scream of emotion, Gunnarr ripped the blade free, jerking Hákon's dead-eyed head off the ground, and brought it crashing down a second time, and a third, until blood began to spit across his skin. His eyes were closed, his mouth agape, and he carried on hacking madly with his blade until his arms began to burn and his blows began to miss and churn up the sand. He dropped the sword, fell to his knees on top of his victim and sank his fingers into the gaping wound that he had torn, snatching through warm innards until he located the hating heart. It still beat feebly, and Gunnarr squeezed and tore it apart with his hands alone, feeling it punctured by his thumbs and ruptured between his fingers, before casting it down and snatching up his sword again. He spat down onto Hákon's corpse. Then he planted the point of the blade with dripping hands through the mutilated chest and down into the sand beneath. The most hardened of those watching did so through squinted eyes.

Gunnarr collapsed backwards and rolled over into the shallows, feeling the cool of the ocean biting into his skin and across his face, amplifying his consuming sensation of release. Unmoving, he lay there across the legs of Hákon's broken body, with bloodied palms pressed into his eyes, lost to the world, speaking to faces in his memory.

They waited for longer than he had expected, but eventually Gunnarr heard swords being drawn, and felt the sand move beneath him as Olaf's soldiers closed in. He ignored them for a few moments longer, focused on the sharp bite of the sea against his skin and the chill breeze whipping across his face. He drew in a stretching breath of air and within it tasted the salt of both seawater and Hákon's blood, yet it felt like the freshest breath he'd taken in his life. Briefly he savoured the burn of it in his lungs. Then he rolled up to face their blades.

He left his sword where it stood like a waystone over Hákon's body and stayed on his knees on the beach. Bowing his head, he closed his eyes rather than waiting to see which one would strike. He was unafraid now that his work was done. In his final moments, he whispered an apology to his son, and then brought Kelda's face into his mind and waited for it to end.

But it did not end. Instead, he felt a hand take hold of him under his wounded shoulder and looked up to find Olaf tugging him up to his feet. The older man's features were fixed with a look of respect, and his sword remained stowed at his waist. He did not speak, but the waiting cluster of soldiers nevertheless heard their orders and lowered their weapons and shrunk away.

'Come with me, lad,' Olaf said quietly. 'I've got something you may want.'

Gunnarr followed the grizzled soldier warily back up the beach, without stopping to retrieve his spent sword or even glancing back at where it secured Hákon's body against the clutches of the waves. He shivered as his soaked clothing clung against his skin, the sun now lower in the sky. Sparks of pain began to fizz from his wounds.

Olaf led up the bank to a clump of swaying ash trees that stood inland opposite the west arm of the bay. Gunnarr had spent his childhood in the branches, spying on the comings and goings from the longhall. Beneath the nearest trunk there was a large object covered in a grey-brown blanket. Gunnarr recognised the manner of shape immediately.

'He was a king of sorts, so I could not just throw him in the ocean,' Olaf said as they drew to a stop. 'I have kept his sword also.'

He bent down and drew back the blanket briefly to reveal Egil's death-white face. His skin was beginning to slacken and his mouth was coming ajar, but his eyelids were peacefully closed. There was a blotch of black blood among the grey hair around his left ear.

'If he is your father, as you say, I thought you may want to see him away.'

Gunnarr knelt down and laid a quivering hand across Egil's cheek. 'Thank you,' he said sincerely.

After Gunnarr had left, Olaf stood for a short while and watched as the young man struggled back in the direction he had come from that afternoon, his footsteps weaving from left to right as he bore the weight of Egil's body away over his shoulder. Olaf doubted he would ever see the lad again. Since the death of the old woman, something had been changing inside him, or maybe he was just returning to the state in which he'd been before he'd forced himself back into the ways of a soldier. No party had been sent out to round up his slaves. To the men, he'd clothed that with swagger and arrogance. 'Give the poor buggers a day's head start.' But in truth, he now doubted he'd ever go after them.

Perhaps he was going soft in his old age, but the plan that he'd devised when he arrived at this windswept place was beginning to fade from his mind. It was one thing to rob somewhere rich and prosperous, where the people were fat and tainted by plenty. In Helvik, he was seeking to wring wealth from folk who were more wretched than most he had seen, whose existence had been miserable even before he'd arrived. All that they could they had given, even rowed overseas and fought for the riches that they could not supply. For that, they had still lost their town and their lives. And now, as if that was not enough, Olaf was seeking to bleed every last drop by stripping away even the liberty of those pathetic few who had survived.

Did he really need to do that? What would he buy with the cost of their lives? More hounds? Another horse he would seldom ride? He had Tyra. He had fulfilled his promise to Hálfdanr and would be rewarded. Maybe that was enough now. If he still wanted plunder from this, his final march into the field, there would be other places where he need only pluck it from the tree, rather than hack the thing down.

As the sun rolled close to the horizon, Olaf returned to the beach, now deserted but for one forlorn figure half submerged in the incoming tide. Removing Gunnarr's sword and tossing it impulsively into the waves, Olaf took hold of Hákon's body and dragged it out into the sea, out to where the water reached his neck, the waves washing a bubbling red trail from the corpse. Eventually he located a strong enough sea-bound current to carry the body out beyond the rocks, and released it.

When he returned to the beach he ordered his men to do the same with the rest of the bodies that still lay around Helvik's streets, sick of the sight and smell of death. By the time that he finally returned to the hall, the sky was the colour of old bones, only the crown of the sun yet to sink below the horizon.

The absence of clouds had led to a cold evening, and he seated himself on a bench and called out for Tyra to bring him something dry to wear. She did not respond, as often she did not, but this time Olaf was tired and in no mood for being ignored. He rose bad-temperedly back to his feet and shouted for her again, before stamping to the master's chamber to fetch her. She was not there. Hissing with impatience, he strode over to the sleeping berth and cast aside the topmost furs, but she was not cowering beneath them. He almost doubled back to go and locate her outside, furious that she had disobeyed his instructions, when suddenly he noticed something on the back wall.

The secret exit through which Hákon's brothers had planned to escape on the night of the assault had been roughly repaired by one of Olaf's men, in order to block out the draft from the sea. Yet, as Olaf looked at it now, he saw small pieces of dirt lying on the floor at its base. Approaching the back of the room, Olaf pulled at the wall and immediately felt the mesh of sticks and straw and mud come away easily in his hands, exposing a low hole big enough to crawl through.

'You bitch,' he muttered. He tore the hole apart and thrust his upper body through and there, directly beneath his eyes, he saw the perfect outline of a footprint in the dirt. He placed his palm down beside it, noting the femininity of its size. It was fresh, barely yet blemished by the wind. Then something else caught his eye, and as he scrambled a little further forward he found another footprint. This one was almost twice as big as the other. A man's footprint. They snaked off down the shingle before him, one beside the other.

Olaf was up and running to the front of the hall.

'You there,' he bellowed to the first man he saw, 'fetch me the horse, now!' and as the man dashed away Olaf ran inside the hall again and emerged with a torch and an oil lamp, dropping to his knees to set about lighting one with the other.

The man returned moments later. 'The horse is gone, Olaf.'

Olaf threw back his head and roared with rage, and then he began shouting to any man that could hear him.

'Light yourselves some torches, and I want every man out and hunting down two escaped prisoners heading west.' His torch burst into flame and he jumped quickly to his feet. 'I'll make a rich man of anyone who catches them before I do!'

He cursed furiously again and then broke into a run, without waiting for the others to follow. His eyes flashed hot and wild like the flames of the torch that danced beside his head. Helvik emptied behind him as his men took like hounds to the trail.

Chapter Twenty-Six

Across the open clifftops at sunset, a horse raced with the speed of one running for its life. Its thundering hooves tore great clumps of turf out of the ground and threw them up high into the air behind it. Gunnarr kept his head of billowing hair low against the creature's surging neck, whispering into his steed's ear to urge it onwards, despite the great extra burden it carried. Across his tensed thighs Gunnarr kept a fierce one-handed grip on the blanket under which lay Egil's body. With both arms locked around Gunnarr's waist, Tyra clung tightly against his back, elated and terrified at the same time by the speed. The rushing wind swept away her tears as they streamed across her cheeks.

Over the barren land they sped, beating a rhythm against the earth, streaking across the distance that had taken Gunnarr so long to cover on foot. Daylight stayed with them but fleetingly and soon it was dark, but their pace slowed only slightly, Gunnarr allowing the horse to guide itself around the drops and obstacles that human eyes could never have seen. Every so often Tyra would look down and see the white of swirling waves beneath her as the beast danced along the edge of the chasm, and she gripped onto Gunnarr even tighter and forced herself to trust.

Eventually the shape of jutting trees became visible against the dull sheen of the fading sky, and Gunnarr allowed the horse to fall back and regain its breath. They trotted across the final stretch, picking their way down the slope of the creaking woods to where the boat lay waiting for them.

The rest of them were all there, grouped together on the shore, and some of the men came running with a torch as soon as they heard the approaching hooves. Ári, Hilario, Bjǫrn and Eiric appeared beneath the base of the flame as Gunnarr clattered onto the stone of the beach, and Hilario reached up to take the bridle, the horse shaking its head and snorting at the smoke in its nostrils.

'Is it done?' Eiric asked dispassionately.

'It's done,' Gunnarr nodded, and he began to heave the laden blanket that rested across his knees down to them. 'I have brought back our father's body, to be given the send-off he deserves.'

Bjǫrn and Eiric looked across at each other and then hesitantly took the body between them, laying it carefully at their feet.

Now Gunnarr spoke with urgency. 'Ári, please, I need a blanket.' His friend nodded without questioning and went away to find one. Gunnarr turned to Hilario, still speaking with haste.

'My son?'

'He's with the women.'

'And my mother?'

Hilario hesitated. 'As you requested.'

'Thank you,' Gunnarr exhaled, and now he reached back and helped Tyra down from the saddle, as Ári arrived back and tossed up a large blanket for Gunnarr to catch. Resting it on the horse's back, Gunnarr immediately bent forward and heaved off the wet armour and under-tunic that by now had set a permanent shiver to his bone, dropping it onto a sodden pile on the beach. The other men gasped.

'Gunnarr!' Ári exclaimed quietly.

Even by the wayward light of the torch flame his condition was plain to see. His left arm looked black from shoulder to wrist, coated by a river of blood sourced from an ugly gash across his upper arm, a chunk of flesh torn clean away. More blood was to be found at his waist of the same side, this wound crusted and oozing, framed by purple rings of swelling. Bruising also dappled the skin of his ribcage, and where it was not dark and beaten the skin was pale and bloodless, beading with sweat despite the cold.

'Start getting everyone aboard,' Gunnarr instructed, rubbing the blanket briefly over his skin before tying it around his hunched shoulders. 'They may be coming after Tyra.'

'What about you?' Tyra asked, her voice high with concern, and she came forward and clutched at his hand.

Gunnarr looked away from her and towards the men, whose faces were poised in the same question. 'Just wait for me as long as you can.' The horse whinnied and its hooves kicked at the stony ground as Gunnarr began to turn it around.

'Gunnarr, we must leave!' Ári shouted, leaping forward to take hold of the bridle just as Hilario released it.

A look of desperation hovered over Gunnarr's face; the look of one who did not have the strength to decline the course of action he was about to take, however selfish or foolhardy.

'Please,' he begged, 'you gave me until dawn. Wait only as long as you can.'

Stones scattered as Gunnarr kicked his legs hard, and the horse grunted and took to the slope, ripping Ári's fingers from the bridle. In moments, all but the sound of the horse was lost in the darkness. Ári sucked at his lip and took hold of Tyra by the arm, leading her away from where she was staring worriedly after Gunnarr.

'We load up the ship. Keep that light hidden.'

Now Gunnarr rode with real purpose, shoulders forward, weight never planted in the saddle. As soon as the tricky slope was negotiated, he turned his steed's head east, and they were away back in the direction that they had come from on so many occasions, back towards the town that they had escaped so many times but never quite left.

A generous handful of stars lay scattered across the cloudless sky, a cut of the moon nestling within them, and their combined glow highlighted sections of the landscape from which Gunnarr could find his path. He drove the beast on as fast as it could make out the terrain, trusting its eyes, making better progress than he could have hoped for. Yet as they galloped up over the crest of a hill, he was forced to break stride and rein the horse to a halt at the sight of the landscape before him.

Lights. Hundreds of lights, planted like jewels all across the distance ahead. He had seen such a scene once before, on the night that he had watched from a distance as an army of flames marched down the hillside into Helvik and burnt it to the ground. But whereas that time they had been in neat, ordered rows, this time they were scattered independently, some large and only two hundred yards or so away, others only just coming into view in the distance. They were stretched far and wide, spreading west like a pox, jerking and flapping with movement as Olaf's men combed every corner and undulation of the land, looking for the man that now watched them from the hilltop.

Gunnarr dropped his left hand and kicked his horse away into a wide loop inland to bypass them and escape their net. Some might hear him, but not see him, and certainly not catch him. Now he did not have much time.

Eventually, with the enemy long behind them, Gunnarr drew up and dismounted and cast around the cliff edge until he found a path that they could pick their way down, and they descended the rocky escarpment towards the shore a short way west of Helvik. Gunnarr galloped the last stretch along the beach and then slid hurriedly from the saddle, leaving the horse to wander across the shingle while he scrambled off amongst the hummocks.

The darkness was thicker at the foot of the cliffs and he slipped many times, but he pressed forward, letting his memory guide him. The air smelt of kelp and wet stone. His feet stumbled up a rise. As soon as he felt he was almost in the right place he dropped to his knees and started to search with his hands, running them frantically over coarse rock and rough scrub, but he couldn't find what he sought and soon through his reckless searching he began to confuse his own senses. From somewhere below he heard the whinny of his horse and fell backwards with shock, and as he did his back crashed against something painful. A pile of rocks.

Immediately he knew that he was in the right place, and flipped over to drag his hands across the structure. It could only have been made by man. Keeping one hand on it so that he did not lose his bearings, he cast around blindly for the tools that he had thrown down so carelessly the last time he was here, but he could not locate them and soon gave up in his urgency.

He scrambled back on top of the pile, and paused, feeling suddenly overcome with nerves. Then he swallowed them down and began to dig.

He tore at the stones with both hands, snatching them up and casting them away around him. Many times he bashed his fingertips and gashed away pieces of his nails in the darkness, but that did not slow him. Eventually, when most of the rocks had thumped or cracked away to his sides, he found earth beneath his palms, cool and compressed under the shelter of the stones. He dug his fingers under the surface and began to lift it away, handful by handful.

At one point the shower of dirt that he cast rained down against something metallic. He dived after the sound and landed upon the spade that he so desperately needed, only a hand's width away from where he had been searching. Now he began to dig with greater speed, feeling the aired quality of soil that had been recently disturbed coming away with ease. The two wounds that he carried began to sing with pain at every motion, and he felt his muscles shivering with fatigue, but that could not deter him. When he had gone as deep as he dared he tossed the spade away again and reverted back to the caring touch of his hands, lying on his chest at the side of the pit and sculpting the earth away. Then, as he was beginning to worry that he had gone much further down than he should have, his hands fell against something much cooler than the soil, and he recoiled on impulse.

He hated himself for doing that. Not now. Not to her. Immediately he crawled forward again and placed his hand once more against what he instantly recognised as the shape of her forehead and cheek, and held it there to pass his warmth into her, feeling the tears erupt from his eyes and his body collapse into crying throbs.

'It's me, my love,' he whispered. 'I wouldn't leave you here on your own.'

Without wiping his tears, he quickly snatched the blanket from around his shoulders and laid it out next to the hole, oblivious now to the cold on his naked chest. He cleared away some of the remaining soil, before reaching down to lift Kelda painfully from the grave that he had laid her in four days earlier, ignoring how different her body felt to touch. He set her down on the blanket and wrapped her up tightly in it. Sweeping her up into his arms, he held her close to his chest and staggered down the hummock back to the horse, guided by the sound of it cropping at the scrub nearby.

His every muscle burnt now, and he barely had the strength to lay her over the horse's back and climb up behind her. This time as he squeezed his thighs the horse snorted and stubbornly took another mouthful, only reluctantly lifting its head after Gunnarr begged and begged. Gunnarr kicked at it violently, jerking at the reins and urging forward with his hips. The horse squealed and tossed its head as if betrayed, tensing and stepping sideways and backwards. Gunnarr kicked again and slapped at its hindquarters with a flailing hand, and this time, with another whinny of protest, it finally broke into a trot and then a canter. It grunted each time its lead leg met the ground and held its head low, lolling its tongue out of the side of its mouth.

It was an ageing creature, and he had near run the life out of it. They made it up onto the clifftops but the steep slope wore the beast down. For a short while it ran along the level ground, moving in a strange sideways motion, and then abruptly it screamed and reared up as if a snake had just flared up in front of it. Gunnarr battled to stay in the saddle as the horse stumbled backwards like a drunkard, and then slipped to the ground with Kelda as he felt the animal's hind legs collapse.

He sat down on the ground with Kelda on his lap, the horse down beside him with its legs folded underneath it, snorting mucus into the grass. Gunnarr found that he was hugging Kelda tightly to his chest, as if she slept. It was so dark around them that he could not see reality. They three could have been the only people in the world and, despite the urgency of his task, Gunnarr found himself strangely comforted, as if, if nothing else were possible, this would do, sitting together in the dark, away from the truth of daylight.

He was not aware for how long he sat there, but eventually the horse rolled up to its feet and began to wander around, and Gunnarr was able to return to the saddle and ride it at an ambling trot for what felt like another mile or so. At that point it stopped again and would not continue. They seemed to be crossing a boggy stretch. The ground sucked as Gunnarr dropped down to his feet again, and an unseen ground bird scattered from somewhere nearby with a flurry of sound. He could hear the ocean off to the side.

For a time he led the horse by the bridle, stumbling through the black. The squelching ground clung to his legs, dragging away his strength, and the next thing he knew he was lying with the cold ground on his face and the taste of peat water in his mouth. He rolled onto his back to look up at the sky. The darkness was thinning, the stars beginning to fade.

A final time Gunnarr climbed into the saddle. He fell forward over Kelda and whispered into the horse's ear, urging it to give one more effort before it was too late, and it went.

*

Olaf held his torch so low that it singed the grass, and crept forward until he reached the nearest of the pine trees.

He peered down the slope that fell away beneath him. It was black as an abyss, but there were voices down there, carried up in snatches by the wind. He kept his eyes trained on the shore, and there, through the darkness, he saw a glimmer of light, a glimpse that lasted only an instant. He snarled.

As the rest of his breathless men began to catch up with him, he directed them around to the other side of the hill, until they had enclosed it in a burning arc, cutting off any escape.

Olaf nodded to the man nearest him and drew his sword. They moved forward in unison, tightening like a snare.

From the ship, Ári and the others crouched against the rail and watched the horizon glowing orange all around them. The women and children cowered towards the back, some moaning with fear as the glow evolved into individual heads of flame that began to march through the trees down the hillside towards them.

'We must leave now!' Bjǫrn appealed.

'We cannot leave him!' Hilario insisted.

'He has left us!' Bjǫrn hissed, and he looked imploringly to Ári.

Ári tried to ignore the words and searched desperately across the surroundings for any sign, but all he could see was the ring of flames coming irresistibly closer, eating up the ground with the patient menace of a stalking cat. He could hear their footsteps now, trampling through the undergrowth, but louder than that he could hear the fearful whimpers of the children and their mothers behind him, perhaps even those of his own wife. Longingly he scanned the empty hilltop a final time. Then he let his chin drop and looked sadly at Hilario.

'Let us go.'

Hilario stared, and then nodded once with horrified accept-ance. Along with the rest of the men he scrambled for the oars, taking them up and heaving them like punt poles against the sea floor, and the boat began to creak backwards. Halfway down the hill, some of Olaf's men noticed the sudden movement, and the torch flames flapped through the air as they began to rush forward. Ári and the others heaved with all of their strength against the oars, feeling the boat lurch slightly as it came free from the ground and out onto the water, gliding away from the beach. Some of the men hurried to seat themselves so that they could begin to row properly and pull away, but suddenly Ári shouted.

'Stop!'

Olaf's encircling men had also heard what Ári had, for they too faltered. The torches halted and began to whip around with indecision. Ári repeated his shout as some of the men failed to respond, and they froze, straightening their backs while the boat continued to glide silently away from the shore.

Now they all heard it: the rhythmic sound of horse hooves galloping thunderously across the clifftop above their heads.

'Gunnarr,' Ári whispered.

Snatching up his oar again, he drove it into the water and tried to halt the boat's glide, already almost twenty yards out from the shore. They heard a whinny, the sound of a terrified beast, and then at a point midway up the hill the burning ring of torches suddenly shattered as something burst through them.

'Gunnarr!' Ári called madly, and then he saw him appear, driving the horse clattering across the beach and into the water without slowing, throwing up an almighty burst of spume. Reacting, Olaf's men began to sprint for the shoreline to claw him back, but the brave horse bounded deeper, slowing gradually with the depth, until it was alongside the back of the boat, only its head not submerged.

'Help me!' Gunnarr cried, from where he sat with his lower half sunk in the water, and he heaved the burden that he carried out for his friends to grab. Ári and Hilario did so gingerly, with a look of sudden realisation on their faces. Just as the horse was forced to break off into a paddling swim, Gunnarr clambered with his feet onto the beast's back and dived the last few yards to where the boat was steadily creeping out of reach, landing hard against the side before snatching hands tore hold of his skin and dragged him over the rail.

A torch came flying through the air and drew a yelp from the women as it clattered into the boat, but before it could get a hold Hilario hurled it back. Now Bjǫrn and the others dug their oars in and they began to skim away from the other torches that dropped out of the sky around them. The horse paddled briefly after the boat, as if it too wanted to clamber aboard, or perhaps just to see off its charge, and then it fell away and was lost in the blackness.

Olaf sank to his knees in the shallows, and let his torch fizzle out beneath the waves.

As Gunnarr sank down to collapse upon the deck, drained now in his relief, Ári went to join the others that crowded around the prow. Like the serpent's head above them, they watched the many lights that now gathered around the water's edge fading slowly into the distance. The oar strokes bit into the waters and sent them flying through the night air.

Chapter Twenty-Seven

Gunnarr awoke when he became conscious of his son's impatient movements under the blanket around his chest. He sat his aching muscles up against the side of the boat and took the infant up in his right arm, rubbing at his eyes with the left. A chubby little hand reached up and slapped him lightly on the cheek, and Gunnarr found the child watching him quizzically, waving his arms as if time was somehow being wasted.

Gunnarr smiled down at him. 'Good morning, Son.'

The sail was up. Its tattered canvas edges flapped gently as they coaxed in the breeze. Sunshine glowed down from above in a sky of pale blue, and below it solaced faces rested across the planks, oars shipped. The adults smiled as they watched the children leaning out over the sides to drag their fingers through the green waters.

Gunnarr handed his son carefully to Tyra beside him, and then stood to pick his way along the rocking spine of the boat towards the prow, greeting those he passed on the way. Eventually he reached the fore, where Bjǫrn was standing with an arm against the prow, frowning into the distance, his cloak streaming gently behind him with the breeze.

'Where are we heading?' Gunnarr asked.

Bjǫrn turned around and smiled. 'Forward.'

Steinthor Anundersson lay with his wife beneath a blanket on the floor of the boat, hemmed in at both sides by gleaming bags of wealth. He opened an eye as Gunnarr re-passed him.

'Bring your lad up,' he said through a yawn. 'Nanna says he'll want feeding.'

Gunnarr nodded his thanks to Nanna and went off to the rear of the ship to fetch him.

Tyra had risen now also and was standing towards the stern, looking out over the empty horizon as they left it behind. She held Gunnarr's son against her chest, bouncing him gently across one arm. The little boy gurgled with enjoyment, studying her with fascination. Gunnarr watched the two of them fondly. Tyra sensed his gaze and turned to flash a smile at him, and Gunnarr returned it and made his way over to her side.

'You are a mother who has lost a son,' he said quietly as he reached her, 'and he is a son who has lost a mother. Nothing would give me greater happiness than to see the two of you mend each other's hearts.'

Tyra's face softened, and she closed her eyes and squeezed the infant closer. Then she looked into Gunnarr's eyes and reached across to take his hand. 'You have also lost a wife,' she said softly.

Gunnarr returned her gaze with an appreciative smile. Then he gently took her hand and placed it back down by her waist. 'But she will never lose a husband.'

He looked past Tyra's sad smile then and across to the covered section at the very back of the ship, where three blanket-covered shapes lay together in seclusion, almost hidden in the shade of the sun-screen erected above them.

Taking his son gently, Gunnarr held him aloft, letting the child study the surroundings. They would pull in to a quiet place on the shore and release them all together, so that they might keep each other company until Gunnarr was ready to follow them.

The child was shifting restlessly in his father's arms. Gunnarr turned him around to face the wind, and the boy's inquisitive eyes looked west.

Acknowledgements

I owe thanks to the following people: to the Harper *Voyager* team for the opportunity, and for the hard work that followed, and to my editor, Natasha, without whom this book may well have stayed under the bed. She championed it when it was nothing, and her skilled edits brought out the best in the story. To my friends for their support, and the various ways they found to help me. To mum and dad, for trusting me in everything and failing me in nothing. And to Rose, Beth, Row and Shan, for a childhood full of inspiration.

Finally, to Marta, my beautiful wife, for all the lonely, boring nights she endured, banished to the bedroom while I worked at this on the sitting room table. For her faith in allowing me to take a chance. And for her tireless love. Thank you.